BRIEF GARLANDS

The Novels of Stanley Middleton

BRIEF GARLANDS

Stanley Middleton

HUTCHINSON
London

First published in the United Kingdom in 2004 by Hutchinson

1 3 5 7 9 10 8 6 4 2

The Random House Group Limited
20 Vauxhall Bridge Road, London SW1V 2SA

Random House Australia (Pty) Limited
20 Alfred Street, Milsons Point, Sydney
New South Wales 2061, Australia

Random House New Zealand Limited
18 Poland Road, Glenfield
Auckland 10, New Zealand

Random House (Pty) Limited
Endulini, 5a Jubilee Road, Parktown 2193, South Africa

The Random House Group Limited Reg. No. 954009
www.randomhouse.co.uk

A CIP catalogue record for this book is available
from the British Library

Papers used by Random House
are natural, recyclable products made from wood grown in
sustainable forests. The manufacturing processes conform to
the environmental regulations of the country of origin

Typeset by Palimpsest Book Production Limited,
Polmont, Stirlingshire
Printed and bound in Great Britain by
Mackays of Chatham plc, Chatham, Kent

ISBN 0 09 179949 X

To David Belbin and Sue Dymoke

Nihil est ab omni parte beatum
(No lot is happy on all sides)
                              Horace

The garland briefer than a girl's
                              A. E. Housman

I

'There's some cloud about,' a female voice instructed him.

John Stone, who had just opened his front door, looked about. He recognised Annie Fisher's tone, and her banality, but could not see her. She must, he concluded, be on the way in or out, for it was rare for her to stand in her front garden or at the gate looking up and down the street. He, on the other hand, often walked out to the front porch, when he'd nothing better to do, where he'd scan the trees, or the sky, sure that they'd provide him with something to think about. His wife had complained frequently. She remembered from her childhood the miners who'd sit in shirtsleeves on the front step exchanging gossip with passing neighbours. 'If you want to look out, do it from the parlour. Nobody will notice you and you'll see whatever it is you want to see just as well.'

Now, on this late August afternoon, he smiled wryly.

His neighbour, Annie Fisher, was waving from a squatting position in one of her borders. He briefly returned her greeting.

'Do you think we shall have any rain?' she asked.

'No,' he answered from his porch.

'Are you sure?' she persisted.

'Yes.'

The brevity and certainty of his answers must have reassured her for she made, without rising, a crab-like movement of a yard to her left and continued to jab at the soil with her brand-new scarlet trowel. Jack Stone moved down the six steps that led from the porch to the garden path. He supported himself lightly on the three-foot brick wall that divided his land from the Fishers'.

Nobody moved in the avenue. The lime tree leaves flourished, a mass of packed green. That must have been the result of the constant rain they'd had in the last two months. Now the sky was delicately blue, and the clouds small and fluffy. It seemed warmer

1

outside than in, but not unpleasantly so. The last three days had been hot, windless, stifling, but today a suspicion of breeze, and from the north, kept it cool out of the sun without robbing the sunlight of its heat. Jack Stone walked down and hung briefly over his wrought-iron gate. On school days this time, 3.45 p.m., would have scattered the pavements with children, the bigger in ones or twos, or groups of young women with the smallest of their offspring in pushchairs and the older children circling around or breaking away. Mothers would talk animatedly, but the children seemed subdued, alert, reduced to whispers and giggles as if the day's learning had taken virtue out of them. Still at the gate, he turned about and looked at his house, now neatly dappled with sun and shadow.

His home was a huge red-brick-and-stone-built Victorian semi-detached villa, the mirror image of the Fishers' house next door. Below ground, though with a window at the back, was the basement, and above that three storeys. The lower two were lighted by wide bay windows with long lace curtains. His own matched, by negotiation, those of the Fishers. The bricks were hand-made, unworn, with lines of decoration; the sash windows rose tall, woodwork freshly painted. The roof above was of Welsh slate. The effect was stately. Inside, the rooms spread large, the decorated plaster ceilings high and snow-white. To the left of Stone's house as he faced it was a deep garden, which merged into an even larger space at the back.

Stone turned for a last glimpse of his gate, the wrought-iron railings, the shrubs.

'Is your wife not back yet?' Mrs Fisher asked.

'No,' he answered. 'Not till Saturday.'

'Has she had a good time?'

'Excellent. Or so her postcards tell me.'

Annie Fisher laughed. He moved so that he could see her. She had turned towards him, but oddly squatted still with the trowel ready in her hand though her back was turned on the bed she was weeding. Her legs were apart and her shortish skirt was tightly drawn up above her knees, revealing stocking tops, strong thighs and a glimpse of lilac knickers. He made no attempt to look away, nor she to conceal herself. He would have expected her, had he thought about it, which he had not, to wear tights.

He could see the dark tops of her stockings, but no signs of suspenders.

'Aren't you gardening,' she asked, 'this afternoon?'

'No. I've done nothing else all week.'

'You'd better have it straight for Peg's return.'

'Have no fear.' He pointed towards her. 'I'm just about to make a pot of tea,' he said. 'Would you like to join me?'

'Oh, yes, please.'

'Where's Harry? Would he . . . ?'

'No. He's fast asleep in front of the athletics on telly.'

She stood up, vigorously brushing the soil from her hands. 'I shall have to wash my paws,' she warned.

'Oh, swill them in my kitchen.' He moved back towards his gate, which he held politely open until she entered. She wished a cheerful good afternoon to a passing couple who half-heartedly returned her greeting.

'That's something for them to gossip about.'

'Who is it?'

'That Congregational minister and his wife. Live next but one to the end of the avenue.'

'He seems a decent sort.'

'Don't know about that. She's a blabbermouth.'

'She maligns you?' Stone asked.

'Maligns? Yes. Me and anybody else she can lay her tongue to.'

'How do you know?'

'People pass it on. That's the idea.'

'In you go,' he ordered, laughing.

He followed her up the garden path. She moved smartly. At fifty-six she was not without a certain sexual animal attraction. She made short work of his steps, and marched along the Venetian terrazzo corridor and into the kitchen. There he filled the kettle and, once he'd laid out teacups, milk jug and teapot on a tray, and begun a search in the larder for biscuits, which he was pretty certain she'd refuse, she washed her hands, dried them on a towel and called out, 'Where are we sitting, then?'

'The parlour.'

'I'm honoured,' she said.

'It's Sunday.'

'I'll leave my shoes outside in the hall.' She did no such thing.

John Stone made tea, though he had no idea why. He didn't usually drink the beverage until an hour and a half later and today he had eaten his Sunday lunch at two o'clock, not at one as on weekdays. Moreover, he had no particular desire to talk to Annie Fisher. True, she dropped snippets of interesting gossip in his way from time to time, but mostly not. She seemed unable to talk to him without punctuating her clichés with squawks of laughter. He smelt her perfume as he walked along the hall with his tray and wondered why the woman steeped herself in expensive scent to go out to weed the garden. When he had placed the tray on the table she immediately rose and bobbed up to ask, 'You'll want me to act as mother, I expect?'

'Who better?' he answered drily.

He moved one of the smaller chairs and sat on it. He did not now face the full brightness of the high windows, but could at least see her profile clearly.

'Is Peg enjoying her holiday?' Mrs Fisher asked again, carrying his tea across to a small table within his reach.

'So I understand.' He pointed to the mantelpiece where he had lined up a couple of postcards.

Annie strutted across, looked the pictures over and read the brief messages. 'At least the weather's good,' she commented, realigning the cards. She sat and continued her commentary. 'I don't know that I'd want to spend a whole month, and August at that, up in Scotland.'

'It's after her sister's husband died. She's been up every year since then.'

Annie frowned and asked her next question: 'How old was he?'

Stone guessed she knew the answer. 'Seventy.'

'No sort of age these days.' She lifted her cup. 'She's well off, isn't she? Her sister? Big house, big car. There's no telling what they get up to. You've been to stay there?'

'Yes. Several times.'

'What was it like?'

'Pleasant. It's on the shore of the loch. Ian had a boat, but his wife got rid of it once he'd died. I went out a time or two with him.'

'Fishing?'

'No. Though I believe he did a bit on his own. When he had

4

me in the boat he drove it skimming along the surface like a lunatic. I suppose he wanted to scare me.'

'Did he succeed?'

'To some extent.'

'He was in engineering, wasn't he?' she queried.

John Stone, drying his lips with a clean handkerchief, made no answer to her trivialities, but nodded.

'What was the best thing about it?' she asked.

'The scenery. Mountains, glens and the loch. It's a beautiful place.'

'And the worst?'

'The midges. They were brutes.' He sighed. 'They much preferred me to Peg.'

'Is that why you don't go?'

'One of the minor reasons. When I'm there, now that Ian's dead, I feel I'm in their way. They have to try to entertain me, to take me to exhibitions and museums, feed me with dishes they think please me, break up their own schemes. I'm uncomfortable.'

'What sort of man was your sister-in-law's husband?'

'Rich. But the only sort of thing he was interested in was his engineering concern. He'd two factories. He started with ships, but long before he retired he'd taken up with aeroplane engines. He retired at sixty-five, that's fourteen . . . fifteen years ago, and died at seventy, a thoroughly unhappy man with nothing to live for. He belted along over the loch in the hope he'd ruin the engine; then he could strip it down and enjoy himself.'

'Did you talk to him?'

'Of course I did. The women used to send us out together.'

'No, I don't mean just generally. You've spent your life in education. Didn't you try to put ideas into his head? Good books, classical music, pictures?'

Stone suspected sarcasm. 'I imagine, Annie, I couldn't help it. But my seed fell on stony ground. He'd listen for a minute, but then he'd drift off. Not to sleep, but to some scheme.'

'What sort of scheme?'

'Well, for instance, he installed a water-powered dynamo that produced electricity. He could heat and light part of the house with it. Not that he'd any need, there's plenty of hydro-electric stations up here. He needed something to demonstrate to himself that he was an engineer and that he'd not lost his practical skills.

5

He'd make detailed plans, and buy materials in Glasgow and search round factories. He acted, he told me, as a consultant sometimes, so they knew him. And he kept himself up to date on cybernetics, computers and the like.'

Annie Fisher nodded, as one already lost. 'I should have thought that would have been enough to occupy anybody.'

'You'd have thought so, but he set off at the same time each morning, at 7 a.m. in his case, to face the day's problems. Once he'd retired it didn't matter much if he decided he'd sort the snag out next week when he found an hour or two to spare. He didn't like it. He thrived – throve – on pressure.'

'And what do the ladies do now that he's gone?'

'Oh, they have their little programmes. They go off on a round of one or two visits in the afternoons and sometimes out in the evening to the theatre or concert hall.'

'That's a long way, isn't it?' she asked.

'Not really, to Glasgow or Edinburgh, but I bet they've spent a day or two there in a hotel, shopping and seeing a bit of the Festival. She, May, showers us with brochures so that Peg can make up her mind about what she'd like to hear and see.'

'Does May know much about it?'

'She's learning, but she regards Peg as the expert because she trained at the Royal Academy.'

'Peg knows her mind.'

'You think so?' he asked sardonically.

'How long have you been married? Thirty years?'

'Thereabouts. Thirty-four.'

'And you don't know yet? My husband knew when I had my mind made up before we'd been married a fortnight.'

Stone smiled grimly, but politely turned his head away. This was a frequent boast of Annie Fisher, this dominance over her husband. He had once asked her if she would choose to have it otherwise. She had screwed up her eyes as if thinking hard and had answered, 'It works out well enough with this man, but whether it would with another I don't know.' The answer had surprised and puzzled as well as pleased him. He had not expected any such subtlety from her.

'You were a headmaster,' she said now. 'You were used to giving orders. And you liked it.'

6

'Are you suggesting that I chose to be subservient at home for a change?'

'I'm not suggesting any such thing. Or if I suggested anything about you, it would be that you don't know yourself.' She laughed, a small sound compared with her usual metallic explosion. 'I see you walking along the street, in your collar and silk tie, and your neat grey suit and panama hat in the summer, your polished black shoes and with such a serious expression on your face that I think you must be praying, and then I say to myself, "I could tell you something about Mr Sobersides there, if I wished." But I won't. You rest content. My lips are sealed.'

Stone smiled at her, as engagingly as he could. He took off and cleaned his glasses. He knew quite well what she was talking about.

Some twenty-seven years earlier he had arrived in Beechnall, newly appointed headmaster of a new comprehensive school in the town. He had been for five years the head of a small grammar school in the north-west where he had raised academic standards spectacularly. Here the county council had decided, after considerable argument, that the new school they were building outside the city in a middle-class area would be 'the school of the future' and they therefore wanted a headmaster who would see to it that academic targets were in favour. The advertisements in *The Times*, the *Guardian* and the *TES* spoke of challenge, new ground to be broken. The school would be large, in its own wide sports grounds, with its up-to-the-minute science laboratories, arts and crafts studios, its own theatre, its music rehearsal rooms. Once Stone had been appointed (there had been three Ph.D.s in the final five candidates), and helped by his three deputies, one already a head, he had set about appointing staff. There would be a small sixth form for suitable candidates from the start, and a full new intake, six streams, into the first form, and the possibility of one class in each of the other three years, provided enough scholars presented themselves. This had been tricky, but his deputies and heads of department had all been well chosen, and the director of education, whose bosom child the new scheme was, had been generous, both with advice and money.

John Stone had enjoyed these short six months of preparation, and had kept his senior staff in good heart and order. They were

7

not allowed to act unreasonably, but the head listened carefully to their ideas. The director had made a brilliant job of his publicity, so they had many more applicants for the middle school than they expected, but it was agreed that they would keep to the original plan of one form only for the second, third and fourth years. This had caused controversy, but Stone could argue a case with strength and had not found too much opposition among his own staff.

The Stones easily managed the move from Cumbria to a new home. Peg was sorry to leave her pretty stone-built house, but had fallen in love with the opportunities offered in the much larger semi-detached villa where they now lived. Peg had friends in Beechnall and had encouraged them to advise her. This present place, then occupied by an elderly academic lawyer, was never put on the market. Hugh Dale, a solicitor friend, told them that the house would be for sale in the next month or two. He mentioned a possible price, and Peg rushed down immediately so that she and Dale could scrutinise the place.

'Beautifully built, beautifully kept. Old Schofield Forbes liked things done properly,' Dale concluded.

Peg was convinced. Her own father had died not many months before, and left her and May a considerable sum, which made the purchase easy, even if they kept their old place in Penrith as a holiday home, a plan Peg suggested early in the negotiation, but which was soon questioned.

'Why should we do that?' her husband had asked her.

'Why? It will bring in rent. It will appreciate in value without burdensome tax.'

'We'll have to keep it in good order.'

'Of course.'

'Isn't this place far too large? I'm going to be headmaster of the Waldeck Comprehensive School, not the managing director of ICI.'

He insisted that she visit Beechnall during the preliminary searches and negotiations. She shared with him his poky flat in the city centre where he had lived, except for weekends, during the few months before the opening of his school.

She worked long and fastidiously, deciding on furniture, on decoration. He listened each evening to her schemes; money now seemed no object to her, but she was in her way just as good an administrator as he was. Peg could hold three or four things in her mind at once and could immediately see what would be the effect of changing one over the others. She was not wasting money. She hunted value. Every morning she set off with an objective, and seemed happy and fulfilled as never before. He was as satisfied as she with life. He still remembered the morning he drove into his new school and saw for the first time the tasteful noticeboard by the main gate. The largest letters in gold on a Lincoln-green background announced that this was 'The Waldeck Comprehensive School' and just below that: 'Headmaster, C. J. Stone, MA (Oxon), FRGS'. This was somewhat diminished by an equally golden, but larger, inscription on the other corner of the board: 'Caretaker, J. Thompson, 24 Primrose Avenue' and a guiding arrow directing strangers which way to begin their search for this official.

The Stones moved in to their new house a week before the first term with pupils started.

'I shall need three weeks to get the house straight and after that I shall shoot up to have a week or two's rest at May's. That means after your first fortnight of school you'll have to fend for yourself for a time.' She eyed him narrowly. 'That will be good, because you'll take your lunch at school and you'll be able to decide what the meals are like.' He had already led her round the shining kitchens in the main building, which she'd judged to be impressive, provided they employed women who knew what cookery was about. Peg had looked distantly, with a Medusa's power, at the chief cook who seemed turned palely to stone under that scrutiny. Later she turned out to be excellent at her job and finished her career, strongly supported by a testimonial from John Stone, as the city adviser on school meals.

These were weeks of excitement; he stayed at school until late, even showed up at the trials of the young footballers and at their first match, a rapidly arranged friendly against another school, on the second Saturday of term. Waldeck won 7–1, but it was reported to Stone that the head of PE had half skinned the defence for that conceded goal. It all seemed part and parcel of that golden age of promise to him now: excellence from the start.

On the same Saturday morning his neighbour, Mrs Fisher, had rung to invite Mr and Mrs Stone to lunch next day. They had exchanged brief words in the two or three weeks they had been in occupation, but now Peg had to explain that she was about to leave for the Lake District on her way to Scotland and her sister's hospitality.

Mrs Fisher said that her husband was away on a golfing weekend and would Mr Stone, then, like to join her? Roast beef and Yorkshire pudding, kidney beans and home-grown potatoes. Mrs Stone accepted for her husband, who seemed not altogether pleased. 'I'm not sure that she's altogether my cup of tea,' he grumbled.

'You'll learn from her what Beechnall's like.'

'I tend to doubt that.'

They embraced and she drove off, at ease with her world.

Next day at fifteen minutes after noon Stone reported next door, as arranged, was made welcome in a large armchair, with a schooner of sherry in his hand. Mrs Fisher spent as long with him as she could spare from her kitchen duties, apparently worried that he would feel neglected. At one o'clock she conducted him to the dining room where she served the meal. They sat at either end of a long, highly polished table.

Whatever else she was, Annie Fisher was a fine cook. His generous helpings on a wide willow-pattern dinner plate he laced with a rich gravy from a matching sauce boat. He ate with relish. For the past few months there had been an air of the extempore, the scratch, about his meals. Now he felt at leisure, with an air of celebration; she kept his glass of red wine brimming. Even when Peg rang, still at the Lake District house, about twenty minutes into the lunch to find out if he had remembered his engagement, he answered cheerfully, describing the excellent meal.

After summer pudding he was led into a small sitting room and left – her words – to fend for himself with a small cup of coffee and a large glass of whisky. Not long afterwards she joined him, bending this time as she passed, to kiss him on the forehead. Far from resenting this, he grabbed at her hand; she fell across him. They kissed deeply. A few minutes later she took him upstairs into a bedroom where the linen blinds were already drawn. In the dimmed light she stripped and drew him into the bed. He had taken off his clothes with slow deliberation; he knew what he was doing was wrong and moreover might well have repercussions that he'd regret on his professional life as a school-master. He sat stark naked on the edge of the bed, as if making a last-minute effort to fight off temptation while she, behind him, stroked his back and giggled to herself, crooned her happiness.

In the end she pulled him over so that he lay facing her. 'That's the boy,' she said, touching him on face, belly, erect penis. His hands fumbled between her legs.

When finally they had made love and he lay inside her he began to think again. He did not move, even as he noticed that her green eyes were wide open and watching him.

'Welcome to Beechnall,' she said.

'That was marvellous,' he said languidly. He knew it was not, that she was not. He had not expected this seduction, and his own reaction surprised and shocked him.

II

For the next few days, he remembered, Stone kept himself busy, dismissing thoughts of his adultery. He had been brought up in a northern puritan tradition and he could not help fearing that his transgression would make the success of the Waldeck School uncertain if not impossible. He instructed himself that this was mere superstition, but he could not see himself, in his first weeks, as anything but one waiting for just punishment to fall. He was invited in to the Fishers' for the second Sunday lunch, but this time Harry Fisher was at home. He was red-faced, well-dressed, rather roughly spoken, but offered Stone to walk with him round the Waldeck buildings and comment on one or two structural problems that Stone had noticed.

'Who's the architect?' Fisher had asked.

'Lionel Spenser.'

'And the builders?'

'Barlock, Bruce.'

'You could have had worse.'

After the meal was finished Stone, perhaps wrongly, had an impression that the Fishers were trying to hurry him out. This week there were no leisurely served cups of coffee or magnificent glasses of whisky. He was both relieved and disappointed that he was not to be pressed into sexual high jinks this weekend and allowed Mr Fisher to head him speedily to the front door where they stood in the September sunshine.

'Beautiful houses, these.' Fisher slapped one of his marble pillars holding up the delicate roof of the porch. 'There are only the six of these semis in the street. And two detached. All have large gardens, but our two the largest of them all because my house is the one where the builder lived.' He pointed across the road. 'Those look much the same as ours, but are nowhere near as big. Your house the builder rented out to his younger brother, but the upkeep proved too much for him and they sold it to the family of the man you bought it from. Jack Langley wanted to keep this road exclusive, or at least his wife did. Professional families only and access at just one end.'

'Is he still alive? Langley?'

Fisher heard the question with astonishment. Stone tipsily wondered why he'd asked anything so foolish.

'You need to take more water with it. These houses were built in 1888. Langley will have been dead getting on for a hundred years.'

'But the street has still retained its professional image?'

'Oh, yes. Either that or business.' He breathed deeply. 'Are you nicely settled? Your wife's off on holiday, I hear. She's soon skipped it.' His face seemed angelic. 'Well, it won't do standing out here. I'd better go inside and see what I can do for my wife.' He winked wickedly. 'I see we shall get on well.'

'And none of the Langley's descendants lives here still?'

'Annie, my wife, was a Langley.'

'I'm talking to a bit of history. That's really interesting. The firm still exists, does it?'

'Yes. Langley, Bell and Fisher. But there's no male Langley working in the firm. Jack Langley's wife saw to it that all her sons were posted off to university, so that they ended up as lawyers and doctors and the like.'

'And does any of them still live in Beechnall?'

'Not to the best of my knowledge.' He did not sound too pleased with his wife's relatives.

Fisher waved his neighbour off his property. Stone remembered tripping over the top front steps and landing face down on the terrazzo floor of the hall, where he lay, uninjured but cursing. Nobody had witnessed his downfall. He pushed himself up, staggered into an armchair in the main front room and fell restlessly asleep.

Now, today, twenty-seven years later, he sat in the same chair while Annie Fisher, knees prettily together, made no move towards his virtue. They had kept the sexual affair going only intermittently over the past years. In a way it had been exactly suited to his wishes. If the spouses were absent, she'd make her move. Sometimes the approach was indirect, so that once or twice,

13

not often, he was able to slip away; at other times she'd point at his genitals and say, 'I fancy a touch of that; come on round.' They had never been out to dinner, or a show together. Their congress – he liked the word – had taken place inside one or the other of their houses, except for one notable Bonfire Night when they had made love in the little wooded hillock at the bottom of her garden, the rockets bursting over the darkening shapes of the criss-cross of branches above them. Neither had found this very satisfactory. She'd vulgarly complained at the time 'My bum's freezing' and he'd had to send a rather elegant light-grey suit to the dry cleaners. Annie still referred occasionally to the adventure – 'our night under the stars' – but they were careful never to repeat it. About these encounters Annie Fisher, who could be a chatterbox, showed a tact that seemed sagely out of character, so that he wondered if she had other affairs on the go, or regarded this, an occasional fling with a strict, successful headmaster, as a small triumph that was the more precious for its secrecy and rarity.

Her meetings from their front gardens or paths were formal on his part and her rather loud, vulgarly cheerful voice elicited no unfavourable comment from their spouses or neighbours. Once, one of John Stone's deputies, a rather impudent man who spoke the first words that came into his head, had said, 'I met your neighbour, Annie Fisher, last night at a charity dinner.'

'Oh, yes.'

'She's a good-looking woman.'

'Yes, she is.'

'And lively. Sexy in her way.' He took the edge off the words with a cough.

'Flirtatious, do you mean?' Stone spoke with cold irony.

'When she dances with you, it's a bit more than that.'

'I've never had the pleasure.'

'She said she thought you rather handsome.'

'She's never told me any such thing. How did she connect you with me?'

'She asked me where I worked and then she said you'd know me.'

She seemed now to have fallen asleep in her chair, untidily, hair awry. Her body slumped shapeless, limp, her chin fatly into her chest. Her breathing was steadily audible and a bubble of saliva moved at the left of her mouth. She, vulnerable, stirred slightly, sighed; he felt, not for the first time, a pang of pity for her. From now on the strength, the optimism, the daring that had made her herself would fade and she'd know it. He put out a hand to touch her lovingly, but decided against it and shuffled towards his chair. The telephone rang out in the hall; he turned energetically to march out.

Eric Woodhouse, a former colleague, his first Head of Mathematics at Waldeck School, was ringing to announce the death of another former member of staff, George Hunter. Woodhouse employed a religiose voice to make the announcement. He gave a brief account of the terminal illness and the last few weeks in a hospice. Stone knew nothing of this and, in fact, in the last seven years since his retirement had not kept up socially with members of his staff, even the older ones. He had been back to school perhaps a dozen times since he retired and found the place untidier than he would have liked. As far as he could make out from the results published in the local papers, the school had kept up to, or near, the high academic standards he had demanded and achieved; the cabinets in the foyer and great hall shone, stuffed full as always with silverware won on games fields and in athletics stadia. Waldeck Comprehensive was as far as he could understand the best, the highest achieving school in the county, in the Midlands.

A year or two ago they had sent him an elaborate history of the place compiled by some old boy. They had printed a photograph of him in academicals, taken on some speech day, and several ex-students had written of the awe they had felt in his presence, the encouragement taken from some few brief words of his, of his kindness, the decisive influence on their lives. He had obviously appeared to his scholars as a distant figure, an ancient of days, though he was under forty when he was appointed, and this did not displease him. The ex-director had written an encomium which strongly claimed that John Stone had made of his school a model of academic and athletic excellence, and that his name would never be forgotten in the city. Stone had read these praises with some pleasure, but never quite believed them. Asked by Peg what he thought, he answered that one thing she could be thankful for was that she hadn't had to wait for his death to hear this length of exaggerated flattery.

'I shall get it twice?' she queried.

'If you live long enough.'

'And it's better the second time round?'

'You won't have the secular saint himself to contend with then.'

Peg looked at him coolly. 'I guess you did them well,' she made her final judgement.

'With your help.' He had felt generously inclined. Peg had been a good wife for a headmaster. She was not there at every event in the school calendar, but when she was she said exactly the right things to encourage staff and pupils. She had no favourites and spoke of her husband to his subordinates as if he were a human being, not a superman or god who could do no wrong.

On one occasion this same Woodhouse had asked for a further period a week for third and fourth form mathematical teaching, and had been misguided enough to raise the matter with the headmaster's wife. 'Why ask me?' she demanded at once. 'I know nothing of the teaching of maths.'

'Oh, I thought that perhaps you'd be interested enough . . .'

'You argue the case with my husband, Mr Woodhouse. You argue your case with him. He has the advantage of knowing what others on the staff are demanding. They will have their good reasons.'

'I doubt it,' the man growled.

'Even if your suspicions are correct, I can't think that an intervention made from ignorance would be of much use, or would be seriously listened to by my husband. I will, however, tell him that you raised the matter with me and he can draw his own conclusions from that.'

'You think he'll hold it against me, Mrs Stone?'

'I think no such thing. He may well conclude that you are serious enough about this change to mention it to me.'

When she spoke to her husband about this he smiled and shook his head. This was insufficient for Peg. 'Come on, now,' she teased. 'Why would he bother to ask me to intervene?'

'He pays a great deal of attention to what his wife says. And she takes a great deal of interest in the small detail of the teaching of mathematics.'

'Does she know anything about it?'

'Oh, yes. She has a degree in maths.'

16

'Then why doesn't she raise the matter with you?'

'She already has. She cornered me one afternoon while she was waiting for her husband.'

'And put a good case?'

'Oh, yes. Very good. But I'd heard it before from her husband and from the historians and the scientists, all those who have an overladen syllabus to work through. Even geographers like me might have argued thus in my younger days.'

'So she got nowhere?'

'No. But I congratulated her on her advocacy. And said I looked forward to the day when she might consider joining the staff and strengthening her husband's department.'

'Which she did in due course, didn't she?' Peg asked. 'I can never quite remember who's who.'

Now, having ascertained the date and place of Hunter's funeral, but still leaving Woodhouse uncertain whether he'd attend, he came back into the room. Annie Fisher had risen from her armchair and was examining her face in the large ornate mirror over the fireplace.

'Are you all right?' he asked.

'Yes. I think so.'

'Good. I don't like looking in the mirror,' he said, 'even when I'm shaving and have taken my glasses off. I remind myself of a potato about to be put in the oven.'

Annie, still close to the mirror, made no comment on his fancy. Without turning she asked, 'Was that Peg?'

'No. An ex-colleague, Eric Woodhouse, telling me that another colleague had died.'

'Who was that?'

'George Hunter. He taught maths. That's why Woodhouse knew all about him.' The explanation explained nothing.

'Will you go to the funeral?' she asked.

'I'm thinking of it.'

She snatched herself away from the mirror, scuttled her path across the room, hurtled into her chair.

'Something's worrying you,' he pronounced.

'Go on, then. Guess what it is.'

'Illness.' She shook her head.

'Harry,' he said without hesitation. Her husband.

17

'Right in two.'

'Is it serious?'

'Is anything? We shan't die from it, either of us.'

'I see.' Headmasterly now: 'I thought he was teetering on the edge of his retirement.'

'He'll never retire. I remember you telling me about Peg's sister's husband and how the only thing he wanted to do was work. Harry's the same. He's pretty well given up golf except for Sunday afternoon.'

'Another woman?'

'I wish it were. He does like the opposite sex. Except for the first year of our marriage when he couldn't get enough of me; then that tailed off. He looked elsewhere. There was a very nice secretary in his office. She seemed to draw him out of himself. He should have married someone like her.'

'He didn't try to divorce you?'

'No. He would have liked to. But he knew quite well that it would have cost him a great deal more money than he could afford.'

'What happened?'

'Nothing. In the end she'd had enough of waiting, and went off and married somebody else. She's the Lady Mayoress this year.'

'It hit him hard?'

'He walked about for a week or two like a ghost. Not that an outsider would have noticed. I felt sorry for him, but any sort of comfort I could give him wasn't much good. Do you know, while they were carrying on' – she used the vulgar phrase without irony – 'he used to write letters to her. Just imagine. Harry writing letters. And he was careless. He'd leave half-finished scripts lying about; he didn't write very fast.'

'Perhaps he wanted you to find them. A cry for help.'

'Not he. He didn't think I'd be poking about in his pockets and drawers, that I'd plenty to do without that.'

'And had you?'

'Apparently not.' She looked up, piercingly, at him, slapping her flat palms together then pointing with her index fingers straight at his face. 'We don't know each other very well, do we?'

18

'What do you mean?'

'Well, when I used to read things you'd said in the evening paper, I could never quite connect them with the man next door. "Secondary Education Lacks Vision." I could hear your voice saying that, but it didn't connect with the neat man in braces pruning in the next garden with all his tools laid out, who would always clear up after a day's work so that the path and the garden were as spick and span as when he started. I wished I could rush out and ask you, "Is there any vision in gardening?"'

'I can tell you now. There is.'

'Yes.' She sighed, as if despairing of his answer. 'I guess I could tell what you were driving at when you spoke about vision and education. I could, honestly. But you, the man saying it to me, were my neighbour in his braces wheelbarrowing stuff up and down the garden. Does Peg connect the two?'

'I don't think Peg takes anything I say in public too seriously. She knows me too well. She's seen me when I'm ill or down in the mouth, or uncertain of what the next move is. If you asked her about me I guess she'd say I was the sort of man who'd muddle through the next crisis without too much trouble.'

'And would that please you?'

'Yes. I think so. But you're trying to edge us away from our subject. You're worried, Annie. What is it?'

'Nothing. Last Friday I was fifty-six.'

'Were you? Did Peg not send you a card? She has a birthday book so she won't forget. And she'll mention her own birthday to me, because she knows I'll forget it. I've no time for these celebrations, my own least of all.'

'I know how old you are.'

'Go on, then.'

'You'll be sixty-seven in October next year.'

'Well done.'

Two large tears ran on to her cheek. He, appalled, gently took her hand. 'Come on,' he said, 'it's not as bad as all that.'

'To me it is,' she blubbered and buried her face in his coat. Somehow, after slow writhing and testing of positions and kind, awkward touchings they ended up sitting on the carpet, backs against the heavy armchair. She laid her head on his shoulder. 'It's all piling up. All proving too much.'

19

'Such as what?'

'I've found a lump in my breast.'

'When was that?'

'Four weeks ago. After we came back from France.'

'Did you do anything about it?'

'I went to the doctor. And he sent me down to the hospital. That was last week.'

'And they said?'

'They'll send a report in a week. Unless it's very serious.' They sat together, uncomfortable, ungainly. He thought that they looked ridiculous.

'Would you like to see it? Feel . . . ?' Her voice tailed off, but she was already unbuttoning her blouse neatly. She moved herself forward to lift her brassiere from her breasts. 'Here,' she said. 'Here.' The beautiful fingers, unmarked by contact with the soil (she wore gloves for any dirty chore indoors or out), with her nails almond-shaped and deeply red, gently searched her left breast. 'Feel,' she ordered. She took his hand and placed it on the breast.

'Yes,' he said. Relieved yet horrified, he had no difficulty in locating the small lump. He'd expected not to find it, fearing it needed some medical expertise as when a doctor flashed an X-ray at you and you could make nothing of it, though he confidently pointed at some slight variation of tone, some misshape. Stone moved his fingers again and again the object – he raked his head for the word – lay under his fingers, a pea, a small bean, not large, but definite enough not to be trawled for. Now he was at a loss; he did not know his next move. He made neither a further caressing nor a squeezing of the whole roundness of the marred breast. 'Yes,' he said again and withdrew his hand. Immediately she lost her listlessness and became almost militarily sharp. She pulled hard at the bra, which seemed to adjust itself into place at once and her blouse she buttoned as if it were part of a race.

'I'm sorry, darling,' he said and laid a long kiss on her cheek. 'Has the doctor made any suggestion yet?'

'No,' she said. 'Blood tests and X-rays and all the rest, and we'll have results this week.'

'Have you been down to their X-ray clinics fairly regularly?'

'No. I should, I suppose. I've been a time or two.'

'What does Harry say?'

'What can he? One of the good things about me as a wife is that I was no trouble to him. I wasn't often ill, or subject to daft whims. When he was at a loss for something, there I was to provide it. When he was short of something to do I'd come up with ideas, book flights or tickets, or invite people in to see us or make a fuss of people he wanted something from. I saw to the house and garden, and if he was ill I'd put him to bed for a day or two or drive him down to the surgery. Now I'm likely to be ill, he thinks it will be all change.'

'And he won't manage?'

'Yes, he's capable and well organised. He won't like it, but he'll do it.'

'What about you?'

'What can I say?' She let out one of her screeches, if diminished, of laughter. 'I'm not pleased. We don't like change at our age, especially change for the worse.' She scrambled to her feet, making a not very good job of it. He tried to help. In the end both stood, she pulling on her skirt to straighten it.

'I'm sorry, Annie. Don't be afraid to call on me. Or Peg. We'll do all we can.'

'I'm hoping that the news will be good, that the growth, or whatever it is, will be benign and that the surgeons will slip it out without any trouble.'

'God, I hope so.' He scratched at his balding pate. She was now facing him, herself again, normal, unafraid.

'Well, my man,' she said, hooking her arm through his. 'Let's have another look at ourselves.' She led him to the mantelpiece mirror where they stood. Their eyes met, reflected during their scrutiny.

He found his breath coming short although there was nothing unexpected to be seen. Annie, if anything, looked the fitter, her face now comfortably relaxed. He drew back his lips and showed his rather uneven teeth. 'Not too bad,' he commented. He put an arm round her shoulder. She drew into him and he kissed the top of her head. 'I'm sorry,' he said. 'You're a brave woman.'

'We'll see about that,' she said, smiling.

'Let's have a drink?' he suggested.

21

'Steady now. But I wouldn't mind. G and T for me.'

'It'll take me away from this ugly mug.'

'I think it's rather handsome. I always did. I do now.' She riffled the sparse hair on his pate. It seemed very like a preliminary move to a bout of lovemaking. Her unblemished breast pressed into him.

The telephone rang. John Stone saw to it that Annie stood steady before he marched out. He returned in under five minutes. 'Peg,' he told his companion. 'She told me the time she arrives at Newark. I'm to meet her there.'

'May I come with you?'

'Yes, surely. She'll appreciate a welcoming party.' He did not understand her request.

'Has she had a good holiday?'

'Very. They've been active and spent hardly any money. I told her about your trouble.' He pointed stupidly at her breast as if she thought he meant something else. 'She was sorry, but said you're not to worry. They can do marvels these days. May, her sister, had an operation on her breast twelve years ago and now she's right as ninepence.'

'Thanks, John.'

She took him by the finger ends to the tall bay window and there they looked out to the two houses opposite, over the buildings, church towers, factory chimneys, clumps of woodland, the distorted shapes of two parks and across the horizon of low hills losing their solidity in a kind of thinly gilded brown mist. The two stood together, swinging now firmly clasped hands like children. They, speechless, seemed unaware of each other.

'Had Peg any exciting news?'

'Not that I heard.'

'No.'

They were both remembering a similar occasion. They had stood by this window on exactly the same spot and stared at much the same landscape thirty years ago. They had come downstairs from a bout of lovemaking that had left them physically tired but uplifted, at ease with the world. He had felt no guilt. Next day he would address the assemblies of both senior and junior schools, and impress on them the importance of honesty and integrity in their lives as well as their school work, and he would mean what

22

he said, believe it to be true and put aside thoughts that this would hardly tally with that naked, pleasurable adultery. If anything, he concluded, as he left the hall next morning at a commanding pace, his gown flying out behind him, his health, his satisfaction with these sexual delights, made it easier to speak with fervour and impress these clichés on the serious-faced children lined up before him.

And that evening Peg had arrived from holiday, by plane this time from Glasgow, and he had met her at the East Midlands Airport; and as they drove back the few miles to their home she had told him, with a slightly humorous bashfulness, that she was pregnant and that he would have to change his ways. 'You'll not be pampered from this time on,' she warned.

'I expect I'll be able to put up with it,' he said.

'I expect you will, but aren't you pleased?'

'Of course I am.'

'You don't look it.'

'I'm just concentrating on driving my wife and her unborn child safely home. That's enough for me.'

'Oh, John. Don't you ever relax? It's all end-of-the-world to you, isn't it?'

'Yes, now and then. Nothing too bad so far.'

He drove her to the front gate. She refused help up the steps. He put the car into the garage and when he came back with two of her larger cases, which he dragged up to the hall, Peg was not to be seen. He went back to retrieve the rest of the luggage and lock the car away. On his return Peg was out again in the garden talking to Annie Fisher.

'Hello, Father,' the neighbour greeted him. Peg had not been slow with her news. Neither was Annie in her turn when the tests and X-rays showed her to be clear. Women do not hesitate to pass on good news.

III

For the next few days Peg seemed subdued.

Unusually, she was not forthcoming with the cause of her quietness. He guessed, but was by no means sure, that she and May, her sister, had quarrelled.

He tried indirect questions to make matters easier for her, but wasted his time. 'Is she calling in on her way down to London?'

'She didn't mention that at all this time.'

'Is she not well?'

'As fit as ever.'

In the end he was forced to put the question to her. 'You and May haven't quarrelled, have you? Not quite seen eye to eye?'

'Every time I go up there we get seriously at loggerheads at least twice.'

'And what were this year's causes of controversy?'

'"Should Scotland be completely independent?" She's against that.'

'And the other?'

'The new director of the Dramatic Society.'

'Well, surely you've no views about either?'

'That's what she thinks. "It's nothing to do with you," she says. And when I argue that if a majority wants independence that should be the criterion, she flaps her hands and squawks like a mad woman.'

'Why?'

'I think she has her own way all the time and doesn't like being crossed. She's always been a bit that way inclined. I know what's what, what's right, so just you listen to me.'

'Well,' he said slowly, as if judging some plausible yarn from a pupil at school, 'you don't care who's in charge at the theatre. She never appears now, hasn't done so for years, so it's not a matter of life and death.'

24

'She wants me to argue. That's part of the beauty of my visits. I tell her she's wrong. She doesn't like it. We both are ratty, or sulky, and gradually, or quickly even, get over it.'

'But this time you haven't?'

'Haven't what?'

'Got over it,' he answered.

'It's not that at all. She's acting ridiculously. She says she's being pursued. Sexually.'

'Happens to many of us. Even those of riper years.'

'Don't you start.'

He dug into his lower lip with his teeth, his expression mischievous. 'Come on, then,' he encouraged. 'Who is he? Let's hear why he's so unsuitable.'

'I haven't said that.'

He did not answer for a moment. 'Let me guess,' he began. 'He's a toyboy. Twenty-three years old. With rippling biceps. Handsome as a Greek statue of Apollo. And moreover he's a conman to whom she's already lent fifty thousand pounds to start a business, which wouldn't make a ha'penny worth of profit even if a real, hard, experienced entrepreneur tried to run it properly. Whereas this man's bone idle, drinks too much, has played havoc with the local lassies . . .'

She held up her hand and he obeyed. 'Stop acting the brainless wonder,' she said. He removed his half-moon spectacles and polished them delicately on a silk handkerchief. 'It's worse if anything than that. He's a widower, a year or two older than she is. Moreover, he's religious.'

'Does he live far away from her?'

'A mile and a half.'

'And she's known him for some time? While his wife was alive, for instance?'

'Yes. All that. They were acquaintances. But it's only since the beginning of this year that he's shown any sort of close interest in her.'

'It's a phenomenon of the millennium, is it?'

She answered that with a grimace of sourness.

'How did he first demonstrate this new interest?' he asked.

'He began calling in. He'd never done that before. On various pretexts. He was going to Glasgow; could he do any errand for

25

her there? Then he'd call in without an excuse; he was just passing.'

'And how did she feel about these visits?'

'She says, and I don't know whether this is true, she wondered if somebody at the kirk had said that she was a bit worried about Mrs MacGregor, all on her own, and if it would be a Christian act to keep an eye on her. That's not uncommon, she says.'

'May's no sort of churchgoer, is she?'

'She'll go for the high days and holidays, Christmas, Easter, Harvest and so forth, and though the minister and the ladies' meeting have tried hard enough to get her to attend more regularly, they've had no success. She'll support good causes and concerts and fêtes, but that's all.'

'But some of her friends are regular members of the kirk?' He rattled his 'r's.

'Oh, yes.'

They paused. Peg seemed to be eyeing him suspiciously.

'Have you seen him?'

'Yes.'

'Well, come on, then. What's his name? What's he look like? What does he do for a living?'

'I might be wrong, John. When I just got there and she told me about him it seemed a bit of a joke. Some grim, unsuitable widower making his awkward advances. By the end of my time there, four weeks, I was beginning to take him seriously.'

'And was she the happier for it?' he asked, headmasterly.

'That's what I'm not sure about. You know what May's like. But one day she's counting the advantages of having a companion, the next she's doing her nut whether he's the right man.'

'Is she sixty yet?'

'Later this year. And he's sixty-eight, but fit.'

'What's his name?'

'Ronald Murray. He's a widower and a retired solicitor. He still will do a bit of paid legal work from time to time, but he does the kirk's accounts and keeps it all in good order.'

'Did you like him?' he asked.

'Not really. He's a bit grim. He's not as tall as you, but thickset. He's very dark, as if he needs to shave about three times a day. But he's a full head of hair and, though it's black, it's not turned yet. There are streaks of grey in it. And he parts it high up and very straight, and keeps it oiled. He dresses in black and his shoes have thick soles. He's originally from one of the islands and he speaks Gaelic, but his English is educated Edinburgh. After university he practised there for nearly thirty years. Then his wife, who came from those parts, was taken ill, and he moved up there for her health and took over his wife's uncle's practice. The uncle was old and wanted to retire, and so was pleased when his nephew-in-law bought him out. He did well, his wife's health improved and all was going swimmingly – they'd settled there about three years – when his wife was ill again and died in hospital, not long before Ian.'

'And did he make no moves towards remarriage?'

'Not that I know. They say he grieved deeply, but worked all the harder. He quite liked it there and it suited his health. He's plenty to occupy him.'

'What do the locals make of him?'

'Pretty well regarded, as far I, or May, can make out. He's judged as a properly serious man. A bit of a heavyweight. Not the sort you'd want to sit down with for a bit of scandal and a dram.'

'Does he drink?'

'Not to the best of my knowledge.'

Stone rubbed his chin. 'Has he either proposed marriage or made sexual advances, however slight, in her direction?'

'No to the first. Hints of a sort. Nothing plain. He doesn't want to look a fool. As to the second, I can barely imagine it.'

'Never mind your imagination. Has he?'

'No,' she snapped at him.

He stroked his balding pate with the finger ends of his right hand. 'But', he said, 'you think May is genuinely troubled?'

'Yes. I caught her crying in her bedroom. It shocked me. You know her. She can keep a stony face if she so wishes.'

'And it was about this Murray business? You're sure of that? It wasn't bad news she'd had? About some medical matter? Or her son?'

'No. I put it to her as plainly as you would to me.'

'Did she seem different? In herself? More nervous, for example.'

27

'Not for a start. If I'd stayed only a few days I don't think I'd have noticed any differences in her. But as time went on and she began to tell me about this Ronald Murray, I could see she was rattled.' Peg had hesitated on her last word.

'You'd not met him until this time?'

'Once. In the market. She introduced us, formally. He stopped for a few minutes' chat. Both said they'd go to a concert on the Saturday. But when he'd gone May seemed to have lost her nerve. She was trembling, shaking all over, you could see it. She grabbed my hand and held it like a frightened child.'

'Had he seemed threatening in any way?'

'Not at all. A well-spoken, polite man. And I looked him over carefully because she'd begun to tell me the story by this time. Again, I was shaken, because I had thought we'd be having a giggle together. She seemed shell-shocked.'

'Well, Peg,' John Stone said. 'If she took up with this man, it will mean a considerable change. She was married to Ian for very nearly twenty years. Then she's been a successful widow for ten years or thereabouts, so it's no wonder she feels qualms at the thoughts of another alteration.'

'When she comes here, will you talk to her, John?'

'If she wants me to. I find it all as puzzling as you do. But I'll tell her to be careful. That's my sole advice these days. To everybody.'

He and Peg made love that night, to the satisfaction of both.

When May arrived three or four days later, John Stone kept a close eye on her, though he had to admit to himself that she seemed exactly as she had always appeared. The trembling woman in the market place had gone. The voice was strong; any answers she gave to his questions were quick and assured. She insisted that they went to see a film they certainly would not have chosen for themselves. It concerned a stalker who for months harassed a rich widow in New York. Neither friends, lawyers nor police made any attempts to advise or protect her; they seemed to write her off as a nervous case; they recommended good doctors or psychotherapists. After terrifying scenes in dark, rain-drenched, dripping alleys, the upper floors of an almost deserted art gallery and once or twice in her own huge home, with its mirrors and threatening stairways and lights more conducive to darkness, all

28

put together competently enough, the film ended with both victim and stalker dead.

'I'm glad to get out of that lot,' Peg confessed on the steps of the triple cinema. 'Did it frighten you, May?'

'No,' her sister answered. 'It's all too far-fetched. Dark trees and towering furniture, and huge, horrible pictures. It's wasted on me. Why don't they put it in more ordinary scenery, offices, or factories, or out-of-door workplaces or suburban homes with ponds and greenhouses, and leave it to the actors to make the impression or terrify their audience? They should be able to demonstrate evil, horror or their fear on their faces or in their voices, by body language.'

'Those Gothic backgrounds add to the effect,' Peg argued. 'Moping owls and ivy-mantled towers.'

'Not with me, they don't.'

'Did you think the woman was terrified for good reason?'

'Well, the man obviously meant to do her harm.'

'Why?' Peg asked.

'Presumably because she ignored him or rejected him. He said so.'

'Love had turned to hate?' Peg mused.

May seemed not at all put out by the film, only rather sorry that she had dragged her relatives to a poor night's entertainment.

'Not my sort of picture,' John pronounced.

'What do you like?' May asked.

'Gilbert and Sullivan,' Peg answered for him. 'Why did you choose that stuff? Did you know what it was about?'

'Of course. It's been reviewed in all our papers, far distant from civilisation as we are. I take it it frightened you both.'

John nodded.

As he and his wife were undressing for bed that night she asked, 'Don't you think she got us to go to the cinema to see that film for some reason? She might have thought she could pick up some tips on how to avoid Murray? Or to suggest to us what a dreadful ordeal she's going through?'

'Her behaviour didn't suggest that. She didn't seem upset by it. If anything, we yokels surprised her because we were disturbed by what we saw.'

'She thinks we're unsophisticated?'

'She may well. You think she's changed her mind about this man? As a possible suitor?'

Each morning Peg, up early, sorted through the post to see if there was anything from Ronald Murray. Every morning before she took the mail – very little – in to May with her morning cup of tea, she allowed John to examine with her the two or three letters in handwriting they did not recognise. They searched without success.

'He's in no hurry,' Peg grumbled.

'He's a lawyer. Won't put more on paper than's necessary.'

'You don't understand her, do you?' his wife pressed.

'No. Neither one way nor another. I can't quite subscribe to your theory that she's afraid of this Murray, or has for some reason begun to resent his intrusions. She seems steady enough in herself, and pressed us to see that film because her local papers had praised it and caught her interest.'

That evening over dinner Peg, in character, introduced the topic of May's suitor. 'Have you heard anything from that young man of yours?'

'No. Not that I expected to.'

'Patient, is he?' John asked, clearing away the dishes from the course.

'This wife of yours is willing on to me', May said, 'a husband, a Scots lawyer all in black, very, very quiet, laconic.' She spoke as one newly introduced to an interesting topic.

'Do you mean,' John said, temporarily replacing the dishes on the surface of the table as if the discussion weighed more importantly with him than the clearing of crockery, 'she's making it all up, or is there an element of truth in it?'

'Well, the man Ronald Murray certainly exists.'

'But he neither cares for you, nor you for him.'

'That's about it.'

Peg, bringing in the pudding, stood listening, her face amazed. In the ordinary way she'd have ordered her husband out with his first course dishes, telling him to get a move on with it. Not tonight. She waited, listening, but could not refrain from comment. 'You can see he's keen on you,' she said.

'You can see it,' May answered. 'I can't.'

'If you changed your mind and decided to marry him, would it make a great deal of difference to your lifestyle?' he asked.

30

'Of course it would. We should have to argue which house to
live in, his or mine. That would raise obstacles, because I've no
intention of moving out of mine. And I guess he might feel the
same. His house is much older, more interesting to historians and
antiquaries, but is less comfortable and convenient than mine.'

'I see. And you'd both be stubborn?' from Stone.

'I would, certainly.' She glanced winsomely at him. 'And
besides, he'd be in the house, under my feet, seven days a week.'

'He'd take you to the kirk every Sunday,' Peg muttered.

'Yes. That's another thing.'

Little more was said that evening and at the end of the week
May set off for the south. Her plan was to stay two or three days
in Farnborough with an old college friend, a widow like herself,
then move to London where she would take up residence in a
bed-and-breakfast house within walking distance of her son's flat.
He had the space to put her up if either of them had wanted it,
but both declined. She got on well with her son, was proud of
him. John James MacGregor, her only child, had attended
Edinburgh University, then accepted a position in a bank in
London where he appeared to be doing particularly well. Now,
at only twenty-six, he earned a staggering wage and had taken,
to the surprise of his relatives, a live-in partner, a girl older than
he by some years, who worked like him at the bank and made
an even more extravagant salary. This change of life had happened
only in the last few months, so that May had not yet seen the
new partner.

'So you've no idea what she's like?' John had asked. He and
his sister-in-law were making an inspection of the garden and were
at that moment standing in the greenhouse gathering the last of
the tomato crop.

'No. They seem happy enough. Not that I hear from her at all.
JJ says she's very good indeed at her job, earns bonuses that are
beyond belief. But she's a good cook and, like him, interested in
the theatre and music. Not that they go out together very often;
they're too busy.'

'Are you pleased?'

'Well, yes, in an ignorant sort of way. They don't approach it
as we would in our day. There's no talk of marriage or engagement. They live together, that means sleep together from the word

go. That surprised me as Johnny had never seemed very interested in girls. He was shy. He'd always seemed too keen on his work at school, at university and then dealing with his banker's exams. He did outstandingly well at all of them. But perhaps because he's doing well and earning so much it's given him confidence.'

'Had she her own flat?'

'Oh, yes. She's let it out. Just in this last week there's been a hint that they're thinking of moving into a house. They're making so much money they could afford to buy some huge manor house or ex-vicarage right outside London in the country. That's what these financial high flyers do in due course. JJ doesn't think they'll manage it for a year or two. When they're certain vis-à-vis each other, that is, when they've lived together long enough, and have enough money coming in to keep up their standard of living after Linda has had and reared a child, then they might choose the house for life. That's JJ's expression. In some ways, she says, in his letters he's that well-scrubbed, get-nothing-wrong sixth-former of a few years ago.'

'So she's pleased with developments on that front?' Stone asked.

'Yes.' Puzzled. The thought of her JJ having sexual intercourse, never mind illicit, seems almost against the laws of nature.

They did not expect to receive any further news from May once she'd moved southwards. There'd be one postcard, Trafalgar Square, the Albert Memorial, an equestrian statue picked at random, with a note on the weather and a coded message – 'I am enjoying all of it' – meaning that she had so far not come across anything radically out of order. Peg could hardly believe her sister's change of mind.

On the morning of the arrival of the solitary postcard Peg was surprised to receive a phone call from Ronald Murray. He enquired after the health of Mary – no endearing shortening of name for him – and seemed surprised to learn that she was not there. Peg explained her sister's route and mischievously invited Murray to lunch the next day. He was over, he had told her, for some legal conference as well as for a visit to relatives he had not seen for twenty-odd years who lived in Leicester.

'Do you think he'd laid all this on so that he could call in here on May?' John Stone asked.

32

'I wouldn't be surprised. I never heard of him attending legal conferences; he's retired. And the sort he'd attend would surely be in Scotland. Isn't their law different from ours? And as to this cousin in Leicester, well, twenty years is a long time. It seems a coincidence.'

'Do you think May will be annoyed with him?'

'Don't know. But I thought if I invited him over here to lunch we might find out what he's doing and why he's *persona non grata* with her. He made no bones about accepting, I can tell you. I thought he'd say perhaps that there were so many lectures and seminars he had to attend that it would be impossible to find a free couple of hours in the middle of the day.'

'Where's this conference held?' John asked.

'At the university, I think.'

They discussed the visit all that evening, not without uneasy hilarity. They decided he'd eat plainly, not requiring piquant sauces nor flimsy puddings. He was due to arrive at eleven and eat at one. Peg and Mrs Sims, her home help, polished away at the main drawing room as well as the downstairs loo, from the floor of which any visitor could have eaten his meal without compunction.

'How's he getting here?' John asked.

'Taxi, from the university.'

'Not walking, then. Saving a bawbee or two?'

'None of that when he comes.'

'I shall be as good as gold,' Stone said, 'and silent as the grave. But I shall expect you to pump him dry.'

Murray's taxi drew up and Stone, neatly camouflaged among the furniture, saw the visitor making his solemn way up the drive in black overcoat and trilby hat.

Peg was at the front door in no time and was soaring into welcome. 'Ah, Mr Murray, how are you? You found us without too much difficulty. This is my husband. John Stone. Ronald Murray.' The two men shook hands. Murray's hands were cold. Stone helped him off with his overcoat and walked away with the outdoor clothes. When he returned from the cloakroom he found the other two seated in the main drawing room and Peg badgering the visitor about tea or coffee. He chose milkless tea, crossed his legs and waved his shining shoes in the air.

'You're at some sort of conference here, I believe?' Stone began politely.

'Yes. Very interesting. It's about illegal claiming of benefit for unemployment or sickness.' He waved a hand towards Stone. 'Disability.' He smacked his lips.

'Is there much cheating going on?'

'More than there should be,' Murray's voice snapped.

'And you are thinking of methods of preventing this?'

'Yes. And yet not making it too difficult for genuine claimants to write an application.'

Stone placed the visitor so that both he and Peg would be able to see that dark face. Murray sat not uncomfortably but not exactly at ease. He would suddenly heave his strong body into a different position, flinging one thick leg over the other. He wore grey socks, a touch lighter in tone than his trousers. He seemed in no sort of holiday guise; this not particularly well-cut suit would have been acceptable at a kirk service, or a funeral, or in his office, or in court. When he moved in his chair his host expected him to groan, though he did not.

'Are you enjoying yourself here in these southern parts?' John Stone asked.

'Well, the course is pretty concentrated. It's meant for professionals. Lectures mornings and afternoons, and what you might call practice in the evenings before dinner, which is at seven thirty, so there's little time to go into town for theatres or concerts.'

'And does this suit you?'

'I get my money's worth. If I want to know about something I want to know it thoroughly. When I retired I determined that I wouldn't let my knowledge of the law perish to nothing. I've done a correspondence course or two in the winter months. When the weather's decent in spring I attend university postgraduate courses in Edinburgh where I worked for many years, or Glasgow. And I've done a bit of locum work in our district for my own old partners and for firms that are afflicted by illness. I was surprised last year at the number so diminished. In my young days in Edinburgh we seemed made up of exceptionally healthy men and women.'

'Is there any reason for the discrepancy?'

'No. Not that I am aware of. I wondered if it were age difference or women who had maternity leave. I took over from an old relative of my wife. He was glad to sell out to me, because he was too ill to travel about, and lost thereby both interest and clients. I had to build up the practice considerably. It's large now, with three separate offices. I have virtually retired.'

'Good.'

'You were connected, I believe, with education?' Murray asked.

'Yes. I was a headmaster.'

At this moment Peg busily returned with his black tea, their milky coffee and a plate of delicious small cakes. Murray was tempted into choosing one of these.

'Don't let me interrupt your manly exchanges,' Peg called out as she finally served them.

'We were each just telling the other how we earned our living,' Murray said.

'You weren't boasting?' Peg asked.

'I expect so,' Murray answered, nodding. 'This tea is delicious.'

'I made it a little stronger than we like it. We're not real tea drinkers.'

They all sipped as if to test the brew, their faces studies in mild embarrassment.

'I'm sorry that May isn't here to meet you,' Stone said.

'I was not exactly sure of the dates of her stay.'

'She perhaps didn't know herself,' Peg said. 'She's often very vague.'

Stone, face more genial now, explained where and how May was spending her time in England. 'At present she's with her son in London,' he concluded.

'Not exactly,' Peg corrected. 'She lives some little distance away in a small private hotel.'

'His flat is not very spacious?' Murray enquired mildly.

'He has a live-in partner.'

'A man?'

'No. A woman.' She stared him out and he dropped his eyes. The next two or three minutes were spent in silent drinking.

Suddenly Peg spoke. 'You disapprove?' she asked.

'Disapprove? Of what?'

'Of a man living with a woman to whom he is not married.'

'I would not do it myself. No. But it is common enough in our parts of the earth. As frequently practised as here.'

Stone laughed and tried to disguise it with a cough.

Murray looked at him with furious dismay. 'Of course one can be serious about the commitment,' he said, his accent more Scottish, 'whether one has gone through a church or a register office ceremony. But such serious people are not many, from my observation.'

'So if you were to think of living with an attractive lady, you would only do so if you were to marry her?' Stone seemed mischievous.

'It's not likely at my time of life, but yes.'

'I often think that people who marry late in life have more trouble,' Peg said. 'They've got into habits which they find difficult to change.'

'My wife was a Highland girl and didn't like the city. She went to university, Aberdeen, but she never felt at ease in towns. She really lived out of the way. But in Scotland it wasn't nearly such a drawback educationally as it would have been in England. I'm not saying she didn't find herself a useful role in Edinburgh. She did herself, and me, proud, but I always knew that she'd like to live out of the city, so that when Uncle Robert began signalling warnings of retirement, she made it clear that I could please her by moving up there.'

'And you were willing to do so? Without a murmur?' Peg asked.

'It was a curious time for me. I was just over fifty, a senior partner in the firm, making a good living. Alasdair, my son, was out of the way just finishing his Ph.D. When I looked about, life seemed all straightforward. Another ten or fifteen years and then my own retirement. I'd be occupied well enough, but at the same sort of work. If we moved up to Tulloch I knew quite well I'd have to shift myself to get Robert's firm in order. But Elsie would be where she wanted to be and I always relished a challenge. That's a cliché nowadays and one I dislike. But I've always been a worker, and I was still active and healthy. It didn't turn out exactly as I envisaged, unfortunately. Three years after we arrived Elsie was dead.'

'I'm sorry.' The pair made sympathetic noises. Peg filled his second cup from her silver teapot. They talked for a few moments about trivialities, the weather, the delivery of sermons (Murray was the only expert), the regularity of break-ins in out-of-the-way Scotland. Murray seemed to enjoy the conversation, became loquacious. Peg suggested that Stone should drive Mr Murray around so he'd have some idea of Beechnall, while she completed preparations for lunch.

IV

Stone drove his guest into town where they dawdled in the thick traffic near the Council House, the great church of St Mary, the castle.

'It's more like a town house of some nobleman,' Ronald Murray commented.

'Yes. That's exactly what it is. The medieval castle was damaged in the Civil War, then pulled down and this place built, and later partly burnt by Luddites in the early nineteenth century. This' – he waved his hand towards the gateway – 'is one of the few medieval bits left.'

'I see. This is built on the site of the earlier fortresses.'

'That's so. This side of the city was Norman, while the other side was Anglo-Saxon. That was defended by a hill and marshes by a river, this by a cliff, which we'll see shortly.'

Murray cross-examined his host closely about the growth and development of Beechnall. They found a place to park and marched into the castle grounds, and from the hill stared over the factories, hospitals, streets, railway and canal.

'A prosperous place,' the visitor concluded.

'Too many high-rise buildings,' Stone said.

'I agree. I don't deny their usefulness and their extremely economical use of land. But the concrete architects never seemed to master their aesthetic problems. Size, utility and window space were their aims.'

'When I was at school,' Stone said, 'I was taught, wrongly, that London would never have the skyscrapers of New York. The nature of the land was wrong, incapable of bearing such weight. But while my old geography master was spelling this out to me the architects had already mastered the problem with their concrete rafts.'

'You schoolmasters have a good deal to answer for, stuffing

38

children's heads with all sorts of rubbish. I remember the senior science teacher at my school telling us that man would never set foot on the moon because the initial velocity required to land there would be so great that travelling through the earth's atmosphere would burn the rocket away.'

Murray was now in full flow about the intelligence of *Homo sapiens*. This, Stone decided, is what the man wanted: to stand and talk. Or rather, walk and talk, for every few minutes he'd march away, ten or fifteen yards to his right without a word of apology to his companion, without checking the spate of talk, and when he reached the new point of vantage he'd stare hungrily out, yet extend his narrative or his polemics without a break in his lawyer's voice. Jack Stone felt delight. He was now giving Murray exactly what he enjoyed: a sympathetic ear and a townscape that was stimulating enough to suggest subjects he wished to dilate on. He followed his companion round and at each new view point would wait for the next pause, deliberately made, in Murray's monologue, then briefly name and newly appraise aspects of the city. Murray would listen, nodding thanks for the information, then continue his own line of argument exactly where he left off or set out on a new trail of reasoning, perhaps suggested by Stone's brief commentary. At the end of the tour of two sides of the castle they stopped and Stone pointed out the university in the distance and, nearer at the bottom of the park, the street where he had his first flat when he came originally to Beechnall, where Lucy, his first-born, was conceived. She died at three months. It was in a squat Victorian tower at the end of a dull brick terrace, nothing very spectacular aesthetically, but the architect who planned this became famous within a few years with buildings that were strong, strutting, athletically Gothic, striking. But here he'd learnt how to make brick walls stand straight and kept time at bay.

While Stone was explaining this, his first speech of any length for half an hour, Murray pushed back his sleeve, glared at his wristwatch hidden under the cuffs of topcoat, jacket, cardigan and shirt, and exclaimed, 'Look at the time. How long will it take us to get back? I'd hate to ruin Mrs Stone's plans for luncheon.'

'She's not one to create a fuss over five minutes.'

'But the lunch?'

'If it's spoilt because of our lateness it will be our own fault. But I don't think it will be so. Peg knows what traffic's like and can hold a meal back for a few minutes.'

'My wife, who was of a nervous type, used to become very uptight if guests were late for a meal.'

'Depends how late. Peg'll blast us if we're half an hour out. We shall be five minutes behind time, if we hurry.' Both men were breathing hard, not relaxing the pace.

They took possession of the car, warm with September sunshine. Once they were seated and away, Murray retrieved his breath and began this time a speech about Scottish nationalism, which he disliked. 'It's not as if we're prevented from doing particular Scots acts or performances, or from carrying out traditions that we wish to put our hearts or brains to.'

'I thought it was extremely popular with most people.'

'So it is; so it is. At one time there were those who thought we should be so wildly rich from North Sea oil.'

'You are, aren't you?'

'Oh, yes. But not as wealthy as if the whole of the income, the taxes, came solely to us rather than London. Some claimed we should be independent and join the European Union as a separate country. Look at Eire, the Irish Republic, they argue, and how prosperous it is.'

'But you still don't want to break loose from the old oppressor.'

'That's right.' Now he outlined the advantages of co-operation. Britain's Premier was a Scot, so was the Chancellor of the Exchequer, so was the Secretary of State for Foreign Affairs.

'That makes you feel anger?' Stone asked sarcastically.

'A Scottish education has many advantages.'

He settled to outline them, but favourable traffic lights did not give him time to conclude. As they entered the front door Peg congratulated them on their prompt arrival.

'Ah, Mr Murray insisted that we shouldn't be late.'

'Have you enjoyed your morning out?' she asked her guest.

'I have not been so happy, so engrossed, for many, many years.'

'Goodness, what have the pair of you been up to?'

'I have talked your husband to death. He is the most carefully sympathetic listener I've ever met. Whatever subject I

40

chose he listened as if he had selected it for his own peculiar delight.'

Peg ordered Murray upstairs to wash his hands and prepare for lunch. 'You'll find a towel,' she said. 'Green with a Maltese cross.' As soon as Murray was out of earshot she dragged her husband into the kitchen. 'Have you been drinking?' she demanded.

'Not a drop.' He breathed in her direction. 'Most of the time we spent up on the castle, from where he looked the city over and harangued me.'

'About what?'

'Anything from Free Scotland to the Kingdom of Heaven.'

'Did he mention May?'

'No.' Stone laughed at her small puff of exasperation. 'If all is well I shall raise the matter over lunch. Then you'll have no cause for complaint. You'll hear it, if there's anything to hear, in his own words and there'll be no exaggeration or misunderstanding on my part.' He laughed, swilling his hands at the kitchen sink.

They started lunch and found their guest a slowish but appreciative eater. In the initial moments before the soup Murray sat, solemn as a judge, without any audience as Stone helped his wife carry the food in. When they had finished the soup, Peg asked her guest if he'd like more.

'I would, I would, but that would be greed on my part.'

'Never mind the greed. John, take Mr Murray's plate out with yours and refill them. Use a tray, won't you, dear?'

'A pleasure,' Stone said.

'I think you should call me Ronald,' Murray suggested.

'Thank you. And I'm Peg, that's for Margaret, and he's Jack.'

'For John.'

Peg pointed her husband kitchenwards for the soup. All three were laughing.

'He's a comic, isn't he?' Peg whispered.

'I don't know whether he means to be. He's very solemn. I don't know if that will suit May.'

'Different from the last.'

Once they were engaged on the main course, specially sought Scottish beef, Murray suddenly stopped and looked directly at Peg. 'I wonder, Peg' – he used the name awkwardly, mumbling it – 'if it had struck you that I was in any way interested in your sister.'

'How particularly?'

Murray scratched his cheek. 'As something closer than a friend, if you understand me.'

'She did say that you called in, or had begun to call in, rather regularly.'

'That is true. Did she mind?'

'She didn't say so.'

'Did she put any sort of interpretation on it?' Murray asked.

'She did wonder if the kirk had delegated you to check up that she was all right. On her own. I know it's getting on for ten years since Ian died, but she guessed that somebody had said something and that in the end you'd been sent as an envoy . . .'

'"A nuncio of more grave aspect",' Stone quoted.

'Oh, shut up, you. Sent to see if she was all right. They know she travels about in the brighter weather, as I do, but perhaps they thought it to her advantage to become more closely involved with the kirk.'

'No. I think the kirk elders in such a case would have sent a lady, or ladies, to visit Mrs MacGregor. I'm almost certain that such embassies were established and the minister himself would visit in the months after her husband's death.'

'But without effect?' Stone asked.

'That seems so. They were politely received, as one would expect, but Mrs MacGregor made her position clear. She would attend church on feast days. She held Anglican Christian beliefs, but she did not feel the need for weekly worship. She was, as I say, both polite and hospitable, but absolutely certain in her mind about how she intended to live. They, and this includes the minister, were, if anything, rather intimidated by her.'

'I can imagine that. May can put her high hat on if she's so minded,' Peg said.

'You call her "May". Isn't her name Mary?'

'Right both times,' Stone said.

'It's what my father used to call her. Our mother's name was also Mary.'

They resumed full-time concentration on the beef, but with a slightly fevered air. It was Stone, the first to finish, who resumed the cross-examination. To his credit he waited until Murray had cleared his plate, thanked and congratulated his hostess, but refused a second helping.

'So,' John Stone began, 'you visited May of your own volition?'

'Yes,' Murray replied, as a man who had eaten well. 'You may say so.' He stopped as if to terminate the conversation, but Stone quietly took up the questioning again. Peg continued eating daintily, but with ears alert.

'You must,' Stone said, 'have looked at May in the interim between the end of the official church visits and your first call on your own behalf.'

Murray nodded, eyebrows raised, but said nothing, perhaps to discourage further discussion. Peg finished eating and said, dabbing her lips with a table napkin, 'Did she show a reciprocal interest?' That sounded vaguely legal.

'It is a long period since her husband died. Six or seven years.'

'Ten,' Peg corrected.

'As much as that?' Murray sighed, seemed disheartened. 'The visitations from kirk members continued, but I was asked to play no part in them. I spoke to her, I must have done, at services and meetings and concerts, and I suppose I admired her. As one does. She seemed different from the others. I put it down to her Englishness. But it went no further.'

'Did you see her in plays at the Dramatic Society?'

'Once or twice. I remember her as a mother in a Christopher Fry play *The Lady's Not for Burning*. She was admirably suited. She has a beautifully modulated voice.'

'You do Fry in your Dramatic Society?' Stone asked.

'Yes. It depends on the committee. And Mrs MacGregor was not the only English person.' He spoke as if they had affronted him for parochialism.

'But.' Stone overdid the emphasis so that it sounded as much like indigestion as encouragement.

'It wasn't until something about six months ago, in spring, I was walking my dog along the shore of the loch when I met her. She was sitting on one of the seats that our local councillors had provided, reading.'

'What?' Peg asked.

'I can't remember. I ought to. It was a library book. We have

43

a really creditable library, with a mobile department. I am on the committee. But, no, I can't recall the title. I stopped to pass the time of day and we exchanged a few words, when my dog ran up to her. She made a fuss of him, asked me his name and so on. I enquired if she was fond of dogs and she said, "Not particularly." We talked on and she said that on a morning like this she, given full choice, would be nowhere else on earth. I looked her straight in the eyes and said, "That is exactly right." The English voice, the sincerity, integrity of it perhaps, impressed me at once. I shan't forget it. She told me she was going to the South of France on the next day, to Biarritz.'

'She'd be going to stay with Bunty Hardinge,' Peg annotated.

'Oh. But she said she did not want to go. "Why leave perfection behind?" she asked. I agreed. We talked for perhaps a quarter of an hour and I began to feel, let us say, drawn to her, attracted. It was as if I didn't want, didn't mean, to leave her. Had we been in Edinburgh I would have invited her to a coffee shop, but here we were miles from anywhere.'

'You could have sat down on the seat with her,' Peg said.

'Yes, I could. But I did not know whether this feeling of affinity was shared. For all I knew she had exchanged a few words, as expected, with someone she knew slightly. I did not want to force my company on her. We talked, friendly enough, and then I said I must go. I did mention that I was going in the direction of her home, but she made nothing of that. I left her alone.'

'Yes,' Jack Stone said, 'it's difficult.'

'It is. I am sixty-seven years old and yet I was as shy as I was at seven, or seventeen for that matter.'

'And then you started to visit her?' Stone asked.

'Not immediately. I thought it over, before I paid my first visit. I found an excuse. We were arranging three or four days in Edinburgh at the beginning of the Festival. Her name was not on the list. I asked if she would like to be included. She declined, saying that you, her sister, would be staying and that you had already booked tickets for that week.'

'Did she seem pleased to see you?'

'As always. Very polite. Provided me with coffee. Said she'd enjoyed our talk. Thanked me for the trouble I'd taken. I said I'd call in again if an opportunity presented itself and she said she'd be glad to see me.'

Peg and her husband took out the dishes and brought in rice pudding, thick with raisins and sultanas.

'Cream or ice cream?' she asked Murray.

'You're like your sister. You bowl me over. I'm not used to such luxury.'

'Have both,' Stone advised.

'I couldn't.'

'You could. I shall.'

'Let Ronald choose for himself. He's a dreadful bully, like all schoolmasters.'

Murray took cream and began immediately to talk of May. The pair of them had got on well. They had much in common. He particularly remembered an animated discussion of Shaw's play, *The Doctor's Dilemma*.

'I don't like his politics, but his style is brilliant. Nowadays we never hear or see his work examined by the young men who write our critical columns. And this annoys her because she admires his plays.'

'He lacks feeling,' Stone said.

'I'm not sure of that. What about *St Joan*?'

'Shaw and his wife drew up a marriage contract,' Peg said, settling to her pudding. 'And one of the clauses was that they should eschew sexual intercourse.'

'I did not know that,' Murray answered. His dark face had become pale. Peg's frank speech seemed to have put an end to the exploration of May's reactions to the frequent visits of her suitor. Stone had also had enough and was glad to give his full attention to his two helpings of rice pudding and cream.

The hosts settled Murray in the main drawing room and took their time making coffee. When Stone carried the tray in, they found their guest fast asleep in his chair, breathing heavily, glasses down his nose. He awoke, startled, scared even, full of apologies. He talked. Peg led Murray to the window, to point out places of interest. As at the castle, this set the man to talk at length, all sleep gone from his eyes. He spoke about American painting and said how interested he had been to find out that in that wild country in the seventeenth century painters worked as if back at

45

home in the academies of Europe. Stone did not understand this. Artists would employ the methods and styles they had been taught, even if the landscapes were wildly different and the natives howling a mile or two away. American painting led him to American language, mores, business, politics.

'How long will it be before people call this world language American?' Stone asked in one of the rare pauses for breath.

'Would you mind if they did?' Murray retorted.

'I suppose I wouldn't. The change would come gradually and by the time it was a fait accompli I'd be used to it.'

Murray left the house soon after five so that he'd be back, bathed and shaved, in time for dinner at six thirty and a lecture on the morals and economics of giving government benefits to people who did not want to work or who could not earn as much from the jobs they were capable of as from their unemployment pay.

'Isn't that what you've been talking about all week?' Stone asked.

'No. We've been examining the everyday rules, the legal principles of the present system. Tonight's the free-for-all. I expect we shall find a few "If they won't work, let 'em starve" clients voicing their prejudices. Thus far we've been finding out the snags in making the existing system work as efficiently as possible. You soon find out that the legal draughtsmen haven't considered all the possibilities and so all sorts of amendments, orders in council, even extra and lengthy legislation need to be added. You see the politicians have to bear in mind whether the laws will make them popular or ruin their chances at the next election. You'd be surprised. And the media have a great influence on the way people think.'

'I have never found,' Stone said, 'any newspaper reported anything I know anything about which is anywhere near entirely accurate. When I was teaching, reporters often came for my views on some matter under public discussion and I'd do my best for them. I spoke clearly and slowly for them. They're so dependent on machines now they can't take shorthand. But when these reports appeared they almost always misrepresented what I said. Sometimes they did it because they didn't know the background and so misinterpreted what I meant, but sometimes they twisted my views to make them more interesting to their readers. I don't suppose what I had to say altered the circulation of the paper by very much, but they get into, or are trained into, bad habits.'

Murray was off at once, after this interregnum of silence on his part, on the importance of accuracy of legal reports in the broadsheets, which were used until cases were officially printed. Even so, errors occurred.

Stone drove him back to the university where he made a rapid, elbow-shaking disappearance into the hall of residence, having completed a disquisition on the advantages and disadvantages of brick over stone in domestic buildings. There seemed nothing he was not prepared to pontificate on.

When Stone reached home Peg sat before a large jigsaw puzzle waiting for him. 'I'm still deaf,' she said. 'He never stops. It would be awful to have him jabbering at you in the car.'

'He's a bit overwhelming, but he's often interesting. He's read so much, and is so certain of himself and his views. I don't know whether he's right or not.'

The telephone rang. Peg went off to answer. Fifteen minutes later she came in, comically staggering. 'Guess who,' she ordered. 'His nibs. Ronald Murray. He was just ringing to make sure that he had not misled us.'

'About his love for May?' Stone asked histrionically.

'No, about early American painting. He mentioned a certain family, the Duyckincks; he spelt it out for me, made me write it down.' She waved the scrap of paper she had been scrutinising. 'He said, when I asked if these early artists were any good, they often concentrated on European engravings for the clothes and painted only the face from life, when they would have done better for us and for themselves if they had concentrated on the sort of straightforward realism that's occasionally to be found. He mentioned an anonymous painting of a Mrs' – she scanned her paper – 'David Provoost. He spelt that out for me as well. He didn't want any mistakes. I asked him if there were any really good painters and he said there were. He said by the second half of the eighteenth century there were two of a high European stan-dard in his view. Hold it.' She lifted her scrap of paper. 'Benjamin West and John Singleton Copley,' she read. 'By this time quite a few had begun to study in Europe.'

'When were these two born?' Stone asked. 'Roughly?'

47

'Both in the same year, 1738. I remember that.'

'Didn't you write it down?'

Both laughed. Peg sat again, staring blindly over her jigsaw.

'Do you think he'll make a good husband for May?' Stone asked.

'It would be like marrying an encylopaedia.'

'And you don't think that would do?'

'You never know with our May. I couldn't make out what she saw in Ian MacGregor. He wasn't at all widely educated. I don't doubt he was a good engineer. And he'd certainly a sharp eye for making money.'

'That's not a bad recommendation to most women.'

'None of your cheap cynicism,' she warned. 'He wasn't a nuisance at home, so that she lived and dressed well. He was not, so the gossip went, averse to carrying on with other women.'

'Talk? Any evidence?'

'I haven't proof, but it was pretty well accepted. He put two girls in the family way. He paid them off and left them little remembrancers in his will.'

'Did May know this?'

'Yes, she did, but I don't think she cared. Cooled his ardour perhaps. I don't think May was physically very taken with him. Perhaps in the first year or two, but certainly not after John James was born. So he took his lustful pleasures elsewhere.' She made a wry face.

'You've not mentioned this to me,' Stone said.

'I have, but you, as usual, weren't listening. It worried me some few years before he died.' She shook her head. 'How much it weighed on May's mind I just don't know. She discussed it several times with me, but she never seemed upset. If it was divorce he was after, she'd make him pay. I think she'd be more ashamed of the actual divorce than disturbed by the loss of her husband. But he didn't move that way. I guess he was scared of her.'

'Were they polite to each other when he was at home in the house?'

'Yes. At least when I was there. I didn't see many signs of affection, but then May wasn't that sort.'

They talked, made suggestions to each other, enjoyed themselves, certain that nothing harmful would affect May.

'Any day now she'll be ringing up to tell us when she's thinking of returning home to Scotland and letting us know if she'll be calling in here on the way up.'

'Yes,' Stone answered. 'Yes.'

'When she rings, do you think I should tell her about Ronald's visit?'

'Why not?'

'She might think that we're interfering in her business. Or worse, trying to influence her in Ronald's favour.'

'No, I don't think so. I'm pretty certain in my own mind that Murray joined this course at the university so that he could be down here and thus have an excuse to meet her here. The course didn't exactly seem to be important to him. He'd like learning something new because he's a real guzzler of new information, but that didn't exactly convince me.'

'Shall I tell her what you think?'

'Please yourself, but if I were you I'd stick to the facts and as accurately as you can.'

'She won't be upset, will she?' Peg acted innocence.

'You seem to think so.'

V

The phone call did not enlighten Peg. May, on her way back, would arrive on Friday and stay with them until Monday. Peg had given her sister a full account of Murray's day with them, but May had seemed not very interested. She was worried, she said, about John James, but would not speak about that over the phone. They'd hear it all soon enough.

Stone met his sister-in-law at the railway station and on the way to his house she spoke cheerfully to him. She was in excellent health, had enjoyed the majority of her holiday, though there had been a small hiccup to her pleasure. It was about her son, John James, but it wasn't important and didn't really concern her. She would spill the sorry tale to both of them together, or better still to Peg who'd pass it on to him and return to her with her husband's views. 'It's a long way round, but seems to work,' she said. 'You're an ideal couple.'

'And speaking of ideal couples, your suitor spent a day with us.'

'What had he to say for himself?'

'He told us how much he admired you, but he was rather shy of pressing his case.'

'Is this true? You and that sister of mine will pitch me any cock-and-bull story.'

Stone guided them round a crowded traffic island. 'I tell you, May, what did baffle me. When Peg came back from staying with you, she had the impression that you quite liked Master Murray, that you look rather favourably on his advances. But she's not so sure now, and I thought you'd gone off the poor chap and announced this over the phone. Now what's the real truth?'

'When she was first with me I was a bit flattered by this development. And perhaps, by way of a wee joke, I exaggerated. Not seriously. But I thought she might be just a bit envious of her

50

crabby old sister who was now being chased by a man of learning with the prospect of remarriage in view.'

'Ah.'

'Then I began to change. I started to look on him as a threat. I had bad dreams about him. All this happened quite suddenly. I had trembling fits and used to dread meeting him.'

'Was there good reason for this? Had his behaviour towards you changed in any way?'

'No. He was as polite as ever. Obsequious even. He loves to tell you things he's heard or read.'

'Not threatening at all?'

'No. I guess he could seem so to some petty criminal he was cross-questioning in court.'

'So it must have been you? Something inside yourself suspected he'd cause some unwanted change in your life and this roused your terror.'

'That's about the exact word, "terror".'

'I don't know. It was strong, this fear of yours?'

'Yes. Physical. Causing me to shudder.'

'Do you, May, dislike the idea of marriage? Think carefully. And don't answer if you don't want to.'

She looked at him for so long that he thought he had been too blunt with this question. 'I'm over sixty and not inclined to change. I'm not particularly lonely; I have friends; like Peg I travel a good deal. But I would have said that I had no reasonable objections to marriage in principle. The right man and the right circumstances. But these shuddering fits this year were powerful enough. They really shocked me. And the nightmares, oh, they were horrible. I can't account for them at all. Before they started I could meet him all on my own, and stop and exchange a few friendly words with him, and be quite unaffected. After they started I dreaded meeting him.'

'All this happened during the six weeks Peg was there?'

'Roughly. It wasn't exactly a smooth progression from one state to the other.'

Stone was now driving uphill towards Laurel Avenue. He swung with scarcely disguised élan into the street. 'I'll let you in by the front door and bring the luggage in through the back when I've garaged the car.'

He was, however, too late. Peg must have been on the lookout for she shot out of the door before her sister had progressed a quarter of the way up the path. She waved her arms and issued orders to her husband. 'Bring the luggage in, John.'

He obediently went back to the car. It was useless to argue against his wife in this excited mood, especially outside, in public. When he lugged the first cases along the path the sisters stood with their arms round each other. May was crying. Annie Fisher from next door had emerged to join the group. By the time Stone came up with the second lot all three women had disappeared. He carefully aligned the suitcases along the hall by the foot of the staircase before creeping back to the street to put his car in the garage. When he returned, coffee steamed on the table, and Peg was shouting questions to her sister over the noise of bubbling saucepans and running taps.

'Anything I can do?' Stone asked.

'Finish your coffee. Then you can lay the table and give May a hand upstairs with her luggage. Lunch will be no more than half an hour.'

Stone and May pulled comical faces at each other.

'She's in a hurry,' May said.

'She's always on edge when she has a guest to look after or cook for.'

'I'm her sister.'

'It wouldn't make any difference if you were the Queen of Sheba.'

'I always think of Peg as on top of things, everything prepared to the last detail, and she without a worry in the world.'

'That's right, but she has to shout and create uproar.'

'Why?'

'To let men, especially this man, know that household duties don't do themselves.'

'Do you think she's sorry about not having a career?'

'No. She might be sorry that I didn't make the money Ian did.'

'I sometimes puzzle myself about Ian. Honestly. Our married life wasn't all rows, but I'm sure I was satisfied with looking after his creature comforts, the house and rearing John James.'

'What was the snag, then?'

'We could never talk anything out. It's always a joke to me when I watch these soaps on television that I'm certain I shall

52

hear somebody say, "We must talk." There were no such sentences between me and Ian.'

'Why was that?'

'I don't think,' May said slowly, 'that it ever occurred to him that one could have one's mind, once it was made up, changed by arguing. In most things – meals, clothes, furniture, decorating, the garden – he let me have my own way unless I was preparing to do something foolish.'

'What happened then?'

'He just stopped it.'

'Did that happen often?'

'No. I had my side of life: clothes, domestic arrangements, holidays. He might offer a suggestion, but on the whole he thought I'd work it out better than he would. At work if he wanted to set a project up, he'd consult, certainly, with various experts, but he'd make his mind up in the end for himself. He was very good at his job, I imagine, knew a great deal about it. But once the decision was made he could see no sense in arguing his view out with somebody for the mere pleasure of it. He knew what he wanted doing and that was that.'

'But,' her brother-in-law asked, 'you would have liked discussion?'

'Yes. I was prepared to learn from it.'

'As Ian was from his experts?'

'I don't deny it. It makes life interesting. I used to envy the way you and Peg argued things out together.'

'Ian wasn't a sociable being?'

'In some ways. He'd enjoy a drink or a dance. He liked female company. But he'd sooner show them what he wanted with his hands than his tongue.'

'Didn't he like gossip?'

'Yes. And smoking-room humour. But he was no good at it himself.'

'Didn't he talk about his work?'

'Sometimes. But very briefly. It was clear what he was driving at, but it was factual.'

'Why do you like this idea of conversation so much?'

'The exchange of ideas keeps you lively.'

'But isn't it possible for a couple who've lived together for years to know what to do next without talking it through?' Stone asked.

'They say so. I didn't find it so with Ian. I told him where we were going for holidays, and he'd grunt and accept my decision. I got him to go abroad. He didn't mind doing that by way of business, but walking around museums and castles and other ancient sites had no attraction for him. But he was willing to please me.'

'When Peg and I discuss something, she does three quarters of the talking.'

'I'm sure.'

'Was there a great deal of conversation going on in your home when the pair of you were children?'

'Not as I remember it. My father, and my mother for that matter, laid down the law and though Peg might protest a bit – she was Dad's favourite – it didn't go too far. I had acquired the notion that somewhere in the higher ranks of society regular family palavers took place. That was from the books we read where the parents used to discuss with the children, for example, where they'd spend their holidays.'

'And, of course,' he said sarcastically, 'they always came across hidden treasure or a mysterious poor girl to be rescued.'

May laughed. 'My mother always had ideas for holidays miles better than any we could come up with.'

Peg returned, ordered them to wash their hands and file into the dining room.

'What is it today?' he asked.

'Chilli chicken burgers with coleslaw,' she answered.

'I hope not,' her husband groaned in mock anguish.

'Lasagne with Bolognese sauce and garlic bread.' May giggled.

'Do you have that stuff in Scotland?' he asked.

'Every second shop.'

'In that case I'll have a tin of Coke,' he said.

'You'll go and fetch it for yourself, then,' his wife said.

She served them soup, pork chops with apple sauce, potatoes, peas and beans.

'These are our first windfalls big enough to use,' Stone said.

'Yes, I hope they're fit to taste,' Peg grumbled. 'They could do with another month on the trees.'

They ate with relish. Peg explained about the old man who cultivated an allotment behind the wall and the copse at the end of the street. He sold her potatoes, peas, beans, green stuff, fruit.

'We're his landlord, somehow. I don't know how it came about. He's an old railwayman and his son's a woodwork teacher, unmarried,' Stone said. 'I go and visit them on Saturday afternoon sometimes. The son has built a beautiful garden hut, chimney, fireplace and all.

'And they send your sister presents in season, strawberries, raspberries, loganberries, and they won't let me pay for them. "They're little luxuries," the old chap said. "You don't charge me anything like what I should pay for this allotment and you pay me more than I should ask for the vegetables, so I take pleasure in sending you a little gift".'

'Do you ever go round?' May asked Peg.

'Sometimes. Not more than once or twice a year. They'd find me in the way. They're both bachelors, widowers. Edwin the son's perhaps forty, if he's that, but looks as if he's the same age as his father and talks in the same old-fashioned way. Both their wives died young. They give me a bunch of flowers whenever I go.' She pointed at a bunch of dark chrysanthemums thickly reflected in the mirror over the mantelpiece where they stood. 'And Albert, the father, takes a bunch up to the cemetery every Sunday afternoon without fail.'

'How sweet,' May said. Her brother-in-law could not place the tone.

They all praised the vegetables; the apples proved excellent. May, eating with appetite, seemed altogether more cheerful than when she arrived. Peg said the weather looked uninviting so that this afternoon she and her sister wouldn't go outside except perhaps a trip round the garden. She needed advice about curtains. They'd scour the house and grounds while John was at his meeting.

'What sort of meeting is this?' May asked.

'He goes out this afternoon to the hospital. He's been asked to sit on a hospital committee. He represents the ordinary man on a committee, mostly of doctors, about the treatment of cancer.'

'Don't they know?' May said.

'What?'

'How to treat it?'

'They think so,' Peg said, 'but they've decided they should look at it from a patient's point of view. There's another lay person, a woman, clever enough, an artist who has had cancer and surgery, chemo- and radiotherapy. Jack's on by chance. When the hospital authorities were setting up this committee he met one of the consultants who happened to be an old boy of his school. He asked Jack to be a member. Jack claimed that he knew nothing about the feelings of patients and this doctor, Jack's old pupil, said, "You don't need to. You'll be there to stop us bullying this lady." "Will you be likely to?" Jack asked. "Very, especially if we're in a hurry. And if she starts to veer away from the topic in hand."'

John Stone did the washing up on his own, then brought in coffee for the women. The sun was bright, but the pair had already made up their minds to stay in. They heard John set off from the front door and watched him on the path. He seemed in no hurry.

'He's got to go round to the back to collect his car. He knew he could leave it out for his journey this afternoon down to the Queen's Hospital. But he doesn't like to park in the street because he's afraid some yobbo might try to break in, and failing that would drag a coin along the Rover so that it needed a respray. He'll park it in the hospital without demur.'

They looked down from the window as he sailed out, trilby hat neatly in place. He stopped and turned towards the next garden. They heard a woman's sunny voice.

'It's your Mrs Fisher next door,' May said.

John reached the gate and stood on the pavement, waiting for Annie Fisher to emerge. The watchers saw the hat raised; the two set out together towards the wide drive and then, presumably, to the garage. Annie flaunted a bright-red dress, and a yellow scarf and a broad-brimmed navy-blue straw hat.

'Do they keep their car round your back?' May asked.

'No. They have a triple garage at the rear corner of their estate, diagonally across the garden, quite a way from ours. No. I guess he's offered her a lift down the hill to the shops or perhaps into town or somewhere. I don't know. She wouldn't take her own car into the city. If her destination was out of the way she'd call a taxi.'

'She's always dressed up to the nines,' May said. 'I'm glad she or somebody like her didn't live next door to us when Ian was alive. He couldn't have kept his eyes or his hands off her.'

'She wouldn't have minded.'

'Does she make a pitch at Jack, then?'

'She fancies any man.'

'But she doesn't get much change out of Jack?'

'Oh, he'll flirt with her in his straightforward old gent's way in public. But nothing further, at least to the extent of my knowledge. Chasing after Annie Fisher would cause complications and he prefers life to be simple. He's always quoting that A. H. Clough poem "A Modern Decalogue":

> "Do not adultery commit;
> Advantage rarely comes of it."'

'That's good,' May trumpeted, rocking in her chair. She repeated the couplet slowly.

'He's a careful man, is John. He does not take undue risks.'

'And what about Mr Fisher?'

'It's said he's like your Ian, always on the prowl.'

'Has he made a pass at you?'

'Once or twice when he'd been drinking too much. I rather like him. He's a hard worker, a building contractor, and will do you a good turn if he can. He found a beautiful Victorian fireplace and hearth, and put it in for me.'

'Is he frightened of you?'

'I suppose so. He looks on me as an educated woman who'll correct his grammar if he's not careful.'

'I read in some magazine that some women prefer rough men like that. They have affairs with plumbers and builders. They go just for the sex, not any real relationship. That brings too many complications. They enjoy the physical contact and that's all.'

'Yes,' Peg answered. 'I've read that sort of thing and I don't doubt it happens sometimes. But not often, I reckon. They make up these stories for their confessional columns. I guess most women would make their joiners or jobbing gardeners go off for a good scrub before they started any hanky-panky.'

'Maybe.' It was obviously not worth arguing. May sat, drawing her eyebrows together. 'I'm worried about John James, though.'

'What, his sex life?'

'That will come into it. It's this Linda Thorpe he lives with.'

Peg made no answer, but left it to her sister to choose her own words.

May had clasped her hands between her knees and began slowly. 'He's been living with this Linda some time now. I thought the live-in relationship had only just started, but there.' May seemed at a loss.

'But aren't they happy?' Peg helped her out. No answer came. 'Is she a nice girl?'

'Yes, as far as I can tell. She came from a poor family, though very few of them are left. Her only brother is dead.'

'Has she no sisters?'

'Yes, I believe she has. She was clever, won a scholarship to a Girls' Public Day School Trust place, did well, but left after A level and went straight into this investment bank. She found her feet at once.'

'She's what they call charismatic these days, is she?'

'I wouldn't say so. She's not bad looking, if you like women tall and thin. But she's quiet, with a slightly Home Counties accent. She's clever, quick with ideas, a wizard at her job and isn't afraid of hard work. They're both at their offices by seven in the morning quite often.'

'And back late?'

'Yes. Nine or ten some nights.'

'Good God.'

'Not every night of the week. And they have the weekend free.'

'And how do they spend that?'

'Catching up on sleep and sex.'

'Don't they go out to the theatre or for a meal?' Peg asked.

'Cinema, occasionally, and sometimes for a not very elaborate meal, which saves them cooking.'

'What about friends? Have they got any?'

'Yes and sometimes they meet. They'll have a couple or three, perhaps, round on Saturday night.' May's choice of numbers ridiculed this pretence at friendship. 'But even when they're at home early, they'll just hang about. They'll take their main meal at a restaurant near the bank at midday. So when they have evenings off they sit about and talk, and do little domestic chores and go to bed early. They've been happy enough with this. They worked such long hours.'

'But now you think John James is getting tired of it? He wants something different?'

'No, I don't,' May almost snapped. 'You know what JJ's like; he's never changed very much. He's never been one for dashing about. As long as he's got an interesting job to do, he'll work on at it until it's done. And however much money he makes he won't throw his earnings away. He's like his father in that respect. "There's no such thing as a free lunch," Ian used to tell me. Though, oddly, he'd let me waste money. Within reason.'

'They're quarrelling about money, are they?'

'No. It's not that at all. And when you consider what they earn, it's not surprising. Their salary and bonus are enormous. Too much for a sane person to contemplate.'

'I shan't ask,' Peg said.

'I wouldn't dare tell you. It's where they live. They were thinking, I told you at the time, of buying some big house in the country. I couldn't understand it, because I thought they'd only just moved in together. They hadn't, as it happened. And that goes to show how I only know half the story. He wrote to me perhaps once a fortnight, but never intimately. Only recently had he begun to mention Linda and even more recently that they were living together.'

Peg sat back in exasperation at her sister's slow progress, but said nothing.

May refused more coffee and began, muttering almost to herself: 'For the last month or two Linda has been feeling off colour. She's suffered from all sorts of pains. She went to her GP who couldn't find anything and he asked her if perhaps her work was stressful. She didn't think much of that for a diagnosis. JJ is very loath to talk about this to me; to him it's like a schoolboy's snitching to the teacher. Anyway, she went off with his connivance to some private hospital where they gave her a thorough examination. It cost a bomb, but they can afford that. They were utterly careful, scans and blood tests and God knows what.'

Peg was made to wait again. May touched her tongue with the end of the first finger of her left hand. 'In due course they got the reports. There were slight dietary deficiencies and that sort of thing. They said there were incipient signs of arthritis, nothing serious, and some slight internal upset. In other words they came down with her own doctor's verdict – stress. She should take it easy with her life. She and JJ discussed this together over a long weekend they took in Paris. He was baffled by it all, didn't know what to say to her, asked if she had any idea of how to relax: gymnasia, health clubs, three days a week only at the bank. She'd seemed so much on top of her work. Then she'd really snarled at him. Their bank, the North European, would only give her time off if she was pregnant or very seriously ill so he wasn't to talk such rubbish. She used to become angry whenever they discussed her health and accuse him of being childishly useless. "You need your mother with you. Somebody to wipe your nose for you. And tuck you up in bed. And kiss her little diddums." This upset him because she'd never acted like this before. Sometimes she wouldn't speak to him for hours on end. She went off once to put up in a hotel for a night, then to stay for two days with her mother. She'd never done that ever since she started work. Then she came back and had made up her mind. She said, and all this without any preamble, that they should both resign from their jobs, buy a little house in the country and live their lives out there, with or without family, that was up to him, and throw off this stress that was killing her.'

'And then?'

'She found out what JJ was made of. He asked her how they'd afford to live for the next fifty years or more. She said they could take little office jobs somewhere close by, if cash became short, and they could buy enough land for a start, they had the money, and grow their own food. He said her work in the bank had blinded her to the difficulties of life outside. She slaved hard, it was true; she was extremely good at it. But she was lucky because the rewards were so high. She was like some pop singer making a fortune, but she'd find that if she looked for a job in the ordinary world these big payments didn't exist for most people.

'It appeared that she wanted them both to resign. He bluntly said "No". If she wanted to give up work herself, that was all right for him. He earned enough to keep the pair of them in comfort, but he was not going to throw over his job. He'd been lucky to find something so suitable so early and he was learning fast. It would be foolish, he insisted, but gently, to throw all this over so soon, to spend his time sowing, ignorantly sowing and pulling, turnips and cabbages every day of the week.

'She was furious,' May continued, her own face now wrinkled, drawn. 'She said he didn't love her. All he thought about was money. He tried to be reasonable, but she was quite unlike the woman he'd first met three years ago. Then she was enthusiastic about her employment, amazed by the amount of money she could make because she came from a not very well-to-do family. Her father worked on the Underground. She helped JJ in all sorts of ways. I think she was the first girl he'd been in love with, certainly the first he'd had sex with. I don't think he could exactly understand, or believe, that such a girl – I say girl though she was five years older than he was – could feel so attracted towards him. It was a kind of miracle. A job that he could do and prosper at, and now a woman, as clever, as attractive as she was, making it quite plain that she loved him.'

May broke off, thinking this over, perhaps regretting she'd been so frank with her sister.

'Did he tell you all this?' Peg asked.

'Yes. Once he'd started, it all poured out of him. I've never known him spill it to me like this since he was a small child. She'd gone out somewhere. Perhaps to her parents' house, or just walking the streets. And twice he broke down and sobbed. Usually he doesn't say or show anything of what he feels. But this had got to him. They'd taken a few days' leave that the bank owed them and spent all the time discussing it, and it had knocked him about.'

'Did they come to any final conclusions?'

'No, and yes. JJ made it quite clear that he thought it utterly reckless to give up his job and had said he would not do it. Linda, according to him, was surprised he was so obstinate.'

'Are you?' Peg asked.

'Not really. Earning a living is important to him and if he's made his mind up about that he wouldn't waver. He told her that having enough to live on was the foundation of a real, lasting relationship together. She argued that he ought to be able to under-stand that she couldn't bear this kind of life any longer. He replied that he wasn't asking her to. He'd go to work, and she could stay at home and do as she liked. "Cook dinners for you and get them wrong every night because I don't know what time you'll be back." He said there was such a thing as a mobile phone. She could go to college and take a degree if she so wished. That would be soul-destroying, she said, to have to go and listen to a lot of boring rubbish from a load of drop-deads who couldn't earn a decent salary between them, professors and all. He'd told her it wouldn't be half as deadly as digging a wintry garden.'

'And that's how it stands?'

'As far as I know. The two days I was there they carried on the argument, if they did, in private. He gave me all these details on my last evening. I hope it did him good to spit it out to some-body sympathetic. You can guess what my time there was like. He spoke to her but she made no attempt whatever to answer him whether I was in the room or not. The atmosphere was awful. She did get us two or three meals. I couldn't complain that she didn't put herself out to excel herself. And she went out both evenings I was there.'

'Didn't you try to talk to her?'

'I did. I cornered her in the corridor. I said I could see some-thing was wrong and asked if there was anything I could do to help. She didn't answer. I said I didn't want to sit in judgement on her or JJ but . . . She said I could sit where I liked, and turned about and went into their bedroom.'

'Did she slam the door?'

'No. Slipped out of the way. Without noise.' May coughed. 'I caught her for a half-minute next morning just before I left, and said she could come and stay with me in Scotland if she thought that might be of any help. She thanked me in a low voice so that I could barely hear her. She said she'd sooner be anywhere else but there. I nearly lost my temper. Do you remember our old cleaning woman? She used to say, "I could have given her a mouthful." But I thought twice. I could see she was miserable. She spoke in this whisper. Whether she always did I can't say. This was the first time I'd really met her. There was next to no expression on her face. And pale. I don't know, but it looked as if all life had been drained out of her. From what JJ says she wasn't altogether happy at home as a child. There had been no encouragement to do well at school, but she persevered, went through as far as A levels and succeeded really brilliantly, swimming against the tide. She could have got in at Oxford or Cambridge, John James says. And now it's all turned sour. She got a job at eighteen that was not the sort people from her class of society usually tried for. They took her on at the bank as a kind of experiment in social engineering, and she proved outstandingly successful. Thinking about it on the train coming up I wondered if it hadn't all proved too much for her. She'd had to work so hard her whole life and watch her "p"s and "q"s in these last twelve years that it knocked the spirit out of her.'

'And what' – Peg spoke with a solemn slowness – 'will be the outcome?'

'I don't know. I wish I did. Linda I've only just met. She might well convince him. He said not, but you never know. He seemed determined enough, but he was always such a quiet boy. He didn't ever wish to cause upset at home. He did well at school and university because he was clever and worked hard. He was never in trouble, with girls or drinks or drugs. He seemed set on pleasing us. I used to think how lucky we were, but I wonder now if it hasn't left him pretty defenceless against somebody as strong-willed as Linda is.'

'What can you do?'

'There's nothing I can do except keep in close touch, be there if he wants to talk to me. I've no idea how this will turn out. I'll ring him tonight if you don't mind.'

'That's sensible,' Peg answered.

'I just am baffled. Ask John what he thinks, will you?'

'He'll tell you to hang on, that you'll have to let the boy do as he wishes.'

'When I think of the two of them trying to grow their own food, I despair. They'd have to learn it all from books. And JJ doesn't like to get his hands dirty. And she's never had a garden in her life. They've always lived in flats.'

'She'd do well to go to a horticultural college and do a year or two before she starts to try to become self-sufficient.'

'I never thought of that.'

63

May threw out her hands in a gesture of despair, at her own inadequacy or the utter impossibility of solving the problem. 'Thanks for listening,' she muttered. She seemed quite unlike herself. She had always lacked Peg's obvious vitality, but made up for it by a demeanour that suggested distance and powers of discrimination. As Peg listened to her sister she heard touches of Scottish intonation and pronunciation she had not noticed before. Perhaps this family trouble had shattered the buttresses that kept her ladylike English accent in place against the constant buffeting of Doric voices.

'I tell you what worried me,' May burst out. 'I didn't know what to say. You'd think I could have fed them – him – some advice, but it wasn't there. I couldn't even get my sentences out properly. My brain had been affected.'

'I don't know whether one can give useful advice in cases like this,' Peg said, her voice tart with common sense. 'They've thought and argued themselves into a complete irrationality. If they were small children you might just be able to shake some sense into them. But you can't with adults. I see that.'

'What shall I do?' May's voice quavered.

'Keep in touch with JJ. Once a week at least. Not more. You don't want him to find you a nuisance. And just talk to him so that he knows the world's bumbling on as usual, however awful his life feels.'

They sat, unspeaking, their minds in paralysis.

Peg looked up suddenly. 'When you'd heard all JJ had got to say, which side did you favour?'

'Why, his. He's my son.'

'Yes, that's natural. But when you thought it over? Given that Linda couldn't help herself.'

'That's what I couldn't come to terms with. Her decision seemed mad. Even if she had been driven quite out of her senses by the stress of the job, or her background or experiences, she could have accepted his offer to work while she rested or did something else.'

'"She should", but that's different from "she could". Her illness – depression, anxiety, despair, whatever – had cut into her so deep that she's incapable of acting rationally. She is capable only of accepting a solution that would make JJ unhappy and that would shatter the relationship between them.'

'Oh.'

'He loves her, does he?'

'He did. I don't know how he feels about it now. He loved her and admired her, and was flattered that she thought so highly of him. He found himself in this ideal situation, then suddenly out of the blue she comes up with this lunatic proposal.'

'Didn't he have any warning?'

'No. Not to the best of my knowledge. I asked him. Until just a week or two ago they were utterly happy. She had been feeling ill for a couple of months, but it wasn't until she visited her doctor and later had the report from the private hospital that she began to argue in this new way.'

Again May threw out her hands as if despairing of her words.

'Come on, big sister,' Peg cajoled. 'That's enough for the present. Let's have a stroll round the garden and then you can give me the benefit of your ideas before John or the gardener set about clearing up for winter.'

Quite out of character, the two set out hand in hand.

VI

May spent two days longer at her sister's than she had intended. Her two conversations on the phone with her son were plain, dull, unenlightening. Neither of the young couple had come to any agreement about their future. Both had returned to work, though JJ had wanted Linda to have more time off. May could not make out whether they continued with their arguments or were enduring an uneasy truce.

Ronald Murray had failed to get in touch with either May or the Stones. This discourtesy was mentioned only rarely and the visitor expressed no disappointment.

'Have you sent him a card to say how sorry you are to have missed him?' Stone asked mischievously.

'No. I'm giving him no encouragement. Nor to anybody.'

'The cruelty!'

May, suffering from a slight cold, decided not to join her sister's shopping trip on the penultimate morning of the holiday. She and Stone prepared the vegetables for lunch together, and talked about JJ and Linda.

John Stone spoke without great force. He did not know the young people and was not sure how strongly life had driven Linda to her conclusion, which he considered unreasonable. 'I have never felt anything so powerfully that I could not resist it. I wanted things, promotion at my work, to marry the pretty Miss Margaret Elizabeth Symmonds, to play as a schoolboy for the county at chess. If I didn't achieve what I wanted, I admitted that I was asking too much. I put up with what I'd got and made the best of it.'

'Did you have a lot of disappointments, then?'

'I suppose you think of me as a successful man,' he said, 'but as often as not I didn't achieve what I wanted. I was ambitious and always put up a fair show at interviews and public appearances.'

66

He breathed deeply. He wore an open collar, corduroy trousers and a light pullover, all neat, all without formality. His face was serious and demanded a suit, a white shirt, a silken, sober tie. She watched his fingers carefully tracing the contours of his face. 'I read about a young woman, pretty and blonde, much sought after by the boys, who had decided in her teens that she should have been a man. You can understand the difficulties, can't you? With her family for a start. With doctors – and I'm not speaking about GPs but about the few experts there were around at that time who often failed her and, in one or two senses, flatly refused after listening to her case to offer any treatment. But she was convinced that she should be a man and searched around until she found doctors who would help her.'

'And what happened?'

'She's now a bearded man, with a partner and a family, and happy.'

'Can she have sexual intercourse with the partner?' They seemed to be learning from Peg.

'No. She cannot penetrate her. But both are entirely happy, so the article said. But though I'm glad of that, all I can say is that I have never felt, in all my life, anything as strong as that young woman's belief. She ran counter to medical opinion, common sense, every sort of prejudice; she was sacked several times by old-fashioned employers, met all sorts of irrational fears in herself and others, but continued on her course, convinced in the face of setbacks and disappointments because she *knew* she was a man. Perhaps Linda has now come to believe she will become her true self as a villager, a market gardener, a poor rustic woman.'

'You think it's possible?'

'I've no idea. I couldn't do it. If I had decided to throw up my headship and become a school caretaker, I'd think I was not using my talents to the full. As to Peg, and what she'd think and say, I know I'd very soon have my mind changed for me.'

'So you don't believe that Peg's love and admiration for you are so great that she'd follow you into your circumscribed, dirty, poverty-stricken life.'

'I do not.' He grinned. 'If my mind came up with any such outlandish notion I'd have pushed it out before ever I'd have mentioned it to her. Because I knew what she'd say.'

67

'Here's the lady in question,' May called from the window. He joined her and they watched Peg's energetic progress along the path.

Some conversation buzzed quietly outside before Peg pushed open her front door and put down the purchase. 'Jack,' she called. 'Are you there?' He appeared at the door. 'Put these away, will you?' she said, pointing at her bags. 'And get coffee for you and May. If you want it.'

'And where are you off to in such a hurry?'

'Annie, next door, wants me to go in for a few minutes. She has something to tell me.'

'And it can't wait?' he asked sarcastically.

'She pressed me to come in.'

'Did she seem upset?'

'No. She looked as always, except that she whispered. None of her usual top-of-the-voice stuff.' Peg wheeled round and, banging the door behind her, gathered speed.

John Stone returned to his sister-in-law's side in the sitting room. 'You heard that,' he said to May. 'Annie wants to tell her something.'

'Does she often call her in?'

'Not that I've noticed. I expect she's found some bargain and needs to boast about it.'

'Is that usual?'

'No. And if she tried it too much Peg would soon put a stop to it. I'd better stow Peg's purchases away or I shall catch the sharp end of her tongue.'

'Do you know, Jack, I've never heard her speak sharply to you in all the years I've known you. And how long's that?'

'Thirty-six years in December. And the reason is that I always do exactly as I'm told.'

'I think she's a bit scared of you. She's never been afraid of criticising someone. She'd come straight out with it and not give a row of beans for the consequences.'

'She's a generous sort.'

'I'm not denying it. She helps anybody out. But she's sharp with her tongue.'

Together, smiling, they put Peg's purchases, as John dubbed them, away. Then they returned to the kitchen, to engage in a small argument whether to have another cup of coffee. The kitchen was warmly redolent of the beef casserole in the oven.

'I don't think I will,' Jack said. 'It will dull my appetite for lunch. But I'll make you one.'

'No, I'll follow your advice. That's what I like about you. If I asked Ian about anything, he was just as likely to answer me with, "Make your own bluidy mind up." In other words it wasn't worth thinking about.'

'But when you'd decided, did he complain?'

'No, mostly not. You know, to me, this house of yours, Jack, is a place of peace compared with most homes. When I came back here from JJ's and Linda's place, oh, the difference.'

'Peg and I don't always see eye to eye.'

'I don't suppose you do. But when you disagree you don't spoil the atmosphere for everybody else for weeks afterwards. Both of you accept it and make the best of it.'

'Especially when Peg's won the argument.'

'No, Jack, that's not true. You seem to appreciate each other in a way Ian and I never did. I think our basis of agreement was never steady.'

'It wasn't as bad as all that, May.'

'I know you liked him, Jack, and he admired you. "Jack Stone's head is screwed on the right way round," he'd say. "He's always worth listening to. And one of the main reasons is that he doesn't make out he knows something when he doesn't. And he knows exactly the extent of his ignorance".'

'You flatter me.'

The front-door bell rang long and violently. May jumped.

'Who's that now?' he asked. 'It's worse than Piccadilly Circus in here.' He marched smartly into the hallway, to find Peg and Mrs Fisher outside silhouetted behind the stained-glass front door.

'I didn't take my key,' Peg excused herself. 'Come in, Annie.' She took her companion by the arm and whisked her past her husband and into the sitting room. By the time he'd followed them in, she had seated Annie Fisher on the settee. 'You know May, my sister, don't you?' she asked.

Both women murmured that they had met.

Peg silently motioned to Jack to settle himself down on the settee by Annie. 'Now,' she summoned them to undivided attention.

'Annie has received some unfortunate news. You'll remember perhaps three weeks or more ago, in the local papers and on TV, that a woman was murdered in Sutton. There was no sign of a break-in and it was assumed that she knew and had admitted the murderer. She had been battered about the head and then strangled. The woman, a Mrs Wallace, was apparently very free with her favours and among those men was Harry. Her husband,' she unnecessarily annotated for May's benefit. 'This morning Annie received an unpleasant anonymous letter claiming that the writer had seen Harry Fisher enter Mrs Wallace's house on the morning of the murder. The writer said that he was a frequent visitor and that unless he admitted as much to the police, she – it looked like a woman's handwriting – would feel bound to tell them. There was good reason why the writer, it concluded, had not done so before. Mrs Fisher should not delay putting all this to her husband and the police. If she did not . . .'

Peg waited, then looked across at Stone for a lead.

'Have you got the letter?' he asked Annie Fisher, who took it, in its envelope with a newspaper cutting, from her handbag and handed it over. He read it, twice, before Peg motioned him to let May see it. Stone thought it over. 'What does Harry say?'

'He doesn't know anything about this. It only came this morning, after he'd gone out.' Annie suddenly jerked herself upright. 'I read it over and over, driving myself mad. I could have rung Harry up, but there might be a quite innocent explanation. It didn't seem altogether likely but I had to give him the benefit of the doubt.'

'Does he always start out early?' Stone asked.

'Not these days. He's half retired.'

'Do you think he's capable of killing anyone?' Stone asked slowly and rather kindly. 'I'm sorry to ask such questions.'

'He's strong enough. He's very fit for a seventy-year-old. But I don't think he's capable, or wild enough. He loses his temper and rages and bawls, but he'd never pick up a hammer . . . But I don't know about murder. People slip over the edge.'

'That's the first thing,' Peg said. 'Show him the letter when he comes back.'

'Do you think so?' Annie asked Stone.

'Yes. Give him a chance to explain.' He stood. 'Could I see the paper once more?' She shuffled in her bag again; he opened the envelope and took the cutting over to the calendar. There he made his calculations. 'It is three weeks and two days since the murder. Thursday, 30 September.' He turned back to check between newspaper and calendar. 'Do you remember anything particularly out of the way about him that Thursday?' He lifted the calendar from the wall and handed it to Annie Fisher; '30 September,' he said, 'a Thursday.'

Annie looked hard at the calendar, stupidly wagging her head. She then dug again into her handbag and drew out a small diary. The other three stared at her, as if expecting some climax. Annie, in no hurry, turned the minuscule leaves, frowned as she reached the searched-for page, lifted the calendar, held it and the diary together, drew in a thoughtful breath before she spoke. 'I remember that day,' she said slowly. 'I went to the hairdresser's. It was not my usual day, which is Friday. Clare, the girl who does me, had to go away that week, so we put the appointment forward.'

'Right,' Stone said. 'That's good. Do you remember anything else specific about that day?'

Annie concentrated, but finally shook her head.

'Do you remember anything out of the way about your husband? I don't mean that his clothes were splashed with blood, just that he seemed troubled, unusually out of sorts.'

The woman shook her head helplessly.

'Think it over. If you can dredge up anything from that day, remember it; perhaps it would be better if you wrote it down, so that you can face him with it when you show him the letter.'

'Yes, I will. Should I mention to him that I've let you read the letter?'

Now it was Stone's turn to think. 'You can, but I wouldn't unless he deliberately asks. It won't help to give him the impression that you've been blackening his name all over the district.'

There followed a pause as if they struggled to bring to the surface some point of importance they had overlooked. Nothing came of it.

Peg, with a gulp, said, 'That's enough for now. We can do without more tormenting argument. The best thing you can do, Annie, is to have lunch with us. You need a bit of company. And we've a beef casserole that will feed you and a dozen like you. And May's just about fed up with the pair of us mumbling on.'

'I'm sure she's not.'

'That's as may be. Now if you want to slip in back home for anything this is the time. Lunch will be about half an hour. Otherwise, sit there and breathe steadily.'

Annie Fisher thanked her hostess for her thoughtfulness and said she would like to go back home to do one or two small chores. Her face was strained, her hair unusually untidy.

'Poor woman,' May said. 'Think of having to show your husband a letter pretty well accusing him of murder.'

'She's fairly resolute,' Peg said on their way back to the kitchen. 'Think how stoical she was when she imagined she had cancer.'

'Would she know about her husband and this Mrs Wallace?' May asked.

'I guess she would.'

'And didn't bother?' Peg made a derisive noise in reply. 'I remember,' her sister continued, 'the first time I caught Ian out. I was shocked beyond measure. It was very typical of him and his slapdash ways. As an engineer he was precise and thoughtful, and checked every point of detail. With this, pah! I had ironed some handkerchiefs for him and was putting them away in a drawer when I found right on top of the other things, with no attempt to hide it, a letter in a huge, hideous, purple envelope. He hadn't even put the letter back in the envelope so that I could see, "My dearest, darling, naked Ian" in big, sprawling handwriting. I looked at it as it lay there and took it out. I suppose it could have been called passionate, but it was so badly written. She couldn't punctuate and she couldn't spell. That made it so much worse. Here she was spilling, celebrating, her love and excitement, and my only judgement was that she was illiterate.'

'She wasn't much good at expressing herself?' Stone asked.

'She was, in her crude way. She called a spade a spade. It infuriated me. I'd no idea. It was an utter shock. And at that time I thought I had a hundred per cent claim to my husband. I did. He was mine and had no right to spread his sexual favours like this. Perhaps I blamed myself. If I were satisfying him as a wife he'd not want to be seeking his pleasures elsewhere. I had John James, then, as a baby and perhaps he, Ian, felt pushed out. And I was

72

up in the night and felt bad-tempered and worn out. My life was a mess without his chasing after other women.'

'You never said anything about this to us at the time,' said Peg from her sink.

'No. I felt ashamed of myself. That I'd been rejected by my husband. That I had chosen to marry such a man.'

'But you got over it in time?'

'It took longer than I care to remember. I got to the stage in a year or two when I thought I didn't mind, that he could do as he liked without troubling me.'

'Did you resume relations with him?' Peg asked.

'Sexual, you mean. Not often. Not very willingly. But sometimes when he was drunk or very forceful, urgent. He was physically very strong, could overpower me.'

'He raped you?'

'Yes. That's so. Though I didn't think about it in those terms. I didn't in those days. I held the view that it was a woman's duty to have sexual intercourse with her lawful wedded husband if he wanted it.'

'The feminists were in full cry at that time, for God's sake.'

'I didn't set much store by them,' May said grimly. 'Not my sort.'

'Oh. Did you face him with the letter?'

'I don't much like to remember what I did. Even now. I feel stupid about it. I sat down with the letter and a red-ink pen, and I corrected it like a school exercise. There were mistakes galore. And red alterations and underlinings all over the place.'

'And you sent it back to her?'

'No. My first idea was to show it to Ian. But the more I thought, the more it seemed to put me in the wrong. He'd think I cared more about spelling errors and grammatical mistakes than about his infidelities. I'd put myself in the wrong. In my own mind. Badly.' May tapped her fingers fiercely on the table.

'So you didn't send it to her?'

'No. I could see no advantage. Not to me. And I don't suppose either of them cared.'

'So, in the end, what did you do?'

'Nothing. I thought of writing an anonymous letter to myself and then showing it to him. I was in a dreadful state. I'd no one to turn to and the baby wasn't very well. He'd started teething. I hid the letter in a place where he had no chance of coming across it. I kept it there for over a week, and I'd take it out twice, three times a day and read it. In the end I burnt it.'

'So he didn't realise you knew about his mistress.'

'No. But that didn't last long, oddly enough. A couple of months later I got a real anonymous letter, accusing Ian of adultery with another woman. This time I did show it to him. I gave him his evening meal when he came in and when we'd finished I passed the letter to him. "This came this morning," I said.

'He put his glasses on to read it. He always did to read private letters. Never the newspaper. He had those half-moon glasses; he looked comical. Anyhow, he read it through, folded it and sniffed, unfolded it, read it again. I stared at him. He looked shifty and he flushed, the whole of his face and neck. He asked, after a time, "When did you say this came?"

'"This morning. After you'd gone out."

'He looked at the envelope, said, "I can't read the postmark."

'"It looks local," I said. "I had this from the Misses Smith up the road."

'He compared the two envelopes. "Yes. It does. Whose handwriting is it?"

'"I don't know. I don't recognise it."

'"Have you had any like this before?"

'"No!"

'He glanced up, then put the letter in the envelope and that into his pocket. "I'll look into this," he said. "I'll ask Jock Laird at the post office. He'll recognise handwriting if anyone can. Or Hamish Brown, the policeman. People have no right to upset their neighbours with filth like this."

'I didn't answer and sat looking over at him. "They need locking up. Some spinster, I'll be bound."

'He stood, stockily, after he had made sure that the letter was safely in his pocket. "I'll get to the bottom of this, I assure you." He pushed his chair with the backs of his legs and took a deep breath.

'"One moment," I said.

'"Ay?" Now he knew there was trouble. "What is it?"

'"The content of the letter," I said. My hands and legs were trembling, but I didn't rise and I held the edge of the table so that he didn't notice my weakness. When I spoke I did it very slowly, one word at a time, to keep my voice steady.

'"Ay, what about it?"

'"First," I said, "is there any truth in it?"

'"You don't mean to say that you believe what this lunatic tells you?"

'I rose to my feet. "Never mind my beliefs. I asked if these accusations had any truth in them."

'"No. Lies. Damned lies." He stared me out. He sat down again.

'I stood. "Why would we get a letter accusing you of those things? Why you? And why this specific name? Jean Graham? I know nobody of that name. Do you know her?"

'"She runs my Glasgow office."

'"So this letter's likely to have come from Glasgow?" I asked.

'"I've told you I haven't the slightest idea where it's come from. It's the work of a diseased imagination."

'"I see. You deny it?"

'"Yes. I said so."

'"You've not had an affair with this Jean Graham? Or anyone else?"

'"No."

'"Very good," I said and sat down. "That's it, then."

'"What do you mean?"

'"There is no truth in this accusation. Or any other. You deny it. So there is nothing for me but to accept your word. I do not think you are a barefaced liar. If this person writes again I shall show it to you."

'"Thank you," he said politely.

'"Will you leave me now? As you can imagine, I'm rather upset by this."

'"Thank you," he said again. "Is there anything I can get you? A drink? An aspirin?"

'I shook my head and sat, chin on chest. I could see that, with the slightest encouragement, he'd come across and put his arms round me or his hands on me. I'd have hated that. Out he went, tail between his legs.'

'And that was that?' John Stone said, speaking for the first time.

'You could say so. Except that I found some weeks later another letter, or part of a letter, from the first woman. It was one rather crumpled sheet, with her address at the top. There it was on the bedroom floor. Perhaps he'd put it away in his pocket in a hurry and it had dropped out. I don't know. It wasn't hidden. It lay on the carpet, clear to the eyes of everybody.'

'Do you think he'd deliberately left it there?' John asked.

'And why would he do that?'

'To tempt you,' Peg said.

'I have not the slightest idea why that sheet was lying on the carpet. I picked it up and laid it in the middle of the dressing table. I straightened it out so that he couldn't miss it. It was half folded, not neatly, when it was on the floor.'

'And?'

'When he came home from work he went upstairs to wash and change because he'd a meeting that evening. When he went out later I crept upstairs. The letter had gone. I made quite a thorough search of drawers, of his clothes, but there was no sign of it. He'd probably taken it out with him and burnt it somewhere else. Nor could I find the rest of the letter.'

'Did you mention it to him?'

'No. Nor he to me.'

'But he must have known.'

'He must have. But you never know what men like Ian think. He might have decided he'd been lucky, that I'd picked it up, that I'd seen his name on it and didn't read it.'

'Little did he know you,' Peg said. 'Did it worry you?'

'Did it? Yes, for months. My mind was in turmoil. Do you know, I've been wondering in these past few days if John James's marital – domestic, rather – problems didn't spring from my distress in those days.'

'But he was only a baby then,' Peg objected.

'I know, but we were together, and I'd sob and scream some-times I was so angry and hurt.'

'Not likely at all,' Peg pronounced. 'What do you think, Jack?'

'No. I wouldn't think so.'

The front-door bell pealed.

'That'll be Annie. Let her in, Jack. And we'll all have a glass of sherry. We need it.'

The meal passed pleasantly. Annie Fisher stayed the rest of the afternoon and when Stone went out on a call to a sick friend the women talked. May gave the visitor a brief account of her marital problems.

Annie left soon after four to prepare her husband's evening meal. 'He'll be back early,' she said. 'He's out again tonight.'

'On the razzle?' Peg queried.

'No. A genuine meeting. Hospital committee. They have some bigwig there today. A professor of orthopaedic surgery from Edinburgh tonight. Jack will be going. Isn't he?'

'You won't ring up to make sure he's there?' May asked.

'No. It doesn't matter. To tell you the truth I don't mind where he is. As long as he doesn't drag us into the public eye.'

'You must be glad that Jack's such a steady man in that respect,' May said.

'Otherwise I might fancy him,' Annie said.

'You're welcome,' Peg answered.

'You don't mean that.'

The women had recovered, to some small extent.

VII

May left for home after breakfast. She had rung her son the evening before, had talked to him for perhaps ten minutes and had reported to her sister that there was no change on that front. Both the young people were at work; both talked to each other about their troubles, but less frequently and more calmly. He had not changed his decision about staying at the bank and was unlikely to do so. May left for the station in Jack's car and seemed cheerful, as if the confessions of the previous day had relieved her mind.

'No rash decisions now,' Peg teased as the two women waited at the front gate for Stone to bring the car round.

'Such as?' smilingly.

'In re Mr Ronald Murray.'

The sisters kissed. Peg had been in sympathy with May more than at most times, perhaps because she felt her elder had been in, and was coping with, real trouble. Peg had known for years about Ian MacGregor's chasing after women; he had once tried to use his hands freely with her, but had rapidly been put in his place. She bore him no ill will; it seemed adolescent behaviour. Anything in skirts he fancied he flirted with, tried sex with, long or short, given the chance, but never, at least in his own mind, lost his respect for his wife, his care for her, his generosity in his dealings with her. He loved his May and that rather solemn, clever child she had borne him. Hanky-panky elsewhere enabled him to carry out his domestic duties more perfectly. That was his opinion, Peg guessed, if he had ever bothered to work it out.

When Stone returned from the station (he had taken May out to Newark) his wife questioned him. 'Did she say anything? Of interest?' she asked.

'Not really. Well, one thing that surprised me. She said she hoped we wouldn't back away if either JJ or Linda tried to get in touch with us.'

78

'Is that likely?'

'I guess she'd advised them to canvass opinions from us. We are, after all, relatives and people who are experienced in the ways of the world, and who use our common sense.' He grinned ironically at himself.

'But we were likely to "back away"?' Peg mocked.

'*Ipsissima verba.*'

'None of your pedantry.' Peg punched his arm, as she did when they were first married and she could think of no convincing answer in a friendly argument. 'What will you tell them?'

'I shall listen first and question them a bit. They're both strangers to me. If I met them in the street I wouldn't recognise either of them.'

'I see.'

They did not have to wait long. That evening Linda rang and talked to Peg for a good half-hour. Stone was out at a meeting at a nearby primary school where he was (for his sins, he jested) on the governing body. 'What did she say for herself?' he asked when he returned.

'She didn't tell me anything very different from May's account.'

'And what did you tell her?'

'Much the same as May: that JJ feels responsibility for her and therefore needs a job and money to meet this. She listened, didn't interrupt and then claimed quietly that he wouldn't accept her solution, life together in the country.'

'And how did you answer that?' Stone asked.

'Just as you would have done. I said that if she had decided that a suicide pact was the only answer she might understand his objection.' Peg sighed, then deliberately drew in breath. 'She just said, in a wooden – no, stony – sort of way, "I haven't proposed suicide. Nor will I."'

'And that was that?'

'No. We talked on for some time and I invited her up here. She said she would consider it, and we discussed times and dates. She's going to ring again. She said she'd like to talk to you.'

A day or two later, while Peg was out, Annie Fisher came round. 'Are you both in?' she asked. He guessed she'd seen Peg on the way out to town and had therefore chosen to call in on him. She was dressed and perfumed for the occasion.

'No. Peg's visiting the Rodd-Walkers.'

She kissed him, with enthusiasm, swaying. 'I wanted to thank you for your kindness to me the other day. I was in a state worse than China.' He wondered if this was an expression picked up from her husband. 'You did me good. I was steady enough to face Harry with the letter when he came home. He read it and looked quite cheerful about it. "I can guess who wrote this bloody thing," he said. "Is it true?" I asked him. "It's quite true that I called in on Wendy Wallace on the morning she was murdered." "You didn't mention it to me," I said. "No, I didn't. I know how you worry." And so it went on. Apparently he was on the way to do a job in Warsop, but he called in at Mrs Wallace's early to drop stuff in for some work he was to do for her at the end of the week. Fortunately, he was seen by a neighbour, while he was storing the panels or whatever they were in the garage, and the same man saw Mrs Wallace with him in the street just before he drove off. This neighbour also saw her later on in the morning alive and well. Harry's man was there, helping him carry the stuff in. He had a full day's alibi out at Warsop. Both his workman, the one who was in the van with him, and the family, an elderly couple at the house he was slaving at, had him in sight all day.'

'At what time was she killed? Mrs Wallace?'

'About noon.'

'Have the police got a suspect?'

'Yes. Her ex-husband. According to Harry he turns up from time to time to beg, borrow or steal money from her.'

'Have they been separated long?'

'That was my impression. Harry doesn't elaborate. He was seen that day in the street by neighbours and later the man next door heard shouts and quarrelling.'

'Who wrote the letter to you? You said he'd a good idea who it is.'

'One of a couple of old maids, sisters, who live opposite. They didn't think very highly of Mrs W. One or the other of them sat spying on her all day behind the lace curtains.'

'Did he seem at all upset by this?' he asked.

'Not really. He said he'd known Mrs Wallace for some years and sometimes did odd jobs for her. That's how he fills his leisure these days, now he's retired. He's kept one of his older men to help out. They have a workshop at the back here.'

'I know. I've seen it.'

'Jim, James Wood, didn't want to retire when he was sixty-five but the new directors insisted. He complained to Harry and he took him on. There's plenty of work about for the two of them and they can choose what they want to do. Harry's never been so happy. He enjoys using his hands.'

'It's not a cover for his other activities?'

'It may well be. But he's seventy now. So surely it's not as important to him as it was. He doesn't look his age, but I think he begins to feel it. And he had Jim in the van with him most of the time.'

'Yes,' Stone said. 'As long as you don't mind.'

'He'll keep me out of these affairs if he can. We still continue' – she smiled at the expression she was about to use – 'our intimate relations. From time to time. Not often. You don't think I should tell you that, do you?'

'It's up to you.'

'You're not jealous, are you, Jack? After all, I'm much younger than he is.' She grinned slily. 'When your sister-in-law was complaining about her husband, and I about mine, I wondered if Peg and May ever thought that you and I did what we shouldn't.'

'I don't suppose so,' he answered in a flat voice.

'You don't think that Peg ever suspects us?'

'Probably not.'

'Would she be angry?'

He shrugged. This conversation had become tasteless. For the moment he looked on her with mild loathing. She was trying to make trouble.

'We don't do it very often,' she said.

'We're getting old. At least I am.'

She looked away, as if thinking. 'I've annoyed you now, Jack, haven't I?' He did not answer. 'You don't mind doing it, but we mustn't talk about it.'

'That seems sensible.'

'Sensible? Didn't you enjoy it, then?'

'If you want the truth, I was surprised that you made yourself so easily available and, in fact, plainly asked me to copulate with you.'

81

'Copulate.' She spoke with her teeth together.

'I have to put it some way. Don't think I underestimate our relationship. It was a kind of out-of-this-world activity for me. Here was a beautiful woman, years younger than I was, offering herself to me.'

'Ten.' In answer to his frown of puzzlement she elucidated: 'Ten years younger.'

'Yes,' he said thoughtfully, groping for words. 'Perhaps it was because it was adultery, morally wrong, against my upbringing, that it appealed. Perhaps because it was dangerous; I could have been dismissed from my headship, or held up to ridicule if the story had come out. And Peg might well have made it public. And, worst of all, left me.'

'Are you sure of that? Wouldn't she have been embarrassed enough to want to keep it quiet?'

'No. Well, I don't know.'

'They wouldn't have sacked you? Scores of the teachers in England would be out if that were the case.'

'Perhaps not, but if it got into the papers and I became a figure of fun, they'd have leaned on me to go.'

'But now you're adding lying and deceit to adultery.'

'That would be fairly usual,' he said, resuming his schoolmaster's manner.

'So,' she answered, 'there'll be no more' – she paused, smiling – 'of our little goings-on.'

'Annie.' He spoke immediately, but slowly, holding up his left hand for her close attention. 'I can't say my behaviour has been impeccable. I don't mean about the sex. I'm talking about what I've said this morning. I'm blaming you and that can't be right. I could have said "No" if morality were all that important to me. But it wasn't like that. Not at all.' He grabbed blindly towards her, took her hand and stroked it. 'Annie.' He spoke very deliberately. 'I owed you something. I still owe you something.' He breathed deeply. His legs trembled. Phlegm clogged his throat. 'If I had to defend our affair, I would have said that it helped me to do my job properly and to keep my marriage steady. I can't deny that Peg would have objected strongly if she had found out, but we were careful she didn't. She wouldn't have been like May.'

'But May didn't leave her husband.'

'No, but she's considerably less volatile than Peg.'

'She would have left you?'

'That's more than a possibility.'

'I knew, Jack, that you would never leave her. I often puzzle myself about us. We gradually practised our sex. That's a mad thing to say; "practised" is the wrong word. We gradually slid or glided into it. I admired you; you seemed a somebody as Harry was not. I guess he had more money than you, but that never even came into it. And we spaced it out. That's the most unusual, and impressive, thing to say about an affair. We weren't chasing after opportunities every hour of the day. Maybe we weren't passionate enough, though again we were both what you could call good performers.'

'You're very articulate, Annie,' Stone said.

'I've thought about it more times than I'd like to count.'

'So have I.'

'And I can't understand how I came to be discreet about it all. I've had other men besides you and Harry. I wasn't exactly promiscuous, but I didn't deny myself either. But you knew that. Ours was different. It almost became a sign of respect.'

'That's not the way I looked at it.'

'Go on, then. Let's hear what you thought.'

'I enjoyed every minute. You were an attractive woman, beautiful. You still are and you excited an old puritan like me. And when we were done I was at ease, rested, refreshed, strengthened. I ought to have felt guilty, but I never could, and the longer we persevered at it the less guilty I felt.'

'You're not quite human, are you?' She giggled.

'No.'

'You've not had anybody else? Some other woman?'

'No.'

'We've not talked like this before.'

'We have not.'

'Will it spoil it, do you think?'

'When anything important happens,' Stone said mulishly, 'I have to go away and mull it over in my head. I'm not one of those men who can make his mind up straight away on the spot.'

'I thought that's what they'd like about headmasters.'

'The authorities, you mean? Or the pupils?' He blew out breath. 'I won't deny I tried sometimes to give that impression.'

83

'You hypocrite.' Annie was back to her cheerful self.

'That's true. You can see it is by the way I've been talking to you this morning. I never thought I'd hear myself putting forward a defence of adultery. It was wrong. Full stop. Even though there could be what you might call mitigating circumstances. But I had you for my own pleasure and yours, I hope. And kept it secret from Peg and Harry and everyone else. That's hypocrisy, if ever I knew it.'

Annie screwed up her face as if she had suddenly sucked a lemon. 'I hope,' she said, 'that when you've gone away and thought your deep thoughts to yourself, you won't decide to give me up.'

'And if I did?'

'I'd be sorry, upset, angry. I don't know the right word. I wouldn't like it. I might even spread rumours about us.'

'That's blackmail.'

'Well, if you will leave the path of righteousness, what do you expect?'

'"Do not adultery commit;
Advantage rarely comes of it."'

'Who said that?'

'A Victorian poet called Clough in "The Latest Decalogue". Decalogue means "Ten Commandments".'

'Always the bloody schoolmaster,' she said, but she moved towards him and held up her mouth to be kissed. He gently touched her lips with his, then drew her in close.

'That'll do,' she said. 'You have to go away and think deeply. Remember?' He nodded, abashed, like a shy boy. 'I've never had a talk like this with any of my lovers. You are quite extraordinary. Even in bed you're polite. You attract me, John Stone. You really do.'

'Thank you,' he said. 'I sound unique.'

She left almost immediately, her purpose for calling round, if it existed, forgotten. He saw her to the door and hummed to himself when she was outside. He examined his face in the hall mirror, found it unchanged, not without faults. He could not understand himself, or his moral attitudes. He had reduced adultery to the

level of, say, buying Annie a drink in a pub, an innocent polite-
ness that might make Peg jealous or idle tongues wag. He frowned,
walked up and down the hall in puzzled ambivalence. All that
afternoon at a committee-meeting his mind wandered from the
charity event they were planning and over to his own hypocrisies.
He wondered as he left the room what the local great and good
would have made of their chairman.

On his arrival home his wife said, rather unkindly, 'Linda's
coming on Friday night and will go back Sunday.'

'Linda?' he asked. 'Linda?'

'JJ's wife, partner, whatever she is. She wants to talk to us.
About her trouble.'

'Very good.'

'I don't see that it is. We don't know her, we've never even
seen her. What good can we do?'

'Well, she'll be away from her home in a new place. We are
observers, she thinks. Spectators on the touchline see more of
the game than the players.'

'If you believe that you'd believe anything.'

'You should have said "No" to her in that case.'

'How could I? And you would be the first to criticise if I'd
done so.'

'And talking of domestic trials and tribulations' – he tried to
lighten the tone by his choice of vocabulary – 'have we heard
from sister May?'

'No. Not a word since she rang to say she'd arrived safely
home.'

'So we don't know whether Mr Murray has popped the
question?'

'No,' she snapped, not pleased with him.

He collected Linda Thorpe from the station on Friday night.
They had, to his surprise, no difficulty in recognising each other.
She stood, tall and slim, with a kind of energy in her movements
as she emerged into the foyer.

'Linda?' he said.

'Yes.'

They shook hands heartily. She made no demur as he carried
her case to the car. Conversation was broken. She had a good
journey, not too crowded, and the train was on time. He pointed

out places of interest, not that there were many and those all misted by street lights, shop fronts and the red lamps of thick, slickly moving traffic.

'We're travelling north now,' he said.

'In the direction of what town?'

'Doncaster.'

'I've never been there.'

He took this to mean that she had no idea where Doncaster was. Her voice was low, with a slight Home Counties accent. She sat beautifully even in the car and her profile approached perfection. A faint perfume delighted him. He edged the car off the main road at traffic lights and up a darker hill. Near the top he turned into his street and drew up outside his front gate under the light of a tall sodium lamp. 'We're here,' he stated.

'You don't live far from the centre of town,' she said.

'All our distances will seem small compared with London.'

He carried her case up the front-garden path, warned her to be careful on the steps up to the door and rang the bell.

A small light slenderly illuminated them before Peg opened the door. 'No key?' she asked.

'Hands full.' He indicated the visitor and her case. 'This is Linda. Linda, my wife, Margaret, Peg. Now I've introduced you, I'll put the car away.' He skipped sprightly down the steps and into the darkness. Peg closed the door behind him.

On his return the house appeared empty, apart from the delicious smell of cooking. He called upstairs but received no answer. He hung up his coat, settled himself comfortably in the sitting room, picked up the morning's newspaper, which he'd not read, and waited for the women to reveal themselves. Perhaps five minutes later they appeared. He jumped to his feet. 'Where have you been?' he barked.

'Been?' Peg answered. 'I've been giving Linda an idea of the geography of the house.'

'I shouted to you when I came in, but there was no answer.'

'We'd be in the small boxroom.' That was that. 'Now do you mind carrying Linda's case up to her room, while I look at dinner?'

'Oh, I can easily manage it myself,' Linda said.

'Let Jack do it. It makes him feel wanted.' Then, in a softer voice, 'Just have a quick wash. We'll eat in fifteen minutes.'

Stone trudged upwards, following the girl. She wore a golden dress, which rode silkily over her buttocks. It looked expensive. She did not speak, but made her way unerringly to her bedroom. He followed her in with the case. 'A quarter of an hour,' he said. 'You know where the dining room is?' She nodded solemnly. 'We'll be on the lookout for you. Shout if there's anything you want.' This time she spoke, thanking him, her voice low and contained. He turned smartly and marched out, closing the door.

He made for the kitchen where Peg busied herself. She was never happier, he thought, than when she was nearing the end of a successful culinary hour. 'Anything I can do?' he asked.

'No. Not till she comes down.'

'And then?'

'Sherry if she wants it. I've got the red wine out. I don't know if she drinks. She can afford it, but may not like alcohol.'

'She's made a bad impression on you, has she?'

His wife looked towards the door. 'No. The very opposite. For one thing, May didn't tell us either how beautiful she was or how well-dressed.'

'Ah, and why was that?'

'She might have been so upset by what was going on that she didn't notice. Though that's not like our May. Perhaps she was jealous and afraid she wouldn't be able to influence JJ against such a paragon.'

'She was well educated, wasn't she?'

'Am I supposed to have found all that out in the ten minutes while you were putting the car away? Actually, May did tell me. She was in a GPD School until A level, doing double maths and biology. I don't know if she reads or goes to the theatre or picture galleries. I guess not; she won't have time. Women when they get on to a subject they like, work at it and don't go frittering their free time away.'

'Did she mention JJ?'

'Not once. Now you just go outside. I don't want her hanging about in the hall. It's not altogether warm, among other things.'

'But it doesn't matter if I hang about there.'

'I'm trying to make a good impression on the girl, not on you.'

'Thank you very much.'

He went out, switched on more lights, stood and examined the pictures. He concentrated on a Dutch print: *The Lacemaker* by Caspar Netscher (1639–84). He breathed deeply as he closely examined the wooden floorboards in the painting. One could faintly see the knots in the wood. The brushwork was delicately accurate, interesting in the variations of monochrome. He noticed that the room had no skirting boards. He wondered at what period these were introduced, but had no idea. How could he find out? He thought of his two encyclopaedias, but did not desert his post. The girl was pretty, but had thick wrists and thus presumably thick ankles under the wide skirt. Vermeer's ladies never seemed to have this instant prettiness.

He heard Linda coming down the stairs.

She wore the same silken gold dress and a small band, also gold, in her hair. Would that be a fillet? He'd ask Peg. He moved nearer the foot of the stairs. She reached his level with a graceful flourish of her skirt ends.

'This way,' he said.

At that moment Peg appeared, bustling, then standing stiffly as if surprised at the antics of the other two.

'Come into the kitchen,' she ordered. Linda obeyed, moving like a queen in front of Stone. 'Has he offered you a drink?'

'Not yet,' he excused himself. 'May I offer you a glass of sherry?'

'Please,' the girl answered.

'Dry? Sweet? Amontillado?'

'Dry, if I may.'

They stood now in the kitchen, which radiated warmth and light compared with the tall semi-darkness of the foyer. They drank together, raising their glasses, smiling their welcome.

'Rather good,' Peg said, concentrating on her glass. 'Show Linda to her place, will you, Jack. And put the lights on. And more heat if it's necessary. Then you can help me bring the soup in.'

He followed instructions to the letter. Linda sat, regally smiling, toying with her sherry. She answered questions politely, said she had not enjoyed a meal as good as this for weeks. 'Our evening meal's skimped and you can tell.'

'Does JJ complain?'

'No. Never. He's quite hungry sometimes, but he's not concerned about what it is he's eating or even what it looks like.'

'His mother's a good cook,' Peg interrupted.

'I'm sure she is,' Linda answered amicably. 'She's a very serious-looking lady.' Stone thought 'lady' carried as much disapproval as 'serious', but said nothing. He quizzed her gently about her work in the bank and she answered freely but never at any length. He decided that these were mathematician's sentences, clear but with brevity predominant. She showed little enthusiasm, though she said she thought it just as interesting as any other work. 'Every job bores you at some time before too long.'

'What's the advantage of banking?' he asked.

'Money. You're well paid if you're anything like good at it.'

'And you are?' Peg queried teasingly.

'Not bad.'

The meal did not last long, but established, at least in Stone's eyes, a thoroughly friendly relationship between the three. Linda did not give away too much about herself and said nothing at all about her domestic difficulties. She drank two glasses of red wine with her beef but refused a second helping of Peg's trifle, a masterpiece.

When they had finished eating, Jack Stone said, 'I'll clear away and wash up, then bring the coffee in.'

'Put them in the dishwasher,' Peg answered.

'No,' he answered and to Linda, 'I quite like washing up. It gives me thinking time.'

'Does he drop much crockery?' Linda asked Peg.

'He's a safe pair of hands,' Peg muttered. 'Or he thinks so.'

'I'd have expected that.'

The women helped him clear the table and made for the smaller sitting room, book-lined, comfortably cosy. Jack congratulated himself on organising matters to his satisfaction. Peg could begin to discuss the important topics with the girl, for she'd do it lightly, easily, making Linda feel at home, not flustering her from the start. He saw that Peg was not altogether pleased to be left with this task, but she'd act sensibly. He took his time over the sink. It was not a long job, for Peg had cleaned up as she prepared the meal. He searched out the best cups for coffee, setting them on a large white tray and this he carried in with the swagger of a hired butler.

'Milk, sugar, brown sugar?' he asked Linda. 'Or black as night?' She smiled gently at him as she chose, her small breasts alive

89

with movement each time she leaned forward. 'Bore at men's eyes,' he remembered the Shakespearean tag. Linda sat upright in her chair, whereas his wife had dropped, flopped, untidily into hers. Peg sprawled shapeless, it seemed, a well-dressed middle-aged woman, making no attempts to impress.

'Do you know what Linda calls JJ?' Peg asked, as finally he sat, straight, he hoped, with his coffee beside him.

'No idea.'

'Jay,' Peg said.

'Half as long. Good.'

'When his mother first referred to him as "JJ" it seemed odd. Not John; not James. I'd called him John so far. I'd heard people on the television refer to men by their initials, but these were usually bosses you wouldn't dare to address by Christian names.'

'Don't you use first names at the bank?' John asked.

'Yes, to some extent, though we are rather old-fashioned and formal.'

They chatted about the change of usage in social contacts. He thought that Linda, with her background, would have little to contribute, but she soon proved him wrong. She claimed that many of the teenaged children called their parents by their Christian names.

'Did you?' Peg asked.

'Never. I called them "Dad", "Mum".'

'Any reason?'

'No, it's what they taught us.'

'Were they clever?'

'Yes, they were. They never attended grammar school, or went to evening classes, but both of them would have done well academically, given the chance.'

'Did they regret it?'

'They don't say so, but they saw to it that my sister and I both had our chance.'

'What does your sister do?'

'She has a Ph.D. in physics. She's married with two children and teaches part-time at Royal Holloway, her old college. She's older than I am. She was in the sixth form when I first went to grammar school.'

'And clever?'

'Yes. Good at maths, like me.'

'That's useful,' Stone asked, 'at the bank?'

'I wonder about that. I suppose it is, but one or two of the best people I work with were on the arts side at university. They're not innumerate by any means, but maths is not their first love.'

Linda seemed not displeased at talking like this. Perhaps she felt she was examining these examiners before the real tests began. She had not long to wait.

As soon as John Stone had filled second cups for all three, he sat and asked, 'And how are you and J getting on now?'

'Yes.' Linda's voice was low, in pitch and strength. 'Not too badly, all things considered.'

'Good,' John purred. 'No developments?'

'Not really. We're treating each other with due care and consideration.' Linda smiled at her own expression.

'You're both still working?'

'Like beavers.' She sipped at her coffee. 'Nor do we argue at home now. When I first suggested that I leave the bank we went at it hammer and tongs every spare minute we had. I dreaded coming home. To tell you the truth I didn't always do so. I spent some nights at my parents' house and I never remotely expected that. I also had a night or two in a hotel.'

'Did you tell your parents exactly what was happening?' John asked.

'Yes. I had to explain my appearance.'

'Am I in order to ask what their reaction was?'

'Yes. They thought as you do, or at least your wife does, that we'd be stark raving mad to throw up our jobs and vegetate in the country.'

'Is there any logical, reasonable case you could raise against their view?'

Linda leaned back, as if she were enjoying this exchange, before she answered again, 'I'm not sure that logic came into it, at least as far as I was concerned. It was purely emotional. I felt trapped, fighting against myself, selling my soul to Mammon, polluting the world if at second hand. That was the important thing to me. But I pointed out to my dad that my position in the bank was by no means permanent. If things went wrong I should be out. Our

91

sort of investment banks are not charitable institutions. As soon
as they decided I wasn't of any use to them, I'd lose my job, out,
bang, slap, wallop.' Again she smiled as if apologising for her
onomatopoeic expression.

Stone smiled in return. 'Is that likely?' he asked.

'Not at this moment, but one never quite knows. Circumstances
may easily, and quickly, change.'

'And if they did are you suggesting you'd be unable to deal
with them and so they'd sack you?'

'I'd be as able as anybody else, I guess. But if they're not
making money they do away with staff. And you're wanting to
ask whether I think I'd be one of those for the chop. The answer
is that I do. I'm a fairly late comer and furthermore a woman.
Our bank is a man-directed place.'

'But if they've appointed a woman, surely that's because they
thought at the time she was an unusually outstanding candidate?'

'Um-ah-er.' She quietly made the comical sound of doubt. 'A
woman's different. If she's unemployed she can depend on a man,
or raise a family. They don't admit these foolish ideas, but the prejudice is there. And you must remember that we all have to show
talent for the work in the probationary period, or we'll lose our
jobs.'

'Is that a great number?'

'Not really. We're well vetted before they take us on.'

'And do you resent all this?' Peg interrupted.

'You know what you're in for. They made it utterly plain that
I was an experiment on their part. A girl from a grammar school
and a working-class family.'

'Why did they do it?'

'Pressure from society. Equal opportunity. If they appoint a
woman they indicate they've no prejudice and thus can't be
accused of being out of step.'

'But they are?' Peg asked.

'They'd deny it. But.'

'You must have done well?' Stone resumed.

'Yes. I suppose so. The job suited me and I wasn't afraid of
hard work.'

'And for how long were you happy?'

'I've been there thirteen years.'

'Quite contentedly?'

'Yes. It kept me busy. And made me plenty of money. I bought my flat outright within the first seven years.'

'And when was it that you began to feel out of place? Did it suddenly hit you? Or come gradually?'

'I had twinges. My sister was an academic high flyer, but she had two children. She obviously put that first.'

'It's stood in the way of promotion for her.'

'Yes and her husband's. He's a physicist like her and has had offers from America, which he's turned down because he doesn't want to drag his wife and children all over the world. He teaches at Imperial and they're willing to keep him on. He's got as far as senior lecturer now, but he doubts if he'll go any further. He's a decent teacher and he does no end of research, most of it published, but it doesn't ring any big bells.'

'Are they happy?'

'Yes, I'd say so. Especially now that Tracey gets some work and the children are at school and doing well. My mother collects them morning and afternoon three days a week, and gives them tea when they get back. I think Trace pays her and it helps my mother run a little car. They fit it in somehow.'

'Is your sister a better physicist than her husband?'

'I see where you're going.' Linda laughed, flung her legs about, though decorously enough. 'I don't know. Probably not. He's been at it full time. But –' she stopped and pointed at Stone – 'I think I'm better at my job than Jay is. For one thing I've been at it longer, though that wouldn't count except that I've more talent at it than he has. He's clever enough, and a worker, but I've more flair. That's my view. You'll have to quizz him to find out what he thinks.' She did not appear to boast.

'You don't know?'

'Of course I do. He's no fool. I didn't notice him very much when he first came to work there. He seemed a neat, polite Scotsman. Rather shy. I had to push him, one way and the other. Even to get him to go out with me at first, to a dance or a theatre or once a party. And certainly three years ago, when I suggested we live together, he was shocked.'

'You both had flats?' Peg asked.

'Yes, he'd just changed his, though it wasn't as good as mine, but I was willing to move into his. I let mine, oh, easily, without any trouble.'

'That gives you an escape route?' Peg asked.

'I suppose so, but I never thought of it like that. It was another way of making money, without too much risk. And I wanted to live with him.'

'Did he want to live with you?' Peg again.

'By this time, yes, he did. And he wouldn't have argued if I'd insisted we had my flat.'

'Did marriage get a mention?' Peg seemed to be monopolising the cross-examination now.

'It never came into my mind, but I guess with his upbringing he thought about it. If he mentioned it I just dismissed it, as an unnecessary chore or expense.'

Peg frowned thoughtfully, rubbing hard at her eyebrow with her left forefinger.

'And how do things stand between you now?' John Stone took up the questioning.

'It's quiet. We don't quarrel.'

'Have you given up your idea of leaving the bank and living in a cottage?'

'No, not altogether.'

'That doesn't sound exactly confident. You're not thinking of changing your mind?'

'I might well.'

'Does Jay know that?'

'I don't suppose he does. As I tell you, we've left off quarrelling about it, but he may think I'm resting for the time, collecting ammunition, getting prepared for the next onslaught.'

'Is that right?'

'I don't know. I tell you what did surprise me and that was his obstinacy and energy in arguing. I thought he'd be weak and give in easily. Or failing that just back away from the whole thing. Sulk, perhaps. But he was hard as nails. It was his duty to earn money for the home. If I wanted to stop working at the bank, that was fine as far as he was concerned. I could live as a smallholder in the country, or go to a university and read for a degree, or anything else; it didn't matter. He'd continue to earn money to keep us solvent.'

'He really set about you?'

'Yes, he did.'

'And did you like that?'

'I'm not one of these women who likes her partner to lay down the law. If you ask me, I know more about most things than he does. I hope I'm not insulting your sister if I say she brought him up in a rather sheltered environment. She took the hard decisions, not her son. But for whatever reason he wants to be master in this one aspect of his life. As I say, it surprised me. It was quite out of character.'

'And did that alter your view?'

'Not really. I wasn't pleased to meet opposition when I didn't expect it. But it made me slightly less confident of my own rightness, I must admit. That's why I asked if I could come up here to meet you and see what you had to say. Your wife's view is that I should respect Jay's argument and do as I'm told at least for the present. That's your decision, too, is it?'

'I never find it very easy to make complex judgements about people I hardly know. I think I agree with her premise. You say a woman's position in business is less stable than a man's, and Jay presumably knows that and wants to make sure that you're not going to be badly caught out. And he'll wonder how you'd manage with your cottage, and vegetables, and ducks and geese. It sounds wonderful, but you're a town dweller, aren't you? You may not like it, or be any good at it.'

'That's always possible. I didn't know when I started whether I'd like the bank.'

'No, but your education had led you, if only obliquely, in that direction.'

'So you think I should drop the idea?'

'Unless you are absolutely convinced of its rightness. I tell you not to pay too much attention because I don't know you or your circumstances anything like well. I must confess that you have made a favourable, very favourable impression on me during our short acquaintance. You seem judicious, amenable to reason, quick on the uptake, able to grasp the view the other person is advancing. I don't know, I admit, how easily you change your mind. There you are. One other thing I'd like to say. My wife and I both gathered from Jay's mother that he was desperately in love with you.'

'Yes,' Peg echoed. 'We did.'

'Did she think we should marry?'

'She didn't say so,' Stone answered, 'oddly enough. But I imagine she thought you should.'

'Why?' Linda's one word was strong, seemed to spread.

'Because it would be a public pronouncement, an avowal, of your commitment. Otherwise you can throw one another over without much trouble.'

'The law might well consider our living together as sufficient witness of our love. They treat common-law wives now to be as much entitled to joint spoils as those married in Westminster Abbey.'

'Um, you may be right.'

'Did you two never quarrel?' Linda now pursued him, eyes twinkling.

'Yes,' he answered. 'Many times.'

'But seriously. I don't mean mere temper spats.'

'We didn't think so at the time,' Peg said.

'Were they so bad,' Linda pressed, 'that you felt like upping sticks and leaving him?'

'Once or twice. Occasionally even now when I think back to them I begin to get hot under the collar. But I can honestly say I'm glad I didn't.'

They talked for an hour and a half, encouraged in the case of Linda and John by the whisky bottle. Peg watched the two with pleasure, joined often in their conversation, saying piously that confession was good for the soul. They went early to bed, before eleven, and Peg and her husband talked past midnight. Both agreed that they had liked Linda and also considered her to be outstanding, a remarkable personality.

'Will you tell May so?' he asked.

'Yes, I shall tell her. I will tell her. But she'll already know. May is not without intelligence.'

Just before she turned over for sleep, Peg asked, 'What do you think she'll decide?'

'I don't know. But if I were JJ I'd fall in with any notion she came up with. He's a lucky man.'

'You're half in love again,' Peg said sleepily.

'Again? Have I been in love so often?' he asked in mock displeasure.

'You've only to spend five minutes in the company of a beautiful, clever woman and you're away, a quite different man.'

'How can you tell?'

'You smile, you wave your arms about.'

'In a way I don't for you?'

'No, not nowadays.'

Breakfast was leisurely. Linda decided that she'd stay the whole day with them and return home after lunch on Sunday. She rang JJ and he made no objection to her plans. He asked her, she said, to pass on good wishes to his aunt and uncle. The two women shopped together at the local Sainsbury's before they and Stone set out northwards to walk in Saville Park, one of the great estates of the county, the Dukeries. The day was not cold and the trees and sharp exercise kept them warm. The old folks, Linda wryly congratulated them, were more used to walking than the girl. She wore sensible shoes, didn't seem afraid to splash in the mud or icy puddles, but her companions' almost robot-like forward movement, elbows working, seemed to intimidate her as if she thought she would suddenly find herself fifty yards behind her hosts. She seemed short of breath, a thin smear of sweat shone on her forehead and the pallor of her face manifested a delicate blush.

'Are we going too fast?' Peg asked.

'I'm out of practice.'

'You'll have to visit us more often,' Stone said, 'and you'll soon be fit.'

'There must be plenty of places in London, parks, gardens, where you can walk.'

'That's true. But if I walk it's along the streets.'

'I'd hate that,' Peg said. 'Give me grass underfoot at any time. It doesn't jar.'

'Does Jay often go out with you?'

'Occasionally. We did walk to work at the beginning of last summer when we decided to lose weight. It took us well over half an hour.'

'Did it do you good?'

'Neither of us was much slimmer. We felt quite proud of ourselves. Something achieved. But this autumn it's rained too hard. I hate to arrive wet through.'

They returned home in the early dark. The house was

comfortably warm, and they sat within minutes to hot tea and delicious buttered scones.

'This is what Saturday evening should be like,' Linda said.

'Is it?' Peg asked. 'I always think we should be off to see *The Marriage of Figaro* or *Waiting for Godot*.'

'What would they do for you?'

'Keep my mind or my heart lively. I've now reached the age when I'd sooner stay at home than go to *King Lear* or Beethoven's Ninth. It's not right.'

'That's what comfortable marriage does for you.' Stone grinned.

'We don't go to the theatre now,' Linda said.

'That's the nature of your life. When I was a headmaster there was pretty nearly always some sort of school event going on at the weekend and we were expected to show our faces.'

'Didn't you mind?'

'No. We enjoyed the plays and the Gilbert and Sullivan. They even had a quite brilliant music hall for two or three years. We were lucky in that we had a very lively staff, bright children and interested parents who'd turn up in big numbers. They laid on charity shows, proceeds to good causes, with the school bus and half a dozen parents' cars picking up old folks from the local nursing homes.'

'Didn't you ever fear that all your spare time, your own time, was being taken away from you?'

'We often complained about it, but whether we believed it or not is a different thing,' Peg said.

'We didn't go to everything. I'd turn up now and again on a Saturday afternoon for a football match or a game of cricket, but I drew the line at the discos they held.'

'And when you look back, now you're retired, do you think that you've spent your life well?'

'I think back', Stone said, 'rather less than you would imagine. Perhaps I'm not old enough yet. And I've kept up my attendance at various committees I'm invited to join. I invariably accept these opportunities in case I get rusty. But to answer your question about my life as a schoolmaster. As I said, we had a good catchment area with bright children and interested and able parents. I think I can say I chose very efficient teachers. The senior men knew what they were about; many of them were O and A level examiners. All this has its drawbacks, like everything else in life. The very well-qualified, bright young men and women would only stay with us three years or so before they moved on to promotion or a post in a more prestigious – I dislike that word – school. The result was we had very good examination results and once word of that gets round you find parents falling over themselves, changing addresses even, to procure places for their youngsters. We managed a good few Oxbridge places.'

'So you look back with a sense of satisfaction? All these great academic results and scholarships as well as all the out-of-school activities?' Linda spoke solemnly, ironically perhaps, John thought.

'Well, yes. But I haven't quite answered your question, have I? I sometimes wonder how much of the school's success was due to me. Would another headmaster, quite different from me, have done just as well as I did?'

'And would he?'

'Yes. Given certain basic qualities. I had to understand the making of the timetable. I could do that. And I didn't add fancy work. We did Russian and Italian, but I didn't have Chinese and Japanese. I sometimes regret that we didn't have Classics proper, Latin and Ancient Greek. I could have done something about it. We didn't teach Greek at all, though there must have been a few students who would have benefited from it. And I was responsible for discipline, in all sorts of small ways as well as large. We were in a middle-class district and so the problems were nothing like as great as inner-city places where they have to wall themselves in and employ security guards all day just to keep marauders out. That's so, but there were difficulties, with staff as well as pupils. These are the basics. These kept lessons running on time, and pupils happy and learning something.'

'Did you expel people?'

'We did transfer a few to establishments they'd find more congenial, more suited to their aptitudes, their attitudes. But not many. And not without warning. I am a middle-of-the-road man. Some heads would try to change the direction of the school. Make it maths or science orientated. I didn't see that as my role. I used to make all sixth-formers at the beginning of their first post-O-level year, as we called them then, write an account of their lives and education so far. It paid off. I learnt a great deal and I think they did. I don't claim I was particularly gifted as a headmaster, but I worked at it and I had the sort of serious face, as well as the balding head, that fitted well with the position.'

Linda congratulated them on their talk, which she had enjoyed, she said, to the full. 'My parents are too suspicious for anything like a frank exchange of ideas.'

'Why is that?'

'Money, really. I once told my father, oh, years ago, how much I earned, and you could fairly see him wince. His body seemed to wither. He did his best to fight, but it was too much. "Even the effing Queen isn't worth that," he said and he wasn't a swearing man. And he's been very quiet with me ever since. I'm from an alien planet now, as far as he's concerned.'

The Stones went down to the station on Sunday afternoon to see her off to London. John carried her bag. Linda kissed them both, whispering, 'I've learnt a great deal from you this weekend. I wish I'd come before.'

'Don't let it be too long before you bring JJ up for a few days,' Peg ordered.

'I promise.'

On the way home the car seemed empty and the two sat silently. Peg tried to rouse her husband. 'That girl learnt a lot more about us than we did about her.'

'That's her way.'

What puzzled them most was that they did not receive a note of thanks for nearly a fortnight. Then one morning a postcard arrived. It depicted a spreading, untidy tree: Piet Mondrian (1872–1944) *Boom II*, 1912, *krijt op papier*:

> Many thanks for those two days in your lovely house.
> Apologies for my dilatory expression of gratitude.
> You're wonderful, both of you. With love, Linda.

'Well,' Peg said in exasperation, 'she doesn't say a word about how she's getting on with JJ.'

'Perhaps she hasn't made her mind up yet.'

'Then it's time she did.'

'You're like her father. He thinks she's an alien.'

'I should like to see a written report from her on us,' Peg said, only half-facetiously.

'You have it. In one word. "Wonderful".'

'I don't believe that. She's trying to work on us.'

They discussed the girl at every meal for a week; the fantastic clashed often with the realities. They frequently surprised themselves by what they said.

'She's shaken us up out of ourselves,' Peg told her husband. 'In two short days.'

'I think that's right.'

VIII

Their neighbour, Annie Fisher, began to speak quite often to Peg about the death of her husband's mistress, Wendy Wallace. The police had called in on Harry Fisher at least four times, so that she had begun to suspect that Harry was more involved than she had originally believed. She had said as much, foolishly, she thought now, to a smart youngish inspector in the CID, who had questioned her hard and then said the reason why he interviewed Fisher was that bits of information kept appearing which threw light on Mr Wallace's behaviour, and as Mr Fisher had had dealings recently with Mrs Wallace – and Annie understood him to mean about building matters, not sex – he might just have learnt something about the Wallaces and their concerns. 'Police work consists of asking question after question of person after person until something appears which throws light on what we've heard elsewhere. It's a long, boring job, but if we bring Wallace to trial it's an expensive business and they won't want to bring the man to court unless there's a fair amount of evidence against him.'

'Will they try him for murder?' Annie asked.

'Yes. Or manslaughter. There's a bit of argument over the pathologist's report.'

'Who'll decide?'

'The Director of Public Prosecutions. Or her office. They'll be pretty careful.'

Now that Harry was out of danger Annie talked all this over with Peg. 'It's frightened Harry,' she confessed.

'Why? He knows he's innocent.'

'All the books and plays on the telly are about innocent people caught up in webs of deceit, or misunderstanding or coincidence. And he's come to believe it. Besides, he feels guilty about this Wallace woman. He knows he was having it off with her. And if the police found out it would be held against him.'

'Do you feel sorry for him?' Peg asked.

'He's brought it on himself. But I could see he was worried at one time.'

'He won't have to appear in court.'

'Not according to the smart young inspector.'

Peg guessed that Annie Fisher took special pleasure in chattering about her husband's shortcomings with her neighbour.

'You don't hold it against him? Or do you?' Peg queried.

'Of course I do. I'd make him squirm, given half a chance.'

All this was passed, in succinct form, to John, who heard it uncomfortably, fearing what might come out next.

A letter from May in Scotland complained of the coldness of the autumn, which had prevented her from taking her daily walks; she had to satisfy herself with short strolls that did her no real good. She occupied her spare hours with reading, knitting and embroidery, but those were, she considered, winter pastimes and thus not welcome as the longer she postponed winter the better for her lifestyle. This complaint took up a good part of the letter, which was completed by two not very long paragraphs. The first informed them that Ronald Murray had called in twice to see her but had not made a nuisance of himself. He had spent two 'quite long' periods in Edinburgh on some business connected with the law, though what it was she did not exactly know. That was just what she would have wanted.

The last paragraph concerned a phone call from JJ, mentioning Linda's visit to Beechnall. According to her son's account, May wrote, Linda had been very impressed by her hosts, who were not only intelligent but knew how to make their guests feel thoroughly at home. She had ordered JJ to be ready for a visit to the Stones' house later in the year. He had no objections to this, especially as Linda had returned from her visit in a very cheerful mood.

'Had she given up her idea of quitting the bank?' he asked.

'She didn't say. So I take it she hadn't. May would have told me if that had been the case.'

'Oh. I'm glad we made a favourable impression,' Stone said.

'Great. She didn't take much looking after.'

'No.'

'I think young company did us good,' she continued. 'We were getting into a rut.'

103

'You speak for yourself.'

'I have to drag you out in the evenings to go to a concert or a play, even for a meal. At sixty-six you ought to delight in such outings.' She smiled now. 'I'm glad she thinks we benefited her to some extent. When you get thoroughly entangled as she is, obsessed with some quarrel or idea rattling round your mind that you can't rid yourself of, it's often the answer to remind yourself that there's a sane world outside, a place where you can see ordinary people getting on with ordinary lives.'

'That's us, is it?' He grinned.

'Yes, at present, though you never know what's going to explode into our placid little corner tomorrow or next week.'

'That's not so likely with elderly people.'

'Don't you believe it. One of us falls over, disables himself, sits in a wheelchair and it's the partner who can't go out, can't leave him for ten minutes, and then they begin to get on each other's nerves. That's worse than Linda's case. Old people know that it's a life sentence, a miserable ending to what started so well and continued over many years until illness or accident ruined it.'

'That's pretty pessimistic,' Stone said. 'It's not happened to us yet.'

'That's not to say it won't begin tomorrow.' She frowned desperately. 'Just look at some of your colleagues.'

'Well, yes.'

'Strokes and heart attacks, multiple sclerosis, Alzheimer's, Parkinson's, dislocations and fractures.'

'That's the case,' he agreed. 'old age isn't a festival for everybody. Not for most.' He assumed a headmasterly air. 'It's not a bad thing to consider these things, but it doesn't do to build our present lives on the prospect of such catastrophes.'

'We have to die,' she said.

> '"Cowards die many times before their deaths;
> The valiant never taste of death but once,"'

he quoted, but harshly as if to make up for the inappropriate nature of the words. Peg hurried off to her next task, which she'd perform, he knew, with alacrity and efficiency. He walked away to prepare a talk he was to give to the city debating society on the usefulness (or otherwise) of examinations in modern education. He had been cutting out statistics for months so that he'd be able to answer the smart alecs who'd take their evidence from headlines in the *Mirror* or the *Sun*.

Peg's final remarks had troubled him. He had always taken it that she, as he, possessed an optimistic temperament that kept her moderately cheerful. What had she heard, read or seen recently that had led to such gloomy prognostications for their old age? She rarely complained about major issues. She ticked him off regularly for untidiness or forgetfulness, even for small infringements of etiquette, or for his laxity in not carrying out repair jobs about the house, or fetching in workmen promptly to do tasks beyond his capacity.

She had never complained about the structure of her life. She had got on quickly with her teaching career, but whenever he moved to better himself she dropped her job and started again in the new place, knowing that in two or three years he might well be searching for new positions that would mean further upheaval, the building of new homes. She had suffered three miscarriages, but when their son, Thomas Alfred Symmonds Stone, was born she stayed at home, relinquishing a post she enjoyed and did successfully to concentrate on the upbringing of the child. John Stone had been grateful, had done his best to play a significant part in the rearing of the boy, but his constantly widening ambitions had demanded frequent evenings out, weekends at meetings or courses, periods away from home. Peg had seen this, he believed, as necessary and had supported him in his climb towards his goal: a large, successful school, a respected, deserved status in society.

He spent much time at his work, wrote a small, modest account of the achievements of his school, which the Education Committee had had printed and distributed not only locally but nationally so that he was not infrequently called to make appearances on educational discussions on both BBC radio and television. There he acquired the reputation of a moderate, not averse to modernism or radical change, but not automatically in its favour. He could always argue a case with vigour and his slaughter – the word used by a fellow headmaster – of a new Minister who had not prepared himself at all thoroughly made him something of a champion within his profession. What he remembered now, and with gratitude, was that when he returned, often quite late, his wife was waiting up at home, a suitable meal prepared, to enquire how his day had gone or to give her own warmly encouraging account of the television programme he had appeared on, which she had carefully watched. She showed no jealousy of his reputation, about which, to do him justice, he was modest enough, but cheerfully supported him. 'I've two babies,' she was reported to have said once to her sister, 'and I don't know who needs the more concentration or cuddling.'

And now she was uncertain.

They listened to the one o'clock news on television as they ate their light lunch. They watched a climber negotiate an almost vertical face.

'I could do with some exercise,' John Stone said.

'What's stopping you?' she asked.

'We'll go for a walk this afternoon if you're not doing anything special.'

'Right. Where?'

'Abbey Park,' he answered without hesitation.

'Your car or mine?'

'Mine.'

They set out immediately they had cleared and cleaned the dishes. He rushed to take his car from the garage while she changed her clothes, 'made herself fit to be seen'. She was not waiting when he drew up outside the front gate, nor was there any sign of her when he went indoors. When she finally emerged downstairs she was wearing a brilliantly scarlet trouser suit and strongly made flat-heeled shoes. She had brought from the wardrobe a white raincoat in military style, which she now donned, together with a dark-green velvet beret. 'Did you put your umbrella in?' she asked.

'No.'

'Then do so. You never know what the weather will be like. Bring my green one while you're at it, please.'

He trotted off obediently and returned, laden.

'Away to the woods,' she said. He followed her down the path, where she walked with sharp purpose like a freshly commissioned

106

officer marching on to the drill square. 'Which way are we going?' she asked.

'North. I looked it up on the map. We'll try the new ring road.'

'Isn't that a bit out of your way?'

'I suppose it is, but we rarely travel in these parts, so I thought I'd have a squint now they've changed the look of the place.'

'Will it have altered all that much?'

'One never knows these days. They knock new roads through fields and line them with factories. Joe Healey was telling me that there are some really modern buildings along here, new workplaces.'

'What do they make?'

'Agricultural products, clothes, mobile telephones, light machinery.'

'Why out here? Miles from anywhere?'

'It may look pretty remote, but in fact we're very close to the motor road so it's easy to send stuff out and get raw material. It's sad that this, which used to be a bit of a country lane through fields, is as it is but people have to live and earn.'

'The whole country will be built over before long.'

'You won't think so once we've escaped from these roads.'

'They seem to go on for ever.'

'Well, yes. We've passed three big islands.'

'That means three other roads crossing this.'

'That's right, but from now on we're rural.'

They slowed down while traffic hurled past, before reaching a B road. He reduced the pace of the car. Clouds speeded over the faint blue of the sky; once a few drops of rain spattered the windscreen. A solitary house, equipped with a double garage and gardens, appeared at the edge of a long series of copses set along the left side of the road.

'I don't know whether I'd like to live right out here,' Peg said.

'No corner shops, that's true.'

'I wouldn't feel very safe. It's a long way from civilisation. Burglars could have a field day here.'

'Yes, they could these days. Before 1969 burglary, that is breaking in to trespass on someone's property, could only be committed at night between, I believe, the hours of 9 p.m. and 6 a.m.'

'You know some comical things.'

They now travelled slowly alongside the wood, dark in the occasional brightnesses of the afternoon. The leaves had fallen, though many remained, thickly, in the hedge bottoms. The trunks of the trees rose slenderly, delicately green where the low sunlight rested on them.

'I wonder if that's privately owned,' Peg said. 'It goes on for a long way.'

'I've no idea.' John drew up. 'Would you wind your window down, please.' She complied. 'No. I thought I saw a noticeboard that might give us a hint as to ownership, but no, it's not so; I must have imagined it. I'm not quick enough with my eyes. I often think I come from the time before the motor car. If I walk I take in much, much more than when I ride.'

'Your parents had a car, didn't they, when you were a boy?'

'Yes. But I didn't when I left home. In the Forces, at university, in my first two jobs, I didn't own a car. It wasn't so easy then. I had to walk and that's when I picked up my slow habits of observation.'

'This wood is very beautiful,' she said. 'Do you think it's useful?'

'They'll be broad-leaved trees, so, yes, it will be. Whether they use the timber or not I don't know. They clearly haven't done much clearing there in the last few years. It may be set aside.'

'You've parked us right in the shadow.'

'Deliberately. I thought we might be able to see what they, the owners, were up to. But I can't. I'll just have to enjoy it aesthetically. And I haven't brought my camera again, as usual. So, with your permission, I'll sit here for a minute or two, taking it all in, in the hope I'll remember some of it.'

'And then?'

'We'll move off. And we'll examine a bit of earlier industrialisation.'

'Such as?'

'The collieries. Not that you'll see anything of them. They've all closed, and the head stocks pulled down and the pit buildings destroyed.'

'What shall we see?'

'They didn't touch the miners' cottages. They're still there. A few rows of terraced houses. Townee places. You step straight in from the street into the front room. They're not elegant, but they'll be comfortable. The miners would be allocated coal, so that in the living room there'd always be a fire in the grate. It warmed the water in a boiler on one side and on the other there'd be an oven where the housewives would do their cooking, and on cold nights they'd take the oven shelves out and wrap them in blankets and put them into the beds. They didn't have electric blankets in those days.'

'No, but they had hot-water bottles, hadn't they?'

'Yes, but they wouldn't waste money on them if they could warm themselves just as cheaply for no extra cost. It depended on the mother. It was important to these people to keep warm. When fathers and big brothers came back in their "pit-muck" from the mine, the majority walking across the fields, they'd clean up in the living room in a zinc bath with hot water from the boiler.'

'There weren't pithead baths, then?'

'Not until later and, some years on, the colliers would own cars and drive home as clean as if they'd been in a solicitor's office all day instead of at the coalface.'

John drove forward, still not hurrying, past a minute chapel and a cemetery cut from the wood. They caught a glimpse of a large house, which loomed to the right on a hill thinly planted with trees.

'What's that place?' she asked.

'Don't know. It has a Victorian look to it. It might have been a mine manager's residence, built when the collieries became big business.'

He slowed at a fork in the road where the village was finally signposted. Houses huddled by the road, built in the last fifty years. The wood doggedly continued right to the village.

'Council houses?' she asked.

'Possibly. Or owned by the pit.'

They drove downhill, now, alongside or between the terraces of miners' cottages, rawly if well built, with utility uppermost. The curtains in the windows all differed; occasionally lace, sometimes coloured dark blue, brown, and heavy against the cold.

'Will they have bathrooms now?' Peg asked.

'Probably. They'll alter the back bedroom or perhaps even the scullery.'

'How do you know so much about it?'

'My first job was in Yorkshire and they were beginning to modernise these little houses.' He coughed. 'I came across some slightly superior places, which had bathrooms and front rooms that opened out into a corridor, but the upstairs bathroom had originally no hot water. If you had a bath you'd have to carry the water up in buckets. Some people, when it became possible, bought Ascot heaters, which eased the situation. Or some larger form to give you your bathwater more quickly. They hissed and gurgled dangerously. I disliked them.'

'How do you know that?'

'My first lodgings were in such a place. I was never so comfortable in my life. My landlady, a maiden lady, cooked like a dream. I had school dinners in a church hall during the week, but Miss Meyrick did me proud on Sunday. Yorkshire pudding first, then beef and vegetables, and finally ginger or fruit pudding in season, spotted dick or apple tart, all thick with custard.'

'And the two of you got through that lot?' Peg mocked.

'Sometimes we had another lodger, an engineer who was up for a few weeks now and then. He was a cousin of the landlady's, a university graduate in mining, but she was a bit ashamed of him. He had a north country accent and he drank.' They were sailing down a narrow road lined with trees. 'We're in the Abbey Park now.'

When they had parked they set off towards the lake. Two swans floated majestically by, sparing them not even a swift turn of the head. Ducks paddled with comical efficiency. The sun sank low and red-raw to the west, scarlet with gold.

'We'd better get on with it,' he said, 'or it will be dark.'

'I could murder a cup of tea,' Peg said.

'I doubt whether anybody'll be open on a winter's afternoon.'

They made towards the last of the buildings. A board outside announced 'Afternoon Teas'. John looked at it suspiciously. It could be turned to promise Morning Coffee. The door was closed but, smiling at his wife, he rang the bell. He hoped for nothing. Peg looked over again towards the lake, disassociating herself from his antics. A girl opened the door eighteen inches.

'Any chance of a cup of tea?' he asked. 'If you please.'

'Come on in.'

She pulled the door more widely open, not without difficulty. Inside were small tables and they were guided to one near the counter. The place seemed badly lit. They sat and John ordered a pot of tea.

'Fancy cakes?' the girl asked.

'Yes, please,' Peg said with schoolgirlish enthusiasm.

John Stone looked about him. One foursome sat at a distance, silently convivial, but at the table only a yard or two away an elderly man concentrated his attention on them. He perched with back straight, in a smart British warm, but his whole appearance was dominated by a large foreign hat. It seemed not furry, but gave the impression that a lady's muff had been carefully dropped or fitted on to his head. It was the size of a small kettledrum and dwarfed the well-shaven face below it.

'It is cold,' the man said. His accent was strong, East European though not immediately recognisable to Stone.

'But the sun was bright,' Peg answered him, smiling.

His face brightened at her immediate reply. 'I don't understand, I have never learnt, to, to, er, predict the weather in this country.'

'No.' Peg, unwilling to interrupt, encouraged him on.

'When I was a boy we could guarantee snow at Christmas. We knew it would be there, and thick, and we looked forward to it.'

'Where was that?' she enquired.

'Hungary.'

'Do you go back there at all?' John asked.

'Oh, yes. Quite often. Once or twice a year.'

The man drummed with his fingers on the table where his gloves lay and poured himself another cup at which he stared with a kind of humorous disdain. He added neither sugar nor milk.

'Have you lived in England long?' Peg asked.

'Since 1956.'

'Do you miss it?'

'Miss? Hungary? No, I don't think so. I settled here quickly. I was lucky. I followed my profession as an engineer. I married an English girl. She was a teacher and I finally worked for the County Council. Until I retired. I hold an English passport now. My children are thoroughly English and speak no word of Hungarian.'

111

'You aren't forgetting it, are you?'

'No. I have the opportunity to speak. There are others around.'

'Is there a Hungarian club in Beechnall?'

'No. There are not sufficient of us for anything as official as a club or meeting place. From time to time we have a social gathering, a dance or dinner, but the energetic man who organised these opportunities has been quite ill.'

'And there's nobody else?'

'Not nobody,' the man said. 'But we are getting older and fewer. Going out to dance is not altogether my cup of tea.' He laughed at the expression and tapped his cup with his spoon. 'And now I am diabetic so I have to be careful what I eat.'

'You'll have to inject yourself with insulin?' John murmured.

'No. I control it by diet. No sugar. I keep visiting the hospital, but I don't suppose I'm very badly affected.'

The girl arrived with a tray, teapot, jug, cups, hot water. Almost on her heels a smaller girl, perhaps sister to the first, stood silently, looking for guidance, holding a glass cake stand which, on a signal from the other, she placed with something of a flourish in the middle of the table.

'They look good,' Peg said. Two chocolate slices, two thickly iced buns, two congress tarts. She was already pouring out the tea, diluting her husband's from the hot-water jug.

'Do you drink tea in Hungary?' she asked, picking up her cup for the first testing sip.

'Yes. It's not the national drink as it is here.'

Peg indicated to her husband that he should take his pick from the cake stand. He chose an iced bun.

'I knew you'd choose that,' she said. The Hungarian laughed.

'Yes. I've liked them since I was a schoolboy.' Stone sank his teeth into the delicacy.

'Chocolate for me,' she said, then, whirling round, 'May I offer you a cake?' she said to the Hungarian. 'To restrain us from greed.'

'No, thank you,' he said politely. 'I am not allowed.'

'Oh, no. I'm sorry. I forgot.'

'It was most kind of you.' He collected his crockery together. 'I must be on my way now. I have been out longer than I expected. My wife will be back from her shopping expedition and she might worry about me. She doesn't quite believe that I have mastered English customs and rules, and thinks I might one day suffer the consequences of my ignorance.'

'Oh, dear,' Peg murmured.

'I think she fears that I shall drive on the wrong side of the road. I took my test in England forty years ago, but . . . She would deny this, and when she considers it rationally she sees there's neither truth nor sense in it, but this suspicion remains, which puts her on edge.'

He picked up his crockery and carried it to the counter, explaining as he passed their table that it would save somebody's legs. He paid his bill and as he returned on his way out he stopped and wished them goodbye. 'It has been a pleasure to talk to you. I hope we shall meet again.' For a minute Peg thought he might sweep his headgear off, but he did not oblige. They made polite noises and watched him walk the length of the room to let himself out by the main door.

'He speaks very good English,' Peg said.

'Excellent. But he still has his accent.'

'Yes. But it's no further from standard English than a good many of our regional brogues. I had no difficulty in understanding him. In fact, he spoke rather more carefully than most native-born English speakers.' Peg also spoke with slightly exaggerated correctness.

In due course they finished their tea, and carried their cups and plates to the counter. 'We're saving your legs,' he repeated. Peg had the four remaining cakes put into a bag. 'It will be a treat for us at home.' Stone paid up and looked pleasant.

'Shall we walk a step or two?' he asked once they were outside. 'It's not dark yet.'

'Right, but not too far. It's a touch cold.'

'Best foot forward, then,' he said. They did ten minutes' sharp walk and about turned for the car.

'I feel quite warm,' he said when they had seated themselves. 'And not too much mud on my shoes.'

Once they drove off, Peg mentioned the Hungarian. 'He seemed a cheerful sort. I wonder how old he was.'

'My age. Older, perhaps. He had a good complexion. Not wrinkled like me.'

113

'I wonder what sort of engineer he was.'

'Electrical, I should think, if the Council employed him.' He had no idea.

Peg stroked her face as they spun through the rhododendron plantations. John waited for her next observation. His wife, he knew from experience, was never short of topics, but she did not speak again until they were out of the main gates and on the major road. 'When I meet somebody like that man and notice how cheerful he seems, I ask myself what we're complaining about.'

'Oh, yes?'

She glanced swiftly, fiercely, at him. 'There's May worrying herself to death about JJ and Annie Fisher about her husband. What would they be like if they were suddenly forced to drop everything and flee their native country?'

'May's husband died. Bereavement's just as bad as exile, I should have thought.'

'May hardly seemed bothered when Ian went. In fact, I couldn't help suspecting she was relieved rather than otherwise.'

'Um. Possible.'

'Bereavement can be bad,' Peg conceded. 'My mother never got over Daddy's death, even though he left her pretty comfortably off. Yet she married again.'

'We all have our own ways out of our difficulties.'

'My stepfather was a thoroughly decent man, but she never recovered from Daddy's loss. It altered her character, her whole outlook on life. Even when she was happy she couldn't help telling us how much Daddy would have enjoyed the event, whatever it was, and how he would always have made it better.'

'Didn't your stepfather mind?'

'He didn't seem to. He acted as though he was honoured to have been allowed to take Daddy's place.'

They drove in silence, thinking this over. Peg routinely began again. 'It must have been awful to have to pack a suitcase and get out of your home and country, knowing that in all probability you'd never see either again.'

'Depends,' he said. 'It depends.'

'On what?' she snapped.

'The alternative. Prison, torture, a bullet in the back of your head.'

114

'Yes. We don't appreciate properly the fact that we live in a civilised country where such injustices don't exist. It's just incredible to us to think that you had to send your children abroad or escape yourself.' Her pronouns scattered in excitement. 'And they would be ordinary people like us, with nice furniture and pictures and gardens, people who went to the theatre and concerts, and read books. D'you know, John, if I'd have been living in Vienna when the Nazis marched in, the *Anschluss*, I wouldn't have believed that anything so dreadful could have happened.'

'You're not Jewish.'

'I know, but they, some of them at least if not most, would have been people like us, with a trust that their society was so organised and well-balanced that racism and genocide just could not exist.'

'I sometimes wonder if some people in this town don't believe that either. There are ghettos on our housing estate where some antisocial families live as if they expect to be arrested and imprisoned at any time.'

'Because they're breaking the law all the time.'

'I wonder,' John said, 'if they see it as such. They've had no chances in life. They're not loved at home, but abused physically or sexually or both. They're not fed or clothed properly. They've not done anything but catastrophically at their schools and when they start work they're dishonest, liars, know nothing of punctuality and so get the sack.'

'It's not the same. These German and Austrian Jews were respected for the work they did, as doctors or bankers or tradesmen.'

'I realise that the comparison is nothing like right, but I'm trying to put myself into the mind of somebody who finds out that society has no time for him or her. More likely a "him" in our country. Of course, many of the Jews, I agree with you, were well educated, and that prevented them from grasping the possibility of such barbaric behaviour from a modern, civilised society or even from a polite neighbour. I'm sure if such a thing happened in this country I just couldn't bring myself to believe it. I wouldn't have dropped my job and scooted off, say, to America with nothing more than I could carry.'

'Do you think that people learn to put up with such extreme circumstances?'

115

'To some extent. If you've ever read, let's say, of the conditions in the trenches in the First World War you wouldn't believe people could survive them. Living in filthy mud, in winter, let's say with no chance to change clothes or rid yourself of lice or wash your mess tins. And all the time the whistle of shells over your head, the next one which might drop on your trench and blow you in shreds to kingdom come, and the chance that your next stumble or careless step will put you in the way of a sniper's bullet – it doesn't bear thinking about. And yet you and I knew when we were children, and later, plenty of men who'd survived that sort of hell and were now decent husbands and fathers.'

'Some didn't recover.'

'True, but the majority did. I'm not saying it had no effect on them. It must have done, but we were never allowed to see it. There was certainly an old chap at the school I went to who used to drop down behind his desk gibbering and firing at the enemy.'

'Did you see him do that?' Peg asked.

'No. He never taught me. It was possible. I believed it. Some teachers talked about the war, but by the time I reached school there was another war in progress. It hardly seems possible now. The human race must be mad.'

Peg saw that her husband's teeth were clenched and his knuckles white. 'I wonder if that man is troubled in any way at all. Nightmares, obsessions.'

'We can't judge that, can we? We hardly know him. He seemed happy enough, but I wouldn't be prepared to make any sort of judgement on such short acquaintance.'

Peg did not speak for some time, as if she needed to think over what he'd said. Stone was worrying himself now about his comparison of Jews or gypsies and political injustice in Fascist countries with criminal families on English council estates. He tried, as he drove on a road that became busier as they approached town, to justify the comparison but he could now see nothing of worth in it. 'I've been talking rubbish,' he said finally.

'I didn't notice.' She grinned. 'This was a most enjoyable little trip.'

'All I'm capable of these days.'

'Cheer up, man.'

IX

That evening after a light dinner the Stones, clearing the table, heard some strong noises in the street outside.

'What's that,' he asked, 'in heaven's name?'

'I've no idea.' Peg was slightly deaf. 'There's a light flashing now.' She pointed to the stained-glass front door.

'Let's go and see.'

'Well, put your coat on. It's cold out there.'

John obeyed orders and went outside. The Fishers appeared at their front door at the same time.

'It's the fire engine,' Harry Fisher said. 'Somebody's abandoned a car and set light to it.'

'I'd better tell Peg,' Stone muttered, returning indoors to shout to his wife who had gone upstairs to find a suitable outdoor coat for a frosty night in a dark street.

Emerging together, they found that the Fishers had progressed no further than their own garden gate. At the end of the avenue, beyond the last front wall, the fire engine held prime position in the middle of the road. Two or three fireman, helmeted, played a solo hose on a car close by but at an angle to the gutter. They'd made short work of their business. There were now no flames, but smoke rose thickly from the wreck. Petrol fumes polluted the air. The firemen worked without haste but with concentration on the car, playing their small hose with ferocious power. A minuscule crowd had gathered, perhaps twenty people, dark shapes under the last street light. Stone recognised only one neighbour; he wondered where these onlookers had come from to this out-of-the-way spot.

The firemen were now checking their work. They exchanged few remarks, but poked and examined with the same attention they had displayed as they doused the fire.

'Hardly worth their coming out,' Harry Fisher muttered to Peg.

'Might have spread or exploded,' she answered.

'Wouldn't have done all that much damage if it had.' Fisher wandered off to quiz some other bystander.

'Nothing he likes better than poking his nose in for the whys and wherefores,' Annie Fisher told her neighbours. 'Look at him now.' Fisher had joined two of the firemen and was questioning them. They answered him, laconically enough it seemed, but Fisher nodded in satisfaction and continued his cross-examination.

'Is that a foreign number plate?' Peg asked.

'I think so.' The plate stood unmarked by the flames, but freakishly lit by the street lamp.

'Is it a foreign car?'

'Yes. Japanese, I think. I'm not sure what sort. And one doesn't know where it was made. They build quite a lot of their cars for the European market in Europe. In England even.'

'It's not a left-hand drive,' Peg stated.

'I never noticed that,' Annie said in admiration.

The firemen were in no hurry; the two discussed their work, pointing down at the wreck. The pavement, they noticed, was littered with glass.

'They must have smashed the windows to get at the fire,' Annie said. 'But you'd have thought the glass would have fallen inside.'

'Perhaps some did,' Peg answered.

A fireman had procured a short broom with which he cleared the pavement.

'Nobody ever walks up here as far as this,' Annie grumbled.

Harry Fisher made his way back to his wife. 'Two young men, they say. They'd stolen the car and then put it up here out of the way to get rid of it.'

'Why did they set fire to it?' Stone asked.

'God knows. Pyromaniacs, if that's the word. Bloody lunatics who can't leave anything alone, but have to burn it or break it.'

'Perhaps they think,' Peg suggested, 'they're destroying clues they've left.'

'Then they've got more respect for the police than I've got. They wouldn't recognise a clue if it jumped up and bit 'em.'

Annie showed her embarrassment, sidling away from her husband. The firemen were now packing away their gear. 'It's cold standing out here,' Annie said.

'Come on in and have a drink with us,' Harry invited his neighbours. Stone was about to refuse when Peg accepted.

'We don't see much of you these days.' Harry spoke with spirit. 'I don't know what you do with yourselves all day.'

They were ushered into the Fishers' hall, which smelt of cabbage. Harry smacked his lips, then led them into the sitting room. The house was a mirror image of theirs. Annie took their coats and scarves. The building seemed warm enough and the chairs deep, shabby and comfortable. With their hosts both out of the room the Stones looked at one another in some confusion. John would rather have been at home with a glass of whisky and a good book; he was trying, not for the first time, to read *The Seven Pillars of Wisdom*, though he had found it less interesting than he had expected on his former attempts, but this time he had made more progress. 'I've learnt the language,' he told his wife lugubriously.

'I didn't think there was a history or geography book written that you couldn't read,' she had answered him.

The Fishers had returned. There had been a consultation in the kitchen, which they could hear though not understand. Annie seemed to be issuing orders. Stone listened hard, but could catch nothing. Quite likely she warned her husband off certain subjects or remarks, or perhaps instructed him as to exactly what he was to drink. Harry Fisher was not the sort of man to pay much attention, but Annie never gave up her attempts to improve him.

When they returned Harry had donned a tie, which he tapped down from time to time as if pleased with this adjustment to convention. 'What can I offer you?' he began, looking towards Peg. 'Beer, spirits, wine?'

'Red or white,' Annie added.

'Have you any orange juice?' Peg asked. Harry looked at his wife, who nodded. 'And sir?' he asked Stone.

'A small whisky and water, if you please. Half and half.'

'And you, m'dear?' to his wife who waved him from the room and followed him.

Peg laughed. Harry Fisher the social man needed guidance, it appeared. Stone drew in prim lips.

'That's an odd picture,' Peg said. 'I've never noticed that before. Picasso, is it?'

119

'Yes. Not the sort you expect them to choose.'

When the hosts returned with the drinks Peg drew attention to the picture. 'Is that new?' she asked.

'Only last week. Harry got two as presents,' Annie answered. 'About a year ago he did some work for a man who keeps an antique shop in Newark. He's also opened a new one in Lincoln, and Harry made the furniture, cupboards and shelves for it. He was pleased with the finished job, but he was more than delighted with the suggestions Harry'd put forward when they were planning it all. After that he quite took to Harry and said he'd give him a special print he was having made. In fact, he gave him two. He had a choice out of six or seven, but they were a bit surprising, weren't they, Harry? They were all what you might call erotic. He said he selected one, this one here, for him but he could have one other.'

'You'd be pleased,' Peg said to Fisher.

'Well, yes. But chiefly because he was so chuffed with the shopfitting I'd organised for him. It saved him a lot of time and a mint of money. But I was surprised. They were sexy, dirty, y'know. I said as much to him and he laughed.'

'They were for special clients,' Annie said. 'Done individually. He'd picked this one for Harry. "Nobody'll know what it's about," he said. "Not even your wife. They'll guess, but they won't be exactly sure."'

'That's it. He had some beautiful things in his shop, but I think from what I gathered he had a cupboard or safe or something in the back rooms with things for special clients.'

'Erotica?' Peg asked.

'You can call 'em what you like. He said he was sure I could frame these for myself. He made some suggestions, but he seemed particularly keen that I should have this picture. I didn't say anything to him, but I'd sooner have had a picture of a steam train or a charging elephant.'

'So you framed this yourself?' Stone asked.

'I did.'

'It's by Picasso,' Annie told them, 'and it's called *Homme et Femme*.'

'*Man and Woman, Man and Wife*,' Stone translated.

'It's colourful,' Fisher said cheerfully. 'I'll say that for it. I wasn't sure about hanging it up here, but Annie told me to get on with it. We had one of a village street before, but this is a lot bigger. Do you like it?'

'Um, interesting,' Stone said. 'I'm no admirer of modern stuff.'

'And you, Mrs Stone?' Fisher pressed.

'No. I don't see much sense in it.'

'Do you think' – Annie looked at Peg – 'that in time I'll grow to like it?'

'I doubt it. I wouldn't.' Peg sounded severe.

'There you are, then.'

All four were standing in front of the picture, uncertain what to say.

'It suits the room,' Stone ventured. 'It's big enough to take it. I'd guess in a smaller place the picture would be overwhelming.'

Nobody commented on this. The silence fell awkwardly.

Stone wondered if they'd been invited in to view the Picasso. He felt bound to speak again. 'And what about the other one, then?' he asked cheerfully.

'We've hung that in our bedroom,' Annie said. 'Go upstairs and bring it down, Harry.' She seemed off-colour, not at ease. Perhaps she expected from her highly educated neighbours some enlightenment and, failing to receive it, was disappointed.

Harry did not hurry over his task. He returned to the room with the picture pulled in to his chest as if to display his success as a framer rather than the artist's achievement. He took up a position a yard or two away from them, before slowly turning the painting. He made a sound of introductory circus trumpets.

This time the picture was nearer realism.

A young girl sat, eyes closed, fingers interlocked on her head with her left leg bent up on a stool in front of her. The right was splayed outwards to the floor on the right of the stool. Her skirt and underskirt were flung back to reveal the full length of her bent left leg and the thigh of the other, and between them the delicate, narrow stretch of her knickers. To the left of her stool a cat lapped at a saucer of milk.

The Stones looked hard at the painting, awestruck.

'This one's called *Le Rêve*,' Annie said and spelt it out to cover the blemishes of her French pronunciation. '*The Dream*.'

'Is that more like it?' Fisher asked Stone.

'It's a very fine painting.'

121

'I don't think,' Peg objected, 'that that girl is asleep. It ought to be called "The Daydream".'

'What's that in French?' Annie asked.

'*Rêverie*?' Stone promptly suggested. 'Who painted it?'

'Balthus,' Fisher answered and he also spelt it out. 'Len Johnson pronounced it in some funny way.'

'No. I've never heard of him,' Peg said.

'Nor I,' Stone backed his wife.

'Len, the man who gave it to me, said he was very famous.'

'When did he live?'

'He died not very long ago. He was very old. In his nineties.' Fisher offered this information with jaunty pride to his know-all neighbours.

'What was his first name?' Stone asked.

'I've no idea. That's what it said on a bit of paper stuck on the back of the picture.'

'How old,' Annie Fisher changed course and addressed her question directly to Peg, 'do you think the girl is?'

Peg approached the picture, staring intently.

Fisher thrust it impudently towards her. 'It depends when it was painted. Girls, adolescent girls, have changed in my lifetime. But I'd guess thirteen, perhaps. Is that right?'

'We've no idea. His Len Johnson might know.'

'Yes, but what do you think?'

'Oh, you can't be far out. She might be anything between eleven and eighteen.'

They sipped their drinks. Fisher put the painting, none too tidily, face down on the chair.

'You like it better than the Picasso?' This time Annie posed her question to Stone.

'There's no doubt about that. It's beautifully painted.'

'I don't think much of the cat,' Annie grumbled.

'He's old, is the cat. Look how he hangs down underneath.'

'Len said he was a great painter of cats,' Fisher said. 'They called him "King of the Cats".'

'Why haven't we heard of him?' Peg asked.

'We can't know everything,' Stone answered.

'What an admission,' Annie gasped, then blushed.

Again there was a pause, which Fisher crudely interrupted. 'I think he must have been a dirty old man, staring up girls' legs like that.'

'Wouldn't you do the same thing?' his wife gibed.

'Chance'd be a fine thing.'

'There is something erotic or out of the way about it.' Peg offered her advice slowly. 'The poor child's sitting there as if there were nobody else in the room except for the cat. And your Balthus should have left her alone, respected her space.'

'He'd choose the pose,' Stone murmured.

'Do you think so?' Annie asked.

'It's usual. He's doing the painting,' Peg said, lively again.

They stood quiet for a time, staring from one picture to the back of the other. Stone then strode across the room, headmasterly and, turning the Balthus over, stood it upright against the back of the chair. 'That's better,' he pronounced. He stared hard at the picture, hands clasped behind his back. The others watched him, waiting for his judgement. 'Beautiful painting,' he said. 'Marvellous contrasts. And the architecture of it all.' He turned on his audience. 'Yes.' He frowned. 'I should like to know more about him.'

Again the embarrassed hiatus.

'Do you know what I find funny about it all?' Annie asked in a kind of desperation. No one answered her. 'It's this. Why did this Len Johnson make a present of these two pictures to Harry?' Her husband smirked. 'Of all people?'

'He was pleased with my work.'

'Yes, so you keep telling me and I see no reason not to believe you. But he could have tipped you in money. Or some bit of furniture or mock jewellery. These prints, which you told me he had specially made, surely he could have sold them. Especially as the subject matter is a bit dicey, spicy. Perhaps he didn't want too many. So he had just the right number made and these were left over. Why didn't he tuck 'em away in one of his cupboards or safes, and leave 'em until a better time came up? I can understand that perhaps he had permission to make only so many prints and if he exceeded that number the owner or the museum or gallery might have taken legal action against him, or, worse, not have anything more to do with him by way of trade. I can see all this, though I don't know anything about it, but why did he choose Harry to have them?'

'You think there's some snag somewhere?' Peg asked.

'There's no such thing as a free lunch, that's certain enough.'

'I don't know. Human beings are odd creatures, and it may be that your Mr Johnson was really grateful and had come to the conclusion, having talked to Harry over a period, that he'd really like these.'

'He came to the conclusion,' Annie answered Peg, 'that Harry was the sort who enjoyed women with lopsided bosoms, or who liked staring up girls' skirts. Is that right, Harry?'

'I'm no worse than anybody else.' Harry grinned, not ashamed. 'I'm no saint.'

'You can't remember talking about such things?' Annie demanded. 'To Johnson?'

'No. We didn't talk about much outside the work I was doing.'

'You didn't pass any comment on pictures he had hanging in his shops?'

'No. Not that I remember.'

'It's a mystery. Well, let's sit down. I'm tired.'

They concentrated for the moment on comfort and their drinks.

'Do you know,' Stone said after a fortifying mouthful of whisky, 'what has struck me? Your Len Johnson had observed Harry and had decided that he would profit from owning and viewing these pictures. It was an educational experiment. Something about Harry had appealed. Perhaps he had noticed when they drew up their plans for the new shop that Harry didn't concern himself only with utilitarian matters, or economic, but with the aesthetics of the whole design.' Stone stifled a smile at his effort. It reminded him of some of the announcements or moral homilies he delivered as a headmaster in school assemblies. It sounded stilted and he could not be sure that it would achieve the desired effect. He steadied himself with his whisky.

'Do you think that's anywhere near the truth, Harry?' Peg asked.

'Shouldn't think so.'

'Neither would I,' Annie sneered. 'He probably thought that there was another dirty old man like him who'd enjoy these.'

'You'd know, wouldn't you?' her husband said. He did not appear unduly perturbed.

'Which do you prefer?' Stone asked.

'That one.' Harry pointed at the Balthus. 'I can tell what's going on.'

They discussed the merits of the pictures with some animation. All four preferred the Balthus. Peg enjoyed herself laying down the law. Stone felt he had done enough for one evening, but accepted a second small glass of whisky and water. In the end he roused himself for a final judgement. 'If you had asked me when we came in,' he said solemnly, 'what we'd be discussing here tonight, I don't think I'd have guessed paintings.'

'You didn't know we had them,' Annie said.

'No. But I'd have thought the burning car would have held pride of place.'

'It shows there's no dumbing down in our society,' Peg said. 'We old folks are preserving standards.'

'I wonder how many people in this street would have been talking about works of art this evening?' Annie asked.

'We don't discuss them all that often,' Harry said brusquely. 'You and me.'

'Don't give the game away. Mr Stone'll put us among the dunces,' his wife warned.

'Oh, no,' Stone said. 'I happen to know that both you and your husband are ex-grammar school pupils.'

'Did you learn Latin?' Peg asked.

'Annie did. I was in the bottom stream and they thought French was quite enough for us.'

'Did you learn anything of advantage to you now?' Stone asked.

'I've a paper qualification,' Fisher said. 'School Certificate. And they taught us to speak properly. Mark you, I had to lose that in the building trade. It's not much use to you there. National Service helped.' Fisher shook his head. 'But I felt I'd been in touch with people who knew a fair amount about the subjects they taught. I started in the grammar school when the war had been on for two years and some of the younger masters had been called up. So we were taught by older men, most of them pretty good. Then the younger ones were women, most of them lively.'

'They didn't have trouble with discipline?'

'We tried to play them up. You know what lads are. But most of them knew what was what. The grammar schools meant something in those days. If we larked about too much, the headmaster

125

used his cane on us. And, by God, he could lay it on. If it happened too often they expelled you.'

'Did you get punished like that?' Peg asked. 'Caning, I mean.'

'Now and again.'

'Did you deserve it?'

'I expect so. The headmaster made sure that you knew why you were in trouble and he asked if you had any excuse. Not that he paid much attention. He didn't spend time arguing with you. He'd hear you out and give his judgements. Three strokes or six. And bend you over and belt you. Then he'd say, "I don't want to see you up here again. Is that clear? We have a reputation to maintain. And maintain it I will. We, moreover, are giving you opportunities you might not get elsewhere. Don't waste them." And that was that.'

'Did it hurt?' Annie asked.

'Of course it bloody hurt. That was the idea.'

'You were pleased you went there, to that school?'

'Yes. I didn't make all I might have of it, I agree. I didn't end up as a professor or a brain surgeon. When I left at sixteen, the war was over and the family business was just beginning to pick up again, and I joined my father. He wanted me to.'

'And you've never regretted it?'

'I wouldn't altogether say that. I've made a good living, never gone short. But you have to work hard in the building trade. I've earned such money as I've got. And besides, I met Annie. Her family were a very large concern in the same line.'

'Were you not at the same school, then?'

'No,' he answered. 'Ours was a boys' school.'

'And were you in a coeducational school?' he asked Annie.

'No. Girls, girls and girls. Besides, I'm rather younger than Harry.'

'Fourteen years,' he said dolefully. For the moment he looked gaunt, almost ancient. Then he grinned again. 'If we'd have had girls I'd have been studying them.'

Both were in favour of the grammar school, it appeared. Annie took an extreme view. The government and the local authorities saw to it that the people who'd failed the eleven plus weren't either properly supplied or taught, and when the grammar school with all its advantages outstripped the rest, the government, on spurious grounds of equality, got rid of them. Stone was surprised at the violence with which she put her case. Her husband seemed to agree with her, arguing that he'd found working-class lads in the army were far from stupid.

'And is that so now?' Stone asked him.

'Ah, well. The lads that joined our firm have no sort of discipline. They turn up when they like and how they like, can't understand a simple instruction, or don't bother to listen. And some of the girls in the office are as bad. They can't or won't take a telephone message down properly.'

'And do you blame the schools for that?' Peg asked.

'They must be responsible in part. You hear such things these days. Not that I go anywhere near schools, but most mornings in the summer I see kids of school age wandering about the streets, up to God knows what mischief.'

'Isn't that the parents' fault?'

'Yes. I heard somebody on the radio the other morning saying that today's parents were frightened of their children and so let 'em do as they liked.'

'I wonder if that's true,' Stone mused.

'Quite likely. I remember when I started working for my dad and I did something wrong, something he thought I ought to have got right, he didn't half tongue-lash me and it didn't matter where it was or who was about. He'd dress me down in front of the other men and the apprentices.'

'Was he short-tempered?' Peg asked.

'Yes. I wasn't the only one to get told off. He had a bit of a reputation for it. I've heard some of the men call him "Biggy" Fisher, for "Big-mouth".'

'But it wouldn't do today?' Stone asked.

'About a year ago, the foreman at Hardcastle's the furniture makers chewed some lad up for something he'd got wrong, and do you know, the little bastard came back that night and set fire to one of the workshops. The nightwatchman caught him at it. Otherwise it would have done thousands of pounds' worth of damage. Even as it was, it didn't half make a mess of the place, what with the firemen and all.'

'The boy must have been unbalanced,' Peg said, 'to act like that.'

'I'd have unbalanced the bugger if he'd been one of mine.'

Twenty minutes later Peg stood and made it clear to her husband that they were going back home.

'That was very interesting,' Stone said, divesting himself of his coat in his own house.

'You didn't say much for yourself,' Peg said ungraciously.

'About education?'

'What else?'

'I was quite pleased to listen to the Fishers. I'm an amateur now.'

'Were they right about the grammar schools?'

'To some extent. When I started my career, in a grammar school, we had staff meeting after staff meeting about people in the bottom stream. After five years of our teaching they often left with very poor School Certificates.'

'Wasn't that because the examinations were deliberately skewed so that only a small percentage of the school population would pass?'

'There's some truth in that.'

'And the equivalent examinations are easier now?'

'Yes. I suppose they are. Or more interesting. In the old grammar school days you learnt what the authorities thought you needed. Now it's more child centred. Not that the students thought that any better.'

Peg marched away upstairs. 'We'll both have a whisky, if you don't mind.'

He had no sooner reached the pantry when the phone rang. It ceased almost at once, as Peg lifted the upstairs receiver. He listened but could make nothing of what she was saying. He prepared the whiskies and water for them both and carried them from the kitchen to the sitting room. The telephone conversation upstairs had now ceased. He sat and picked up the newspaper, cast a casual eye over a front-page boast that the paper had forced the government to act over compensation for miners suffering from pneumo-coniosis as a result of their work on the coalface. He had been down a mine, pit as they called it here, but once and what he remembered most was how careful he had to be not to trip over the cables sprawling across the ground. He had worn a pair of old walking boots. Some of the party had sported polished shoes and decent suits, and one foolish woman high heels. He had not enjoyed it. It had seemed dangerous, wet and filthy dirty. He shook his head, reread the article. The walls seemed ready to advance in and on to you. He did not touch his whisky until his wife appeared. He heard her coming energetically down the stairs. She was wearing a bright red tracksuit he had never seen before.

'Ah,' he said, 'the scarlet woman.'

'You're as bad as Harry Fisher.'

She picked up her whisky and raised it to his health. 'That was Linda.'

Stone waited, asking no question.

She pursed her lips as if in rebuke. 'She asked if they could come up this weekend. Friday night to Sunday afternoon. So that they could talk to us. They wanted, she said, to get to know us better. She had had such a comfortable time here and reported so favourably on us that Jay was pressing her to invite them-selves up here.'

'And did she say anything about their domestic affairs?'

'Hardly a word. She was too busy buttering me up.'

'Did she overdo it?'

'No, not really. Neared the margin, sometimes.'

Peg drained her glass and stared down at its emptiness. 'Not a very generous draught,' she said.

'No, a *chhotá peg*, as they said in India.'

'Who did?'

He was already out of the door and on his way to the kitchen.

X

At first the young visitors slightly disappointed their elders. They ate heartily; they praised their hosts; they offered and gave help at every opportunity, but said little about their domestic troubles. On the Friday night the four had dinner at about eight thirty soon after Linda and John, as Peg called him, arrived. They had had a hectic week, they claimed, so that Peg bundled them off to bed before ten thirty. 'We're early birds,' she said. 'And you need sleep. And there's no hurry to get up in the morning.'

'What time do you have breakfast?' Linda asked.

'About eight. But we'll put it back.'

The pair were down by nine, dressed in jeans and sweatshirts. Jay's was pure, but Linda's read 'We love Arsenal'. Both looked thoroughly clean as if they, and their clothes, had been scrubbed with a hard brush and carbolic soap. The casual clothes suited them; the boy looked young and eager, while the girl had what Stone described later to his wife as 'extraordinary beauty'. They had slept like logs and had never occupied such a comfortable bed. Jay said, hesitantly, that it was like Paradise. The sun shone with sharp brilliance through the large dining-room windows.

'This is a beautiful house,' Linda said.

'On a morning like this,' Peg answered. 'This sun sharpens everything up.'

After breakfast they took a turn round the garden. The Stones put on outdoor clothes, but the young people walked out unprotected.

'Don't you find it cold?' Peg asked them.

'Not at all,' JJ answered very politely.

'It's November,' Linda backed him up. 'But the sky's like spring and there are still some leaves on the trees.'

'Do you hear fairly often from my mother?' JJ asked Peg.

'She phones quite regularly. She doesn't write often.'

'Do you know anything about this new suitor of hers, the clergyman?'

'Not really. She's mentioned him, but casually, humorously if you like. I've no idea whether she's serious about him.'

'She's no chicken,' the boy said with a fierceness that belied the phrase.

'Sixty-one.' JJ bit his lower lip. 'She should know her mind at that age.'

'Why so?' Stone asked. 'She's probably very comfortable and doesn't see much advantage in change. This man is not the first to cast a favourable eye on her.'

'Besides,' Peg came in quickly, 'I wouldn't have said her experience of marriage was altogether favourable.'

'You mean my father was by no means an ideal husband?'

'I do,' Peg answered. 'Does that contradict your impression of him?'

JJ considered this. 'I didn't always see eye to eye with him. And quite often I used to ask myself how my mother came to marry a man like him. But he was a worker and he left her comfortably off. I was still at school when he died.'

'Cancer, wasn't it?' Stone enquired.

'Yes. He had had it for about a year, perhaps longer. He wasn't the sort of man to make a song and dance of his illness. I was surprised that he died so soon after they'd taken him for the second time into hospital.'

'He wasn't old, was he?' Peg asked.

'Seventy. He looked very ill by the end. He'd retired at sixty-five and he couldn't really find enough to do, or at least to satisfy himself. He put his hand to no end of things at home, but he liked big affairs, civic or national schemes, not renewing the central heating or rebuilding the greenhouse twice as large as before. He'd been called in as a consultant now and again; for instance, he advised them at the church about rebuilding the roof and church hall, saved them no end of money and ran rings round their pet architects. But he'd been used all his life to be out working for twelve hours a day. And my mother was pretty demanding. She was a woman who knew her mind and wasn't afraid to speak it.'

'And how did you get on with him personally?' Linda asked this question.

'All right. I wasn't exactly his sort of son. But I did well at school and he always encouraged me in that, though I think he was never enamoured of schools and universities, which he regarded as places that stuffed your head with useless knowledge. He liked to be seen as a practical man.'

'And had you any idea that he was out chasing women?' Linda pursued her subject.

'Not when I was still young. No.'

'You sound doubtful,' Linda said.

'No. That's a truthful answer. He never mentioned his women to me even in a jovial manner. Even as an oblique boast.'

'Made jokes, you mean?' Stone glossed.

'Yes. Never.'

'But,' Linda pressed. 'But.'

'What do you mean, "but"?' he asked.

'I know you well enough,' the girl said. 'You're holding something back.'

The party made slow progress down the garden path. Stone thought Linda's whole mien bespoke triumph. The boy seemed embarrassed, dashed, kept his head down, answered questions in a lower, lifeless voice.

When they went indoors Linda disappeared upstairs to change for the morning's outing, and Stone bustled outside to the back step to clean shoes and boots.

Suddenly JJ went across to his aunt, touched her arm. 'There was something,' he said. 'About my mother and my father. But I wasn't going to tell her. She's ruthless. She'd never let me forget it. I think I can tell you.'

'There's no need.'

'No. I've never told anybody before. It upset me at the time.'

'Just think about it first and then, if you wish, you can tell me later.'

'No. I'm going to tell you now. I know you're good friends, both you and Uncle Jack, of my mother.' He paused, then braced himself. 'I'd have been about fifteen at the time and it was probably in the school holidays. I can't be sure. I'd been reading and I went into the kitchen to get myself a glass of water. And my mother was sitting on one of those high three-legged stools we had. That was unusual. She rarely sat down when she was at

132

work. She didn't hear me, but then turned about suddenly and I saw she was crying. I had never seen my mother cry before. She snatched some tissues from a box she kept on the table and dabbed at herself, trying to hide her tears. I asked her what was wrong and she said, "Oh, nothing, nothing," but I could tell from her voice that wasn't anything like true. I went up to her and put my arm round her shoulder as she sat. I don't know why I did. We weren't a demonstrative family. She put her arms round me and began to sob. Her whole body shook. I'd no idea what to do.' His voice was now unemphatic and he could not look eye to eye at his aunt.

'I kept asking her what was the matter. In the end she stopped crying suddenly. That was typical. All at once she regained complete control over herself. She grabbed the tissues again and wiped her eyes. She stood up and faced me.

'"It's your father," she said. "He's committing adultery."

'"With whom?" I asked.

'"Betty Campbell." She looked up. "You know what adultery is?"

'"Yes," I answered.

'"And he's parading her round the streets at all hours."'

JJ tottered, almost out of his mind. His hands shook; his eyes were closed; his skin shone unhealthily; his lips trembled. He still managed to make his voice heard, but only with effort, breathily, scratchily.

'I said that I would speak to him. I don't know why I said that. I was not likely to criticise him, had never done so. If I had he would have clouted me, though I was taller than he was. He wasn't the sort of man you'd choose to argue with.

'My mother made a kind of small, gasping sound and said, when she'd sufficiently recovered, I mustn't even mention it to him. She pressed me to promise her and that was it. She said she'd be all right and that she'd made a fool of herself, but I must forgive her because she hadn't been well. We were never to refer again to this conversation.'

JJ stood now, presumably waiting for comment.

'You don't do well in kitchens,' Peg said.

'"If you don't like the heat, stay out of the kitchen",' he quoted, recovering, smiling at himself.

133

'Did you ever speak about it again?'

'No, not at all. I'm not certain about this, but I think my mother regretted confessing this or breaking down in front of me. She seemed stiffish, not ever talking freely. She was always rather that way inclined, not given to easy confidences, but now sometimes she seemed frozen, as if she felt afraid of giving herself away again.'

'And you?'

'It shook me. For one thing at that age I didn't think anyone of my father's advanced years would be interested in sex. He was, and looked, a lot older than my mother. He'd always seemed an old man to me, older than other people's fathers. And here he was in his sixties screwing some woman.'

'Did you know her?'

'By sight. She never came to our house.'

'And what was she like?'

'I only met her the once to speak to. My father sent me to her home on an errand. I was to take a stool, a polished little thing, for some sort of raffle or auction she was holding for the cottage hospital, I think.'

'This was before the upset with your mother?'

'Two or three years.'

'So the affair must have gone on for some time?'

'I've no idea. It's possible.'

'And did you like the look of her?'

'She was scented. My mother might use lavender water or eau de Cologne, but Mrs Campbell's was stronger, more exotic. She dressed rather boldly, in bright colours and always low-cut, showing her cleavage. She was pleasant to me, gave me chocolates and had a strong Glasgow accent.'

'Was her husband alive?'

'Yes. He'd retired from some sort of grocery chain in Glasgow and they'd moved out. He died some little time later. I think he and my father used to have a drink together. They had something in common, but he was never invited to our house. He died after a car accident, while they were abroad.'

They heard the door open and Linda, carrying her outdoor clothes, barged in on them. 'He's very slow,' she said.

'It's my fault, I'm afraid,' Peg answered. 'I kept him talking.'

'Do you know he'll hardly say a word to me for hours on end.'

'Love doesn't need it.' Stone had reappeared to lay down polished shoes by JJ's feet. 'There you are, sir,' Stone said. JJ muttered embarrassed thanks.

'Hurry up and change them,' Linda ordered, 'or we'll be waiting for you.'

'No rush,' Stone said pacifically, as JJ slunk out, shoes in hand.

Later in the day, after a hectic short tour of the city, a pub lunch and a run out to the Dukeries, Peg signalled her husband into the kitchen. 'Will fish be suitable for dinner?' she demanded.

'Depends what sort.'

'Trout.'

'Have you time?'

'Yes. And the young people will be hungry by seven when we eat.' She pulled a wry face. 'How did you find them?'

'They didn't speak to me much, never mind confide.'

'No, we tried too hard. The weather's been too good. If it had been pouring with rain all the time, it might have been better for staying indoors and baring our souls. What do you think of Miss Linda?' Peg asked.

'She gets on to him a bit. She seems quite different from when she was here on her own.'

'She's got it in for him; it's nasty.'

Peg repeated briefly JJ's account of his mother's weeping over her husband's infidelity.

'It seems to upset him still, just speaking about it?' Stone asked.

'Yes. He's sensitive, I think, but she likes to goad him. He said he had not told this story to her and he wasn't going to. He seems frightened of her.'

'So you think the partnership isn't likely to last long?'

'I don't like to lay down the law about how people are going to behave. They don't seem matched somehow. She must be in charge.'

'He stood up to her about leaving the bank, from what we hear.'

'Yes. He did. And it's to his credit. But I don't see it lasting. She'll be coming up with some other madcap scheme to establish her superiority. And next time he might well cave in. And' – she spoke portentously now – 'moreover, I'm old-fashioned. If a couple are going to live together on a permanent basis they should get married.'

'Why's that?'

'They make a public and legal announcement of their intentions. Then they're serious.'

'Even so, marriages seem to break up at an alarming rate. You wouldn't make divorce more difficult, would you?'

'I'm not here to argue. What are we going to tell them?'

'You tell me first. I can see you're bursting to.'

'John Stone, I don't know how we managed to stay married for so long. I think we should ask them if they love each other and see what they come out with.'

'Together? Or do you ask John and I Linda? Or vice versa.'

'Never mind the fiddling detail. Even if we get an honest answer out of them, or one of them, it won't resolve the difficulties. The only thing we can claim is that we tried.'

'I guess you're right, if you're suggesting our intervention will mean anything to them. But we'll try. The world will condemn us for it ever after, but we tried.'

Peg aimed at him the sort of swipe she employed when they were first married. They laughed outright and he put his arms round her. He acknowledged her warmth with a clownish kiss on the cheek.

He seized his opportunity to question Linda when they sat together after dinner. JJ uncharacteristically had ordered them to stay where they were while he helped his aunt to clear the dishes and wash up.

'That's not fair,' Stone objected. 'Your aunt ought to sit down. She did the cooking.'

'It will do you good to do as you're told for once,' Peg said. 'While I enjoy the company of my handsome nephew.'

As they sat together Stone, swirling the last of his Chardonnay in his wineglass, spoke only half seriously to the girl. 'I suppose,' he said, 'I ought to ask you how things stand between you and JJ.'

She lifted her glass coquettishly to him. 'No change. Or nothing radical. We get on each other's nerves. When we're together at home I invariably wish I were somewhere else. It's better while we're here. Jay seems more interesting, more assertive. Back in our flat we come home tired out, with nothing to say to each other, struggle to get some small dull meal down us and then loll about until we go to bed. Nothing exciting happens there, either. We doze off, knowing that it won't be long before the alarm wakes us at six, and we have to roll out and get ready for work.'

'Is your work stressful?' he asked.

'I suppose it is, but that's what's attractive about it. It's about the only thing in my life that is interesting.'

'So work should be. You're involved in it ten hours a day.'

Linda smiled at him and he fetched the opened wine bottle from its cooling bucket to fill her glass.

'You'll have me drunk,' she said.

'Does it happen often?'

'Never. I'm always mindful of that six o'clock reveille.' She raised her glass again cheerfully.

'What I couldn't understand, if you don't mind my saying this, was your proposal to leave the bank and live in the country on your own produce.' He made a pause. They had now reached the heart of this matter. 'Were you serious about it?'

'Why do you ask?' Linda's voice chilled.

'From what I hear you are extremely good at your job and it is the sort of work that our society chooses to reward very highly. We're acquisitive. Money means power.'

'You can easily see from us that it doesn't mean happiness.'

'Is that because you'll never be happy?' he asked. 'Individually or as a couple?'

Linda burst into a bray of laughter. 'Probably, in my case. Jay will do well. He likes money, will enjoy earning and learn to spend it. So he's in the right place. I'm not so sure of myself. You asked if I was serious about throwing up my job at the bank and setting myself up as a peasant. Well, I thought I was at the time.'

'But not now.'

'I'm not so sure. I guess I'd have been perfectly satisfied as long as I stayed in good health. But if I were ill, there'd have been no insurance behind me, no private consultations or even time in hospital provided by the firm.'

'You hadn't saved sufficient to keep you afloat?'

'I guess you'd think so. I'm not so sure. I might live to be ninety.'

'So it's stick to the bank, is it?'

'This one or some other.'

'And what happens to the two of you?'

'I haven't the remotest idea.'

This answer silenced him. He was convinced that she was doing her utmost to speak the truth, that she didn't know what would happen. 'You're doing your best to stay together?' he asked.

'No.'

'You, or he?'

'He may be, but I'm not. It hardly seems worth it.'

'Then what will you do?'

'Carry on with things as they are and if it all gets too unbearable I shall scuttle out, leave him.'

'Won't you run across him every day at the bank?'

'Possible. We don't work together. I can keep out of his way.'

'Can he do anything to prevent your partnership breaking up?'

'I shouldn't think so. We've been through every argument that exists. I think he just needs mothering. He's quite good at sex, though. He's learning.'

She did not look him straight in the eyes this time, but held her glass under her nose and knitted her brow. He could not make out whether or not she was emotionally concerned.

'Does this not upset you?'

'No.' She rubbed her cheek. 'When things began to go awry, it knocked me about in a way I didn't think possible. I had crying bouts, couldn't sleep, even had pains in my arms and legs that couldn't be anything but psychological. And we had blazing rows. I threw things at him. I didn't know I was so involved. We first lived together at my suggestion, and it seemed comfortable and pleasant, no skin off anybody's nose, and now here we were, fighting like cats.' She held up a hand, traffic-control fashion. 'But.' Linda waited for him. He sat quiet. 'I don't mind now. It doesn't seem to matter. If we can hang on together, that'll not trouble me. If I have to leave, I shan't fret either.'

'Won't you feel sorry for Jay?'

'He'll get over it. He's that sort. We all have to suffer at some time or another. And when you look at these third-world people lost in earthquakes or floods or civil wars, what are our little domestic differences?'

'I never found that other people's troubles, however awful, brought any comfort to me and my bits of setbacks.'

'I don't much talk about this, but when I was twenty I was in love with a marvellous man. He could do anything: play the piano, paint and draw, write poetry, run like the wind, beat everybody at tennis and badminton.'

'He hadn't any faults?'

'One, in my eyes. He was married to somebody else. He was a mathematician and I went to a class he ran. Most of the other pupils were university science honours students, or postgraduates. There weren't many of us. Fifteen for a start, but some dropped out. If you had to miss a lesson or two you were lost. It was exciting; it really was.'

'And you could keep up with these university people?'

'Yes, they weren't mathematicians proper. Or at least I don't think so. We used to go for a drink afterwards and he gave me a lift to my tube station.'

'And?'

'He asked me if I'd go out with him for a day. He'd told me he was married with a couple of children at school. We'd go out to the country and once we went to Margate.'

'Every weekend?'

'No. Not more than half a dozen times altogether. Once for a whole weekend. Friday night, Saturday, Sunday. That was in the beginning of his summer holiday. He was due to start another course in October, but it was cancelled. I ran into one of the other students by chance and he told me Julian, Dr Toone, was ill. He died just before Christmas. Leukaemia. It seemed very quick. He was so fit. I don't understand it to this day.'

'Did you never write?'

'He said there was no need. We saw each other once a week. I read his name once in the newspapers when he'd won some badminton competition. That sort of thing. He wrote me one note in that last summer holiday, saying he was ill, but he hoped to be back to teaching by the beginning of term. I heard no more. He must have got worse and quickly. I went to his funeral. There were plenty of people there. The student, the man who told me Julian was ill, took me. We saw his wife and family, and two people, a professor and a cousin, made speeches about Julian.

They all said how brilliant he was, and how good at everything, a "Renaissance man" the cousin called him. He came, it appeared, from a well-to-do family and had been bright from the word go. They spoke about his family life, how he never neglected his dependants however many tasks he took on. Our class even got a mention from the professor, a chemist, who'd once said to Julian that some of his students would profit from a firmer grasp of mathematics and so the class had been set up. There was no mention of days out with a twenty-year-old girl from a bank. I didn't expect it. I cried a bit; I couldn't help it, but his wife, though she looked pale, showed no signs of emotion. She stood at the door and shook our hands. I said I was a student at his evening class. She said, "Are you a chemist, then?" and I said, "No, a banker."'

'Is that the end of the story?' Stone asked.

'Yes. That was that.'

'Did you go to any other classes?'

'I did. And they were interesting enough. But there weren't any more Julians about.'

'You've got over it now?'

'I suppose so, though I shall never completely recover from it. It was so marvellous. We had sex. I wasn't a virgin. He never made any allowances for me in the class, nor showed favouritism, so that when he praised me I knew he meant it. I shall never forget him.'

'Were there others between Julian and John?'

'Yes, there were.'

'Would you like children?' Stone pressed her. 'I hope you don't mind my asking these questions.'

'No. I don't particularly see myself as a mother. Except, as I've said, mothering Jay, I've not felt any great stirrings of the maternal instinct. When I meet my sister's two, and they're bright enough and pleasant enough, I can't see myself looking after their likes every hour of the day or night. So you see, as far as your efforts are concerned I'm a hopeless case.'

'One never knows.'

'I do. I like you. You seem straight. I think that if I wanted advice about life I'd ask John Stone. But I take decisions and then it's up to me to put up with them or change them.'

'That's not always possible.'

'I know that. I think of Julian Toone. There he was with a job he liked, a family he loved, outside activities at which he excelled, a young mistress and then, bang, he gets leukaemia and he learns he hasn't long to live. He'd taken his decisions, I dare say, but they were wiped off the slate. It must have been terrifying.'

Stone was just about to answer, or attempt to, when Peg and JJ returned smiling and red-faced from the kitchen.

'Any wine left?' Peg asked.

He nodded. 'And there's plenty in the cellar, I'll get you two glasses after your labours.'

They sat, Linda still at the table, the other three scattered in armchairs, and drank, though moderately, for the rest of the evening.

Stone noticed that Linda and JJ went up to bed hand in hand. 'Is it a good sign?' he asked his wife.

'Can't be other,' she said, then contradicted herself. '*In vino veritas.*'

In bed he gave some account to Peg of his exchanges with Linda.

'Did you like her?' she asked when he had finished his eager discussion.

'On the whole, yes. She seemed really decent, pleasant. But then suddenly she'd give me an ice-cold answer. I couldn't quite make it out. She wasn't consistent. It's as though she has her defences ready in case people go too far.'

'You didn't? None of your headmaster's stuff.'

'No. She talked freely enough. About her earlier affairs.'

'Will she leave him?'

'She hadn't made up her mind.'

'I quizzed JJ. He thought she would probably go before long. "We don't have a great deal of leisure time," he said, "and she thinks she could fill hers more profitably." That was his line.'

'Doing what?'

'Sex. Some sort of mathematical studies and she's beginning to take an interest in music again.'

'Again?'

'Yes. She had piano lessons as a child. Oh, and by the way, she thinks you're sexy.'

'Not one of her better judgements.'

141

'She didn't make a pass at you, then?'

'If she did I didn't notice it.'

They fell asleep, unusually, in each other's arms. Peg felt that her husband had prised more information out of Linda than she had out of JJ. She was enjoying the weekend, but was totally unsure of what the young couple would do next. She decided it did not matter, was on a par with some interesting snippet from the newspaper. It gave you something to think about, but didn't much alter your way of life.

The house seemed empty after the young people left on Sunday afternoon. Peg and John wrote letters, but separately, and in the evening they held their bedtime investigation over again, in more detail, as if their words would suddenly throw up some hidden meaning, illuminate their puzzlement. Nothing came of the hope. They enjoyed the conversation and their glosses on it. She congratulated her husband on his success in worming the truth out of the girl. He did not think he deserved her praise, but he basked in her approbation. They walked out into the garden.

'The nights are drawing in,' she said. 'I hate it.'

Lights shone from Harry Fisher's workshop and the sound of his happy, energetic hammering struck amiss on the still air.

'Fisher sounds busy,' he said. 'I suppose he's preparing for one of his little bits of building next week.'

'It's more likely that Annie has got him to work on some improvement in the house. She always complains that there are half a dozen things to be done at home, but he'll never find time.'

'To no effect?'

'Not so. If she threatens to call the firm in, he might stir himself. He likes working, especially if it's slightly tricky and he thinks he can manage it. But he prefers it away from home where he can flirt with the women. Typical of him, she says.'

They listened to the violent blows and the faint squawk of the accompanying radio.

'What energy,' Stone said. 'The noisy devil.'

XI

On the next morning, a Monday, Peg drew back the curtains of the bedroom just before eight o'clock. Outside the Fishers' front gate she saw an ambulance. Surprised, she squealed out to her husband who was in the bathroom shaving. He ran in, wearing only pyjama bottoms.

'It must be Annie or Harry,' Peg said.

'Unless they have someone staying with them.'

'They never mentioned visitors. And Harry was making enough clatter in his workshop last night.'

A paramedic stepped down from the back of the ambulance, walked round to the front and almost immediately the vehicle drove off. The street in grey light stood emptily quiet.

'We must go round,' Peg said, 'to see if we can do anything for them.'

'Yes.'

'How long will you be?' she asked.

'Ten minutes at the most.'

'I'll go round right away. If I'm still there when you come down you could call round. I don't like to think of either of them there on their own struggling. I wonder who it is.'

Peg bustled downstairs while he, without hurry, finished shaving. When he had dressed and had examined himself in a mirror, he went to collect an anorak from the cloakroom. Now fully prepared to make an appearance outside, he was interrupted by the rattle of the front-door key and Peg's return. 'What's wrong?' he enquired.

'Harry's had a heart attack. They've taken him to hospital.'

'Which?'

'Queen Elizabeth. That's where the casualty department is. They weren't sure. They could have had more beds in Bagthorpe.'

'Is it bad?' he asked.

'Well, I'd hardly call it good. Annie'll be round in a few minutes; she's not had anything to eat. Then you and I can drive her up there when she's had a bit of breakfast.'

'How's she taking it?'

'Well. She's upset, but she's keeping calm. She'll be here in a minute.'

It was twenty minutes later when Annie arrived, make-up in place, dressed to the nines, ready to go out. Stone kissed her and she hugged him athletically, nothing of the poor weak woman about her. Her scent drenched the room; Peg hated that. Over breakfast, as Peg bullied her neighbour into eating, Annie gave Stone a brief account of the attack. Apparently she and Harry slept in separate rooms – John did not know that – and she was woken by his calling out.

'That wasn't like him. He wants to be up and about, if not away, by the time I stagger down. I dashed in and he was dressed, but half sitting, half lying on the bed, clutching at his chest. He had a fearful, tearing pain in his heart and in his arms, he said. He thought it was getting worse. When he had got up and washed and shaved he first had this pain. He took a couple of indigestion tablets and dressed himself, but it didn't go away. Then he called out to me. He was sweating and pale when I got in. I asked if it was a heart attack and he'd no idea. I gave him half an aspirin and propped him on the bed with pillows so that he was half sitting, half lying. Then I rang the ambulance. Harry didn't want me to; he said he thought the pain might be going away, but I wasn't having that. When I rang 999 and I was put through to the hospital they were very good. They made contact with an ambulance and told me it wouldn't be much more than eight minutes. It was less.

'Then somebody started to talk me through it all. Where was Harry? How did he seem? Was he dressed? Was the room warm? That sort of thing. Then they told me how to make him comfortable. It seemed a long time to me, but the ambulance arrived in just about five minutes. There were two young men, and they asked a few questions and then got him downstairs into the ambulance. They were serious and cheerful, if you know what I mean. They kept us going by chatting. "These old houses have proper wide staircases," they said. "It makes our job easier." They said they'd get him into the ambulance. "We've got the wherewithal," they said. "It's the modern way. We bring the hospital to the patient, not the other way round. We can deal with an emergency." They were very good.'

'And how was Harry all this time?'

'I think he was relieved. He was frightened by the time they came and his face was ashen. But these young men were so efficient and normal I think it comforted him. They spent quite a lot of time in the ambulance connecting him up to this machine and that. "Get in early," one of them said to me. "That's the secret of our success." They told me I needn't go with him unless I wanted to. "He'll be all right," they said. "You go back home and get your arrangements made. You'll do it more comfortably there than on payphones on hospital corridors." Then when all that was done I was to come up to the hospital and bring his things. "He'll be kept in?" I asked. A daft question. "Afraid so," they said. "But for a start they'll be assessing him."'

Annie talked her way quietly through this account. The Stones could not but admire her. She had dressed herself carefully for breakfast in her neighbours' house and doubtless she would complete the process before she went on to the hospital. She ate, with Peg's encouragement, a bowl of cereal and two slices of toast. She drank a large mug of coffee. Stone knew she would be scared. The Fishers' house had been a place without a great deal of illness and Harry's sudden attack, disablement, incapacity must have caught her out. But she had not been at a loss; she had administered the half-aspirin. Had she read that in the newspapers or had some acquaintance told her what she had done in an equivalent situation? Once breakfast was over she offered her hosts help with the dishes, but Peg ordered her back home.

'You go in and let people know what's happened. Relatives, Harry's workman . . .'

'I've already rung him.'

'Good. You've done well. But just sit down on your own with a slip of paper and a pencil, and work out what's to be done. You'll be able to get a meal, a proper cooked meal, in the middle of the day at the hospital, and you'll eat this evening here with us, I hope, after you've finished all your visiting and arranging.'

Annie kissed her neighbour. 'You're very good, to me, Peg,' she said.

'How long will you be before you'll have it all cut and dried, and are ready for the hospital?'

'Three quarters of an hour.' Without hesitation.

'Good. I'll have John outside in the car. And remember. When you want to come back give us a ring and we'll pick you up.'

'There's no need. There's a good bus service or I can call a taxi.'

'You can do as you're told for once.'

The two women kissed again.

Stone listened from outside the kitchen door.

'You heard all that. Three quarters of an hour to get the car out.'

'Yes, ma'am. You're a good woman.' He liked to praise. A word of commendation from the headmaster in the old days had worked its short-term magic often enough. Peg grinned at him.

Exactly on the appointed time Annie appeared, smart as ever, though her lips seemed tight. She talked cheerfully enough, but once or twice she faltered.

'I'm going to park and come with you at least as far as the information desk,' he said.

'It's a waste of your money.'

'I don't know.'

He stood with her while the girl took details, made two phone calls, finally tracked Harry down. 'We get there in the end,' she said. She gave lucid instructions how to find the ward. Stone took Annie's arm; they used a lift. Stone hated lifts, felt they took his opportunities for healthy exercise away from him. Without trouble they found D3, Harry's ward. They accosted a nurse who said Harry was already in bed.

'He's lucky,' she said. 'Available beds have been in short supply all this week. But he's come in on a day when hardly a thing's happening.' She looked them over. 'So far. Don't be afraid to see him all wired up.'

'Is he doing well?' Stone asked.

'Yes. It's early days. There'll be other tests. The consultant's already looked him over.'

'And they've decided on his treatment?'

'We work for safety, other things being equal. What I mean is

146

we make him comfortable, and then we'll continue with tests. But come along and see for yourself.'

She led them into the ward proper. The patient was not too far from the nurses' office.

Harry, stripped to the waist, was connected to some sort of machine which gave out a series of high-pitched short notes. A younger nurse bent over touching the controls. The curtains were drawn.

'Visitors, Harry,' the first nurse announced. 'Your wife. And friend.'

Fisher opened his eyes. He looked ill, his colour was that of putty, but his expression showed boredom rather than fear. Stone was surprised how thin he was, his ribs countable. He must have strength without fat.

'They've examined me, oh, about half a dozen of them, and given me an echo-test.'

'What's that?' Annie snapped.

'It's an ultra-sound thing. They did it next door on my way up.'

'Did it hurt?'

'No. They put grease on you and then rub this machine up and down you.'

'Were you lying down?'

'On my side. This machine here shows whether my heart's regular.'

'How do you know all this?'

'They tell you what they're doing. They'd got one of these going buckshee so they decided to put it on me for a bit. By the way they talked they hadn't got many patients in. These young doctors seemed quite glad to scc me. Something to do.'

Fisher answered questions quite lucidly but without his usual energy. He kept his eyes closed much of the time. When Stone said he would leave, Fisher thanked him, almost courteously, for ferrying his wife.

'Makes us retired people feel useful,' Stone answered.

He inquired of Annie whether she had further instructions, tore out a slip of paper from his note-book on which he wrote carefully and large his telephone number.

'I've got it down at the back of my diary,' she said.

'You never know when it might come in useful.' She did not answer. 'Don't be afraid to ring us.'

She asked her husband if he needed anything. He raised his eyes. 'No, you put it all in when I came first thing.' Now the poor man looked worn out, as if answering a simple question proved too much for him.

Stone made his way from the ward. Patients looked gratefully at him: some sat by their beds; some read the newspapers, one a book. Stone nodded to those who caught his eye. They returned the silent message with interest. Once outside he took his bearings. The hospital corridors were quite wide and decorated with large pictures of seaside beaches or rustic landscapes not unlike old railway posters. Their quality he thought little of, but then he asked himself what the intention of the hanging of these prints was. To catch the eye of the patients, as they were wheeled along the corridors to the operating theatre or the X-ray studios? He doubted it. To guide or amuse visitors hurrying breathless with anxiety, or embarrassment, to visit relatives? His senior English master at school had spent time in hospital and had reported that what he had most missed were pictures on the wall. 'I never looked hard at those at home, never, but since I've been back I've stood in front of them one by one for minutes on end. We don't know what we miss,' the man had complained.

This newish hospital seemed to Stone like any other public building. The notices detailing the wards and departments were neat and unobtrusive, unlike the huge authoritative boards in the old hospitals. These were seven or eight floors here, so perhaps the need for instruction was less than in one-storey buildings with wards branching off each side. He remembered his first hospital, closed now, where he had visited his mother. That seemed puritanical, utilitarian; steep steps of cold stone with iron railings and the walls, dark blankness broken with sets of pipes, running purposefully, orthogonally. You were in there to be cured or killed, not amused. He imagined those patients carrying their few necessities in small shabby suitcases, toiling upstairs for the last time for the next day's operation from which they would never recover. The walls and barenesses offered no comfort. It was a serious place.

He arrived at the huge foyer where he and Annie Fisher had received their first instructions. He walked round it, one of many wanderers. Here there was a restaurant and a fast-food bar, a bank, other shops where one could buy groceries and confectionary, toys and clothes. It was more like an airport lounge; people hurried or paused, harassed or laughing outright. In the older hospitals he thought one saw more nurses; no one in uniform made much impression here.

When he told this to his wife she asked, 'Which did you like better?'

'Neither. The old hospitals used to smell of hospital, if I remember properly. Perhaps they all used the same disinfectant. I don't know.'

'And what's this place smell of?'

'Nothing much. Not that I noticed.'

Annie rang before three to ask if John Stone would pick her up. 'I had to ring you,' she said. 'I'm so frightened of Peg.'

'So am I. The car's standing ready. I'll come over at once.'

She reported that Harry seemed fairly well settled. They kept fetching him out for tests at intervals and said they would continue to do so. The consultant would make up his mind tomorrow. 'About what's wrong and what they do next.'

'Good.'

He had been instructed to ask her if six thirty would be a suitable time for the evening meal. 'I can't tell you what's on the menu,' he said.

'I shan't go back to the hospital today. I was just in the way.'

'Right. Six fifteen for six thirty, as they say.' She thanked him. 'And don't be afraid to come in before if you're lonely.'

The meal went well and all three talked with animation. Stone and Annie dealt with the pots, deliberately ignoring the dishwasher. Annie had spoken almost brilliantly of the jobs she had done in the two or three hours she had been left on her own. She had sorted out matters that had been in abeyance for months.

'It was as if I had a new dynamism,' she said, 'something like Harry's. Whether that was because I had hated the sight of him in bed, looking so vulnerable. He's the sort who likes to have his day's work planned, and his tools and materials set out all ready the night before. "No use leaving it to Jimmy," he'd said often enough. "He could give any plumber a few lessons in forgetfulness." But he sits in his bed so helpless now. The longer he's there the more frightened he gets. They wouldn't be doing all these tests if they didn't think there was something seriously wrong with him. He said as much to me. He didn't complain, but he needed me to comfort him. I said that nowadays doctors were so frightened of litigation that they had to do all sorts of things they wouldn't have considered just a few years back, so they've got the answers ready for some hostile lawyer's cross-examination. I told him to lie still and co-operate. I'm sure he does his best, but a hospital's the last place he'd want to be.'

Annie left at nine thirty, saying she wanted to get to bed early. Stone accompanied her back home in the darkness. He kissed her on the mouth once she was inside her house. No iota of eroticism displayed itself. Her face was warm and perfumed, but her lips were dead to him. She kept up a babble of thanks for their kindness. He instructed her to let him know when he'd be needed again to drive her to the hospital.

'It won't be in the morning,' she said. 'That's the day they spring-clean this particular ward. Move the beds. Put polish into the floors. So they won't allow us in before 2 p.m.'

'I'll be ready. And if you have to go anywhere else.'

'Thanks, Jack.'

When she had closed and bolted (he heard it) the door he stood outside and stared out over the north-west edge of the town with its strings of light and behind these the dark country beyond the motorway. The November sky was light enough – the moon shone nearly full – to show the separated shadow lines of low hills, with hidden valleys erased. Stone knew the landscape well enough, had examined it with field glasses often enough, from their bedroom, had walked there a few years ago, travelled through it by car. Small lights sparked distantly out there but dispelled none of the early darkness for him.

He could not see a single star, yet the moonlight stretched strong. He would have been thankful for something celestial he knew, the Plough, or Orion, but they made no appearance. It seemed not too cold, though a small wind faintly disturbed the twigs. From the equivalent spot on his own garden path, pausing again, he stared out. Nothing showed any difference. A kind of milky darkness spread over the sky. Why should it be different? Because Harry Fisher three days ago was knocking hell out of materials, good, solid, enjoyable hammer blows, and now the man was confined to hospital, his body scrutinised by the latest medical technology. Annie had changed. She, the fly-by-night as he'd sometimes considered her, more interested in underwear than understanding, acted now with a kind of balance, of control, sorting out difficulties, knowing when to lean on neighbours and when not. She had learnt sense, and intelligence, and taste even in the course of the few short hours of her husband's illness.

'What are you standing out there for?' Peg chided. 'Without a coat or scarf or hat?'

'Studying the stars,' he said.

'There aren't any. At least not at the back.'

'But they're still there.'

'Ugh.' She expressed contempt for his schoolboy argument. 'Are you taking her in tomorrow morning?'

'No. In the afternoon. Tomorrow's the big clean-up day. No visitors allowed until two.'

'You're learning your way around, you and our Annie.'

How wrong she was hit home a week later when Harry Fisher, who had seemed well and was being prepared for an operation, suddenly died. The day before when Stone chauffeured both Annie and Peg to the hospital, Harry had sat in his bedside chair, smiling at them and claiming to be bored stiff.

'Shall I bring you something to read?'

'I manage to work through the *Telegraph*. I've learnt quite a bit just lying here with nothing else to do. That's the paper we have at home, but there I barely look at it.'

'Any pretty nurses to make eyes at?' Peg asked.

'You'll get me into trouble with my better half, you will. They're all pretty presentable and there are two smashers.'

'I bet they'd thank you for that designation,' Peg said.

'Are they busy?' Stone asked.

'Rushed off their feet.'

They came out of the hospital much cheered, certain that Fisher was getting somewhere near his old state and ready for any operation they'd put him through. Annie thought the stay in hospital had done him good. 'He knows his limits,' she said, 'as he never did before.'

In the early hours of the next morning he died.

151

It happened with such suddenness that they could hardly grasp it and Stone, shocked, wondered if someone had not made a dreadful error.

Clearly the same suspicion had crossed Annie's mind and she'd put it bluntly to the consultant. 'How is it when you've done all these tests, you didn't find what was going to kill him a day or two later?'

'That's exactly what we plan to find out. I've been away, as you know, at a conference at the Royal College, but my subordinates did all I would have done and, as far as I can find out, did it well. Neither I nor they expected any complications before the operation. The valve we were to deal with was leaking, but I have seen many worse among patients who have lived. The body is a highly complex entity and it is possible that some weakness suddenly became more marked; it's always possible. That's why I have asked you to allow a post-mortem on your husband, to which you so courageously agreed.' His phraseology reminded her of John Stone's, though the doctor was younger. 'My senior registrar, Mr Frobisher, a conscientious and gifted young man, fought for three hours to keep your husband alive. We do not like to lose our patients. And he admired your husband as a man. "A cheerful stoic" is how he described him. I'm really sorry about what has happened, but I will keep you in touch with any conclusions we reach.'

The consultant spoke earnestly and, when he had answered her questions, led her by the arm to the door. She dissolved into quiet tears in the corridor, but the reaction was soon over, as Peg took her arm.

That morning just before six, when she was lying awake wondering whether it was worth getting out of bed to make a cup of coffee, the telephone had rung. A quiet voice from the hospital asked her name, then informed her that her husband Henry had been taken very seriously ill during the night and was not likely to live long.

The brutality of the message from this low official voice battered her. She, on one elbow in bed, trembled as if she had been pulled from freezing water. She heard herself making small noises, like croup, of grief. Leaping out of bed, she nearly fell. She swayed, hung on to a chest of drawers. Her mind lacked clarity. Should she ring her neighbours at this early hour of the morning? They had pressed her to do so at any emergency and this was. She rang, remembering the Stones' number, and stood listening to the repetitive signal. She was through. They must have been sound asleep for it seemed an interminable time before Peg answered. Annie gave her message and found she was crying.

'We'll take you,' Peg said. 'Jack's downstairs making us a cup of tea. You get dressed and come straight round. You must have a drink before you go out, that's certain. We'll get dressed at once. I'll shout down to him; I don't know what he's messing about at. He'll get the car round. It'll be quicker than ringing for a taxi. Are you all right? Are you sure?'

Annie washed, cleaned her teeth and put on the trousers of a tracksuit, then pulled them off again as unsuitable. She now chose a blouse, skirt and jacket. The thought 'Shall I wear my pearls?' flashed into her mind and was dismissed. She stumbled downstairs, clinging to the stair rail, and once below she stared about her, not knowing her next move. She struggled out to the kitchen, snatched a half-glass of water which she swallowed. Moving rapidly nowhere across the kitchen she knocked her head on a cupboard door she had left open. Agony creased her brain like explosive light and she swore loudly, a filthy word more suitable to Harry on a building site. Tears splashed again. Weakness creased her knees.

By the time she went round to the Stones' house they were waiting for her.

'I know you want to get there, but I don't suppose five minutes will make much difference. So sit down with this cup of coffee. I've made you a slice of toast.'

Annie did as she was told. Her slice of toast was buttered and cut into fingers. She did this sometimes for herself when she ate a boiled egg instead of a cooked lunch. It reminded her of childhood. Peg had put on a tracksuit, looked motherly.

'We're both going with you,' she said, 'unless you've made other arrangements. I'll stay with you. John here will come back and do any errands, and pick us up and run us about the rest of the day.'

Stone appeared from outside. He wore a tie, though he was unshaven. He put a hand on Annie's shoulder as he passed. 'Ready at any time,' he said.

Annie struggled, but could not finish her toast. She apologised.

Peg brushed her murmured words aside. 'Are you ready, John?' she called. 'Time we were off.'

The journey in darkness to the hospital was not passed in silence. They commented on the traffic or lack of it, on the beginnings of light. Peg embarked on some tale of all night travel to catch the morning ferry to France. There was little point or relevance about the story, but a sympathetic voice sounded, keeping desperate thoughts at bay.

Stone drove well. Outside the hospital he asked, 'Shall I park the car and come in with you?'

'No. We'll be all right. You go home and get yourself shaved, but don't wander far from the phone in case we need you.' A faint tang of humour, or bluff common sense, coloured the words. In the car Peg had been holding Annie's hand; she held it still as they entered the wide doors.

The two women hurried up to the ward and announced themselves to the staff nurse, a slim, swarthy young man.

'I'm afraid he's gone,' the nurse said. 'I'm very sorry.'

'From the ward?' Annie queried.

The man jerked back, in alarm. 'No,' he said, shaking his hands towards them. 'I'm very sorry but he died. About half an hour ago. We haven't had time to move him yet. It came quite suddenly at the end. I was there. And the registrar and the house surgeon. He wasn't on his own.'

'Is he still here?' Annie asked, as if she didn't quite understand the information.

'Yes.'

'Can we see him, then?'

'Yes. They'll be taking him away quite soon, I expect. He died peacefully, without pain or stress.' He looked at them both, speaking low as if his last sentence was some sort of mantra to render their ordeal bearable. 'This way.' He led them from the office to the nearest bed, where the curtains were drawn. He eased back one corner and led them in. Annie seized her friend's hand, as they edged through the narrow opening. The nurse stepped back to complete the closing of the curtains.

Harry Fisher lay neatly in the middle of the bed, covered with a sheet. The young man gently lifted this from the face. The two women stood close, not knowing what to do next. Fisher's eyes were closed; he might well have been deeply asleep. He did not look ill, only rather older than in real life. This stillness removed his likeness to himself; he had always been on the move, dashing off to the next task, complaining or joking. They could not judge his colour in the dimmish lights of the ward. Annie let go of Peg's hand, shuffled a pace or two forward, bent, with her palms down on the mattress, to kiss her husband's lips. She straightened with a little cry, then bent again. Peg moved close, so that next time Annie stood, she put her arm round her friend's waist to still the trembling.

The curtains were slightly drawn back and another young man, this time in a white coat, eased himself in, snatching it behind him. 'Mrs Fisher?' he asked.

Annie turned, almost regally.

'I'm sorry,' he said. 'I'm the senior house surgeon. The porters are here to take your husband away.'

The wife did not seem to understand, stood aghast. 'Perhaps,' the young doctor continued, 'you'd just like a moment or two with him on your own.'

'Yes, please.'

The nurse, then Peg, then the doctor slipped out. The porters with their trolley were waiting, this time middle-aged men with solemn faces. They looked with a kind of professional sympathy at Peg, but the doctor signalled them not to move. The little party, six people, stood uneasily, unspeaking, not knowing where to look. There were stirrings now among the other patients.

The doctor drew in a slow breath, glanced towards Peg, said in a whisper, 'Perhaps we should fetch Mrs Fisher now.' He held back the corner of the curtain and called in a low voice, 'Are you ready, Mrs Fisher?' He moved in and shortly afterwards the two emerged, he with his arm through hers. He motioned to Peg to take up the other side.

Annie's face was straight, as if set in wax. A silver trickle of a tear glistened on the left cheek.

'This way,' the doctor said.

The three moved off funereally. Annie leaned with a great weight on her friend's arm. Her legs gave no support, but she made no noise, looking ahead, her mouth slightly open.

155

'In here,' the doctor said, indicating a door a few yards down the corridor. They entered a small storeroom with shelves on one side. A chair was pushed forward for Annie. She took it. The doctor brought a second; on this Peg parked herself.

The doctor stood, leaning back on a cupboard. 'I'm very sorry about this,' he said. 'We'd all come to like Mr Fisher. He didn't complain, though I used to think he saw some of us as too young or barmy. But he took the tablets and went through all the tests without a murmur. And he was used to talking to people, one could see that, and he used to cheer some of the others up. Some people seem suddenly disorganised when they are put in hospital, but Harry would talk to them, make them laugh; they'd listen to him and feel more settled. He was just the sort we'd have in the ward all the time if we had any choice. Makes our life a lot easier.'

Annie, nodding, looked up, stared hard and asked, 'Was his death unexpected?' She spoke with some hostility.

'Well, he was very seriously ill when they brought him in, but I must confess I was surprised. The senior registrar really battled for him, tried everything.'

'Was he in pain?'

'Perhaps at first, but well before he died he was peaceful.'

'Unconscious, you mean?'

'Oh, no. He knew what was happening. He kept looking at us, puzzling it all out. And then at the end he went easily as you could wish. One minute he was alive, the next he was gone. No noise, no discomfort. The senior registrar had another go at him. He never gives in, that man, but your husband was away.'

Annie now wept openly, but silently. To her surprise Peg felt tears trickling down her own cheeks. She found a clean handkerchief, mopped as unobtrusively as she could.

The house surgeon was talking again. 'Have you any questions?'

Annie, bemused, looked over at Peg who said, 'I expect there are papers to sign and so on?'

'Yes. But we'll deal with them in due course. And this is one of the mornings Mr Holmes, the consultant, comes in early. He'd like to speak to you. We had a message. He hasn't spoken to me, of course, but I think he'd like to have a post-mortem if you agree. I mention it so that you'll have time to think it over, or

discuss it.' He pointed vaguely towards Peg. 'But all in due time.
I think your best plan is to get a cup of tea, or even better to go
downstairs and busy yourself with a little something to eat. You
can stay here if you wish and we'll provide you with tea, but I
think it will be better if you had a bite of something. I know at
times like this it might seem heartless to be talking about bacon
butties or toast and marmalade, but take my word for it. I can
see you're a brave woman.'

Annie appeared shaken by this advice. Peg was surprised that
a young man of this age – he'd be twenty-four or -five – had the
nerve to deliver these possibly sensible judgements like this. Did
he realise that Annie had just been parted from a husband of
nearly twenty-five years, a blow of sickening proportions, and
could still tell her to go and eat toast so that she would be here
and ready, fortified, for milord Mr Holmes, the consultant, to
speak to her when he arrived?

'Would you like to go downstairs?'

Annie sat, dazed, not in this world of clattering footsteps
beyond the door. 'As you think best,' she whispered.

'Come along, then.' Peg took her hand.

The houseman said that when they had finished down below
they'd perhaps be kind enough to come back up here, say in half
an hour or so, and Mr Holmes should then have arrived. He courteously held open the door for them. Annie led the way, but turned
right not left.

'The other way,' Peg warned.

Annie paid no attention and moved on into the ward where
she stood looking down at her husband's bed. It was already
stripped of mattress, blankets, sheets and pillows. The nurses had
wasted no time. 'They've taken him away?' she queried, voice
subdued.

'Yes,' the doctor said. 'Before the rest are up and about. We
try not to upset them, or as little as possible. Harry was very
popular.'

Again the answer, Peg thought, was sensible, but delivered with
no consideration for Annie. They'd bundled Harry to the mortuary
as they'd wheeled out his bed linen to the laundry. One or two
patients now trotted about the ward with their washing kit and
towels. Annie looked at them without expression. Peg took her

157

companion's arm and led her out to the lift. All around the hospital began to hum. Men and women walked swiftly and talked. Machines clicked. Lifts flashed and sounded. All the people seemed to know exactly where they were going and why. Annie sniffled softly to herself but made no attempt to wipe her face.

'Do you want the loo?' Peg asked. They went in together. When they emerged, and Annie had made no attempt to make up her face, Peg settled her down slightly out of the way of the morning's growing rush. 'I'm going to have fruit juice and two slices of toast. What would you like? Would you fancy cereal?'

Annie shook her head. 'The same as you.' She appeared baffled by the question.

Peg moved towards the short queue; no one seemed in any hurry. She looked back towards her friend who slumped on her seat. It was impossible that a smart, sexy woman could appear so vulnerably alone. Orphan Annie. The phrase presented itself and Peg was ashamed of herself. She organised two trays, grapefruit juice, toast, butter, marmalade and milky coffee. She left her tray behind, with permission, and whisked Annie's across to her. By the time she returned with her own breakfast, Annie had begun to butter one slice. Neither ate with much appetite, but both managed to swallow something. Peg had, in fact, cleared her plate and cup, and again felt a touch of shame. She glanced at her watch. 'It's just past eight,' she said.

'Time goes slowly.' That surprised.

'There's no hurry. I suggest that I return our trays and then we'll go to smarten ourselves up for the consultant.'

This time Annie carried her own tray. They weren't sure where to leave them.

'I'll see to 'em for you, duck.'

A uniformed cleaner took possession. In the washroom this time Annie made some attempt to repair her face. She wasted her time, Peg thought, but they walked steadily up the last flight of steps to the ward. Here they announced themselves to a nurse who did not appear to understand them.

'Ah, Mrs Fisher.' A smart voice from a stiff-backed sister. 'Just come in with me and I'll ring to see if Mr Holmes has arrived.' She completed her enquiry and led them out and through the length of the ward. She said nothing, but Peg felt guided, guarded, cared for. Outside the ward in a wide foyer the nurse knocked on one of three doors. 'His secretary won't be here yet,' she said.

A male voice asked them in, and they passed through an outer office and a second door.

Peg eased Annie forward. The consultant rose from his desk, a tall middle-aged man in a dark suit. His gingery hair was smartly styled and his face suitably troubled as he raised his eyes to scrutinise the women. He rounded his desk, murmured 'Mrs Fisher' and shook her by the hand, and she, almost with sangfroid, introduced her companion. He shook hands again politely. His hands, Peg noticed, were warm, well manicured. He expressed his sorrow about Harry Fisher's death, said how much they had all admired him, praised his senior registrar for his efforts and then, in the same level, rather deep voice, asked if they had any questions. Annie enquired again if her husband's death was unexpected. He answered that, and afterwards one or two supplementary questions, before he raised the matter of a post-mortem.

Annie listened to the reasons he gave why this would be beneficial to his work, then said in a strong, level voice, 'Yes. I would like it myself. And I think he would.'

When Peg gave an account of this interview to her husband, she said how surprised she had been at Annie Fisher's demeanour during this interview.

'When we first got to the hospital she was very shaky, cried from time to time and made little crying noises. She hardly seemed to understand what anyone was saying to her. I don't know whether she's a bit deaf, or if what had happened had confused her. When we were eating our toast she was like a child, playing at it, crumbling it, couldn't find the plate. I watched her; it was amazing how she'd changed from a grown-up rather jolly woman, in charge of herself and others, and now there she was, snivelling like an infant. But do you know as soon as we got up to the ward her back stiffened; she walked past Harry's bed like a grenadier. She looked at it, but it didn't wreck her this time. And when we went in to see Holmes, the surgeon, she was steadier than I was. Her voice was as strong as usual; she answered him and questioned him.'

159

'Did she lose herself again?'

'Not really. Holmes handed us over to his secretary, who'd arrived by this time. She told us where to go and what to do. Then she sent us to see somebody else. There were papers to sign and so on. They were very clear, these women, and sympathetic. When we'd got it all taped, I went off to ring you to fetch us. We had another cup of coffee, but by this time she seemed tired out. She hardly said a word as you were driving us back. She's coming in for lunch at one. I told her to go and lie down, never mind letting people know. I said she was to put her feet up and if she could drop off she was to do so. She'd been up and about since soon after six. I don't know what she'll do. She didn't seem to want me to stay with her. It was as if she wanted to come to terms with what had happened. I don't know. It's all a bit beyond me.'

XII

For the next fortnight the Stones kept a close eye on their neighbour. At first they invited her in for meals and offered to accompany her on her trips to the registrar's, the undertaker's and to the vicarage. Annie proved exceptionally efficient; she'd been brought up in a 'business' family, she said, and had been used to this sort of work. She sent off printed cards, announcing the death of Harry and the date of the cremation, done at speed by a cousin, in large numbers, inserted short, sensible obituary notices three times in the local evening newspapers and once in the *Telegraph*. She organised a post-funeral buffet at her house with a caterer. These kept her both bright and active, though once Peg told her husband that she had found Anne – she had resumed her baptismal name during this time – in tears. 'I expect she's had a few quiet bouts of weeping when there's nobody about.'

'She was genuinely fond of him, do you think?' he asked.

'I'd guess so, or used to him about the place.'

On the few occasions Stone saw her on her own, she gladly hugged him, held the embrace, but when he put his hand on her breasts she shoved it brusquely away, saying nothing but dismissing him with a shake of the head. Propriety ruled. On the day before the funeral their son Laurence, a big, serious young man in rimless spectacles, arrived from New York where he ran an accountant's office. He was in his early thirties, was said to be doing extremely well financially and was accompanied by a striking American wife. He brought her round to see the Stones soon after his arrival. Karen, the wife, charmed them both, said she and her husband would be staying for at least a week because she would like to get to know the provincial environment where D. H. Lawrence had been brought up. She had visited England several times before, but had spent her time trudging round museums and cathedrals and castles, and the Lake District.

161

'Laurence won't mind staying over here?' Peg asked.

'No. He wants to look over his father's affairs with the solicitor.' She laughed. 'I've used the English term. With us a solicitor's someone who calls round at your door trying to sell you something.'

'He'll know all about investments and that sort of thing?'

'He surely will. If there's been any defaulting by anybody he'll root it out at once. He's made quite a reputation over in New York.'

Karen seemed proud of her husband, not afraid to praise him. Stone remembered Laurence as a schoolboy, good at rugby and cricket, articulate, grown up, seemingly, from the age of eleven. He seemed quite unlike his parents, but never looked down on his father when the old man appeared in his working overalls. He seemed serious beyond his age, did well at university, then qualified in accountancy and was invited over to the States by an American he met casually on holiday. He was supposed to stay for a trial year and return home, but he found himself in congenial surroundings where his qualities of quickness and conscientious application were appreciated and he remained in New York, rising steadily in the firm.

The funeral seemed oddly stilted or subdued to the Stones. The vicar was impressive, but distant in his towering Victorian church. The organist played Bach's E flat Prelude and the Saint Anne Fugue with massive authority before the solemn entry of the coffin. The church was almost full, for obviously Harry's firm and the Langleys were well known. But to Peg the hymns and prayers were as cold as the high roof, the Gothic windows, the grey walls and the pews. There was no choir and the singing was vague, unenthusiastic, though the organist accompanied this inconclusive and embarrassed humming with brilliant registration and surprising harmony changes. But for all the technical skills, virtuosity and fire, the organ seemed to neglect or even repulse the congregation's feeble efforts.

After the service John Stone met the organist, a small, neat young woman who taught at the university. When he commented on the lack of response in the singing she said sharply, 'People don't know hymns these days. I blame the schools.' In view of her disdain Stone felt he was at fault. 'Churches sing choruses

162

nowadays, but when Dick Hewitt-Jones asked me to play I said only if he let me choose the tunes and made sure there were no recordings of "I did it my way" blaring out.' Her choice was odd, in Stone's view: two Orlando Gibbons songs, number one, to words he had never heard before, slightly modern in an old fashioned Boy-Scoutish, public-school way which ended

> Brave living here: and then, beyond the grave
> More life and more adventure for the brave

and, better known, 'Forth in Thy name' to Song 34. She redeemed herself by playing the coffin and congregation out to a Purcell trumpet tune, more usually heard at weddings, her nod in the direction of popularity. Stone thoroughly approved of that, but was not surprised to learn from the vicar that he was about to lose this marvellous musician. She was to return next year to Oxford.

'You'll miss her,' Stone commiserated with him.

'She doesn't play every Sunday, only on special occasions and then only when it suits her.' She gave recitals all over the country, apparently, was making a tremendous name for herself, could play any man off the organ bench.

Laurence Fisher gave the address. He delivered it in a rather monotonous voice unlike his usual speech; he had obviously decided to adopt a tone suitable to the occasion and the surroundings. After listening to a string of platitudes Jack Stone began to realise that the young man admired his father, praised him but could not find the exact words to describe the old man's success. The boy saw that his father was as clever as he was and, inside the limits of his chosen trade, had done well, made enough money to leave his wife in considerable comfort. The last few years Harry had returned to the actual making and mending as opposed to the organising and planning that had occupied much of his career. He described how Harry had made him as a child a most beautiful rocking horse. 'To see my father with a hammer and chisel in his hands was to see something out of the ordinary,' Laurence proclaimed. 'These tasks are not mere artisan's routine, they demonstrated an art, perhaps not a high art but one above the abilities or ambitions of most people.' This was the climax of the speech. Laurence decided that if everybody had done as well as his father the world would be a better place. He muttered his conclusion without much conviction, then stared round the church, as if daring the mourners to contradict him and, when no one did, ostentatiously folded his notes, thrust them into his inside pocket and stepped cautiously down from his lectern, three steps, and resumed his seat.

The vicar read his final prayers and the congregation stood, knelt or crouched as the spirit moved them. Nobody seemed quite sure what to do next. The signal had been given, but the undertaker's mutes had not noticed or some accident held them from their duty. In time they appeared, rallied by Purcell, lined up round the trolley and were led forward, out towards the great south door. The family, properly instructed now, followed. The small group of relatives and close friends moved quickly into the limousines, making speed for the crematorium. The congregation broke up at the door into huddles or moved funerally homewards. Peg and her husband walked three streets away where they had parked their car for a strategic escape. They had promised Annie to be back in Laurel Avenue to act as hosts until the Fishers returned from the service, for close family only, at the crematorium.

The Stones did their best with handshakes, offering directions towards cloakrooms or lavatories, but the caterers were excellent and soon handed round welcome cups of hot tea. By the time Annie and Laurence, with the two or three relatives who had attended the final rites, returned from the crematorium, most of the guests were seated and eating heartily, or queuing to have their plates filled or replenished at the caterer's board. The talk was loud until it was realised that the widow had arrived; the sudden hiatus of silence in the hall and two rooms seemed a just reward for Annie, who was dressed in black and seemed a completely different woman from her everyday self. She and Laurence moved around the house with real dignity, even when they managed to carry, as they did, a plate of food. She thanked Stone and Peg with a kiss and a pat on the arm, saying all had gone well. Laurence, on the same mission, asked what they thought Harry would have made of the service.

'He would have appreciated what you said.' Stone smiled. 'Because it conveyed in a short space what he was like. I remember that rocking horse; it used to stand in your sitting room in a place of honour by the window after you'd outgrown it.'

'We have it in our apartment now in New York,' Karen said.

'He sent it over to us when we were married,' Laurence added. 'He'd painted it up so it looked as good as new.'

'He travelled over for your wedding, didn't he?' Peg asked.

'He did. And thoroughly enjoyed himself. I remember what he said to me. "I like weddings because everybody means well".'

'And when did the rocking horse arrive? Before or after?'

'Just after. It looked wonderful. I'm preparing myself for my part.'

'You mean you're pregnant.'

'Yes. But I'm not saying much to anybody else yet.'

'I bet Annie's pleased.'

'I don't think she'll be overjoyed to be a grandparent. But there.'

'Did Harry know?'

'No. We've only just discovered it ourselves.'

'Is your mother pleased?' John asked.

'My mother died three years ago. Just before I married Laurence.'

Stone began to enjoy the occasion. He and Peg had introduced themselves to new arrivals. 'We're the neighbours, delegated to make you feel at home.' At least two had said, 'Ah, the head-master,' suggesting that the Fishers had spoken about him to the relatives and friends. Peg's idea was that once Annie had arrived back from the crematorium they should quietly slip back home, but clearly she was relishing the company as much as her husband.

Stone moved around, reintroduced himself. The atmosphere was noisy, unlike the awkward quiet that leadenly sobered the church congregation. Here it was warmer, lighter; people laughed out loud; one or two spoke strongly, making themselves heard against the constant chatter. Almost all began with the same senti-ment: that Harry would really have appreciated being here.

'He would,' one man said. 'If Harry enjoyed anything it was chuntering to his friends, especially when there was a bite or two to eat. He always used the old expression "buried with 'am". That'd be from the days when you had ham once a month at most, and then only on Sundays. And he liked a drink with it. Yes, he'd be in his eye'oles here.'

165

'For all you know he is,' the man's wife argued. She looked towards the ceiling as if expecting to catch a glimpse of the deceased's spirit floating about their heads.

'He's not making his presence felt much, then, is he?'

They laughed, the three.

Elsewhere in a corner a middle-aged man was haranguing a group about his own father. He waved a battered photograph of his old man as a young sailor. 'He died six months ago, just after his eightieth birthday. He was one of those not properly recognised for what he did in the war. He was on the Murmansk run. They used to send convoys round the top of Norway, and that was occupied by the Germans, so they could bomb our boats, torpedo them at will. I remember him saying that they used to sail right north above Iceland, and join a convoy up there and then set off east.'

'What were they carrying?'

'Supplies. Arms. Tanks. Guns. Aircraft parts. Whole aeroplanes. Ammo. Food for the Russki troops.'

'How many ships were there in a convoy?'

'Varied a bit, I think. Between thirty and forty, usually.'

'Quite big?'

'Yes. It was no bloody use going all that way to just hand over a couple of rifle bullets and a hot-cross bun. They carried all sorts. One ship carrying petrol got bombed one night and it went up like a torch.'

'Wouldn't the weather be bad up there?'

'Bad? According to my dad it was bloody awful. There were great high waves that crashed over the boats, even the escorting cruisers and destroyers. And it was so cold. Freezing miserable all the time they were. He was only a lad, eighteen or nineteen, strong as a horse, could stand anything they could throw at him, he said, but it was no picnic. They were crammed down in the 'old like cattle, he reckoned. You talk about factory farming. It would have been bad even if the Huns weren't having a go at them all the time. Great squadrons of Fokkers bombing them.'

'Hadn't they got anti-aircraft guns on the boats?'

'Of course they had. They were banging away, but there were too many there, mainly keeping out of range. We shot some down. And you'd think it was better at night, but no. There'd be

166

submarines. They'd go right into the middle of the convoys and let their torpedoes loose. It was no holiday. And yet he used to say it was an experience he wouldn't have missed. Just recently some MPs have been trying to get them, or such as are left, a medal for this campaign, the Arctic Star or something like that, but the government or the Navy won't wear it.' The inappropriate metaphor passed without comment.

'How long did it take 'em to get there?'

'Don't know. Can't remember. He must have told me. Two or three weeks, perhaps. Then less than a couple of days and you were back in the boats and off home again.'

'Why won't they give 'em medals?'

'I don't know. Perhaps there aren't enough of 'em. Some committee decided who'd get what and for what just after the war. And the present government won't change their decisions. I've written twice to my MP. And he answered and said he knew what a dangerous and valuable job these sailors did, but they work now on the assumption that the original decisions were taken by people who knew, at first hand, the exact ins and outs of the campaigns they were assessing. Nice letters, they were, but nobody has done anything. I suppose it's getting on for sixty years since all this happened and they think most of the men who survived have died off.'

There were murmurs from the group who had gathered to listen to this. John Stone stood at the edge, in judgement. The speaker was obviously used to telling the tale and thoroughly appreciated the growing size of his audience. The listeners, with one exception, were all male. The female, a stout, middle-aged woman, concentrated with a face of stone. Perhaps she was the orator's wife. She wore an unsuitable black straw hat with three bobbing cherries.

'It's a shame,' some tall body intoned.

'It is. And even if they'd made a move now it wouldn't have given my dad much satisfaction up in the Northern Cemetery.'

The group slowly broke up, hesitantly, perhaps expecting more. As Stone turned his neighbour muttered to him, 'Amazing what some people had to put up with. Was Harry Fisher in the war?'

'I don't think so. He wouldn't be old enough. Might have done National Service.' Stone thought of his own two years. If people asked him about it now, he said it had been a waste of time, but he wasn't sure this was so. He continued his circuit of the room, smiling at people, making sure they knew their presence was acknowledged. Conversation sounded animated, but the subjects were trivial: preparations for Christmas, grandchildren, holidays, the price of things, the inefficiency of workmen. Two serious men, small with bristling moustaches, brushed crumbs from their lapels as they discussed football management. Two women, heads together, caught Stone's interest as he passed.

'No,' one of them said. 'His son committed suicide last year. He was only sixteen.'

'It broke his wife's heart,' the other answered.

Stone crossed the corridor where the caterer's table stretched and went into the other room, just as crowded, perhaps even noisier. Annie stood with Peg and a knot of women. All were laughing freely, without reserve. At first this seemed wrong to him, inappropriate. Annie looked especially elegant now she had removed her hat and coat. The vicar on the perimeter of the women's group beamed as broadly as the rest.

Stone made towards Harry Fisher's man who had taken up a position on his own by the window. He wore his best suit, now slightly tight on him, and a faded black tie. 'Good morning, Mr Wood.'

The man looked pleased that Stone had recognised him or remembered his name. 'Good morning, sir.'

'A sad occasion,' Stone said.

'Not by the way some of these are going on.' Jim Wood's tone was surly.

'Isn't that the usual way with funerals? Long faces in the church and then pleasant talk, jollity, afterwards?'

'I don't feel cheerful.'

'You've lost a good friend.'

'Harry Fisher? He was a decent boss. He wanted his pound of flesh out of his employees, but if you did your work properly he treated you well. I didn't want to retire when I was sixty-five, I'd nothing else to do. But the firm, Langley, Bell and Fisher wanted to make changes and didn't see why they should keep me on rather than some younger man. But Harry, with these small jobs he did privately, employed me. He knew a skilful workman when he saw one. He was a craftsman himself. But I knew that as soon as I grew too old or stiff for the job I'd be out. So we got on pretty well.'

'What'll you do now?'

'Well, I'm seventy. I've promised Mrs Fisher I'll finish off such of his outstanding jobs as possible. But it's a purely business transaction.'

'She'd be grateful for your offer, wasn't she?'

'She didn't seem to know what I was talking about.'

'That may have been shock or grief. We none of us expected him to go off like that.'

Wood shrugged his shoulders. When Stone invited him to fill his plate up again he shrugged even more violently. 'I've had plenty, thank you. When we were out working, Harry and I didn't eat much in the middle of the day. Bit of a sandwich, something of the kind. As long as there was plenty of hot tea to drink we were all right.' He made a dismissive gesture towards the rest of the people. 'The way some of these eat you'd think they'd been starving for a week.'

'Perhaps they have,' Stone said.

Jim did not smile at the pleasantry, seemed to withdraw into himself. Stone wished him good afternoon and was answered with a curt nod.

A small woman accosted him. 'Mr Stone,' she began. 'I didn't know you were a friend of the Fishers.'

'I live next door.'

She coughed. 'My son was at your school many years ago.'

'What was his name?' he asked. She had not offered the information.

'Derek Tomlinson.'

'Yes. I remember him. He was captain of the school. A mathematician. He went to Oxford. Did well there.'

'That's right.'

'What's he doing now?'

'He's just been appointed professor in Reading.'

'Very good. Give him my congratulations when you're next in touch.'

'I will.' She fiddled in her handbag and pulled out a purse. She opened this and carefully extracted a small folded rectangle of newspaper. This she straightened and handed to him: 'From their local newspaper.' It showed a photograph of a man barely human in doctoral robes. The caption read: 'Dr D. J. Tomlinson has recently been appointed Professor of Applied Mathematics at the university. Dr Tomlinson who was Reader in Mathematics at Sheffield University is married with three children.'

'A family man,' Stone said. 'Very good.'

'He married a girl who was a student at Oxford when he was.'

'A mathematician?'

'No. She did languages. Russian, I think. A very nice girl from Farnham.'

'He's done well for himself on all counts. Congratulate him for me.' One could not overpraise.

She very gently slapped his forearm, stroked it, thanked him and slipped away. He suddenly felt pleased with life. Out in the corridor a few people were still collecting food. One ribbed Laurence Fisher: 'Don't starve yourself.'

'I'm thinking of my sylphlike figure.'

'I'm thinking of mine, but that's as far as I get.'

Stone edged his way round trying to contact Peg to suggest they went home, but she seemed always engaged, caught up in animated conversation with people not known to him. He concentrated again on listening. Two well-dressed women were expatiating on the difficulties of buying slacks suitable for holidays: 'If they fit round the waist then they're not long enough.'

'I asked them in Marks about standard sizes, but the girl seemed vague. All she knew about was the price on the ticket.'

'They're doing badly, aren't they?'

The next pair spoke about supermarkets. No one, he noticed, talked about cultural matters. No book, play, opera, concert rated a mention. He did not expect the women to discuss football. That was the Saturday afternoon when they got rid of their husbands and then had to comfort them if their team had lost. They made no mention of schools, although some were young enough to have children of that age. Money, the spending of money, seemed central. How to rid yourself of your surplus wealth on cruises, exotic foreign holidays, seemed to obsess them. They told with admiration the spending sprees of people they knew who had converted factories in the Lace Market into luxury apartments,

170

or how one man had bought an aeroplane and in learning how
to fly it had killed himself. There was no sense of hubris in their
telling: the accident was a pity, but the man had died in the right
place. If he'd been killed by a bus, that could happen to any fool,
but this man died spending big money, buying and flying, or
failing to fly, a private aeroplane.

Annie Fisher was seen to be pointing at him, pushed him into
the corner by the stained-glass door. She held his arm, caressing
it. 'Jack, I want to ask you a favour.' He indicated his willingness
to accede to her wish. 'Laurence should have done this, but at the
last minute he won't. He says he spoke his piece at the church
and that's enough. "Ask Jack Stone," he advised. "He won't take
too long over it, and won't bore us all, and he'll put a bit of Latin
in it." What I'm saying is this. Harry always joked that at his
funeral we should be given a big glass of champagne, and drink
his health in this world and the next. What I'm asking you to do
is to propose that toast. It'll happen in a few minutes because the
caterers are ready with the bottles and glasses, and we'll hand
them out. It shouldn't take more than ten minutes or a quarter of
an hour to do that. Will you propose the toast? It needn't be long.
Two or three minutes at the outside. It's just to remind them really
what we're here for. Will you do it for me?' She clutched his arm
all the tighter. He immediately agreed. Headmasters were used to
speaking off the cuff. 'We've put a little box at that end of the
hall and you can make your speech from there.' She kissed his
cheek. 'You're a treasure,' she gasped as she hurried away.

Within a few minutes the chief caterer had banged hard with
a gavel, had removed his tables with one exception on which the
champagne glasses were crowded. 'When you've all got a glass
there will be a toast to the late Mr Fisher.' This final preparation
took rather longer than expected and Stone noticed that most of
the men tested the quality of the champagne with a surreptitious
sip. The hall was now crowded, as were the doorways off the
hall and the stairs. A fair amount of excited noise kept the crushed
onlookers lively.

'Good job it's a big house,' the man next to Stone commented.
Stone, immersed in his speech, nodded.

The caterer banged on his table with the gavel. The sound was
extraordinarily loud, like the crack of a rifle. 'Have you all got

full glasses?' He looked around, made sure all was well, then announced that Mr John Stone would propose a toast. Stone stepped up on to his little rostrum; it did not shake. He was breathless, but in no hurry to start. He stared into faces he did not know, which seemed on account of the occasion unsmiling, even hostile. Annie stood four yards away by a wall. He could not see her son and daughter-in-law. Suddenly he noticed Peg, whose brow was puckered, at the front door. She must have been standing on a stool for she seemed six inches above the men round her. She concentrated hard on him and it cheered him. He filled his lungs.

'My dear, dear Annie, Laurence and Karen, ladies and gentlemen, or better, my dear friends.' His mind swooped with a dive into the past. As a child of five he had recited at the Sunday School anniversary what they called 'the collection piece' an appeal for the congregation to give generously when the basket came round. He had not trembled then, even though his audience had been much larger than today's, but had spoken loudly and slowly, as he had been carefully drilled, opening with the words 'My dear friends'. Such an address was unusual in those days from a small boy to his elders, but he had carried it off with aplomb, so that some notable had said to his father, 'Your boy, he was the star of the day.' This memory appeared in a flash and was gone, leaving its trace of confidence.

'I am here today' – the opening of his childish oration – 'with an unusual task, one which I did not expect: to propose a toast to an absent friend. I am doing it because Annie asked me to. She came to me because Harry Fisher had suggested that he'd like his friends to see him off with a glass of decent champagne. He'd not mentioned a toast, but Annie made it clear to me that the toast would remind us what we were here for. I'm not going to give you a list of Harry's virtues. Laurence did that well enough in St Andrew's. I was moved when he described his father as a superior craftsman, a view reinforced a few minutes ago by Jim Wood who worked at his elbow over many years. I remember the rocking horse when it was brand-new, now it's in America. It shone. It shines, I expect, today. It was extraordinary; it was perfect. Harry would have pooh-poohed our praise. Any competent joiner could have made that if he'd taken sufficient time and care. That was

172

not true. He'd made it, as he joked then, out of his own head. Oh, he planned it. Meticulously. And then carried out the plan to perfection. But I don't think that's what he regarded as the highest consideration. Whenever he did a job for you he was there to time, made less mess than most builders in your house and garden, did you a first-class job and never overcharged. That was the secret of his business success over many years. That was the Harry Fisher I knew. And I can pay him no higher compliment.'

Stone paused, eyes downcast. Someone began to clap. Others joined, hesitatingly at first. Stone allowed the applause to continue before he raised his hand.

'We know now what we're here for and I have nearly finished. When the evenings were light still, my wife and I would take a turn round the garden. And more often than not in the last few years we'd hear from Harry's workshop the sound of hammering or sawing. We knew exactly what was going on. He was preparing his materials for tomorrow's jobs, be they at home or out elsewhere.' He stopped with eyes shut tight. 'Harry Fisher was taken suddenly from us. Annie did not expect it, nor his family, nor did you. But I guess he was, as always, prepared. Death did not catch him out. He was ready for any contingency. Whenever in the future I hear the sound of confident hammering or the squeal of a modern drill, I shall think of Harry Fisher, that craftsman, that careful man, ready for any emergency, an example to us all. He lived his life properly.'

He looked down. There was no glass for him. He signalled to the chief caterer, who appeared baffled. 'A glass,' he said. The caterer handed him his own, but it took time. Nobody spoke during the hiatus. If they thought him unprepared, they made nothing of it. He raised his wine high, at full arm's length.

'I give you . . . Harry Fisher.'

His voice was, he thought, over-loud, but the listeners reacted to perfection. They almost shouted as they raised their glasses. 'Harry Fisher.' The sound was barbaric in the confined spaces of the house. Stone sipped, said 'thank you', lost in the commotion. Before he stepped down he noticed a middle-aged woman near the front, unknown to him, whose cheeks glittered with tears. She made no attempt to hide them or wipe them clean. He wondered who she was. One of Harry's mistresses, perhaps.

173

Annie came towards him, threw her arms round his neck, kissed him. 'Thank you,' she said. 'Thank you.'

'Annie.'

'I wish he could have heard you. He would have been proud.'

'He was as I described him. I didn't need to exaggerate. He was a good man.'

Laurence and Karen came up. The young woman kissed him with enthusiasm. Laurence shook his hand. Stone thanked them. He'd done his best and hoped it fitted people's expectations. A bald-headed man punched his biceps, said the speech was just right and not too long. A tall lady said it had sparkled like the champagne. '"Bring me a bottle of Bach",' he answered, at which she beamed, missing the allusion. As he worked his way to where he thought he'd find Peg, he was congratulated on all sides, was praised beyond his deserts, he felt. Champagne helped his admirers. When he finally reached the door, Peg had gone. He found the stool on which she had stood but she was away. He mounted it himself and glimpsed his wife at the other end of the corridor, talking to the chief caterer. They must have passed each other in the corridor. That was next to impossible, he decided. It must be his fault; it had happened. Peg would have had no difficulty in spotting him; the speech, the praise, the champagne must have unsettled him. He struggled back, again much thanked by strangers. Peg and Annie were now making trivial conversation over the heads of others. He forced his way through, excusing himself, reached his wife who looked him over as if to see he had done up his buttons properly and not spilt his drink.

'Another glass, sir?' the chief caterer interrupted them.

'No, thank you.'

'A very fine speech, if I may say so, sir.' The man looked towards Peg for confirmation.

'Yes, very good,' she said. 'You got it just about right.' She left that comment until the catering manager was engaged elsewhere. 'I didn't know you were going to speak. You didn't mention it.'

'Annie asked me.'

'I guessed that. I didn't think you'd stand up and start speechifying on your own account. Though you never know.'

When half an hour later he and Peg went home, he was still concerned with what he had said. He felt a slight elation, but put that down to the champagne. He knew from experience that in speeches of that sort one must always exaggerate the virtues of the person to be praised, but without appearing to do so. Certainly Harry Fisher had always appeared chipper, gave good advice about building problems when asked for his opinion, had done several repair jobs in the Stones' house very efficiently at reasonable prices. The rocking horse was worth a mention. That had truly impressed him. It was huge, far too big for the young Laurence so that the child had to climb up to his seat, but the finish, the paintwork was eye-catching: the dappled grey of the horse, the red reins and seat with its golden studs, the white flowing mane and tail. It had dwarfed young Laurence; once, Stone recalled, the boy had thrust his whole leg through one of the stirrups, terrifying himself.

Not long ago Annie had mounted the seat and gripped the reins, and seemed to have comfortable room. Again, quite recently, Annie had stood stark naked by the charger. Stone shuddered. He had praised Fisher, but had cuckolded the man. Annie had tempted him into that in the first place by outrageous behaviour. And there she had stood, an hour ago, the modest widow, in black, her face expressing thanks to them for coming to her aid in the hour of need. With how many of the men present had she betrayed her husband? How many of the women had Fisher pleasured? These were disposable thoughts, unfit for the occasion. Fisher had paid for his sins by dying; that would do. But certain people there would add these footnotes to Stone's banal solemnities. He shook his head, leaned on the nearest door frame, staring out into the darkening afternoon already pinpricked with lights.

'You all right?' Peg asked, passing.

'Yes. I think so. I don't like death.'

'Good God,' she said, shocked. 'Annie was pleased with your speech.'

'Good. I'm glad.'

'She looked the part, didn't she?'

'What part?'

'The grieving widow. Do you think she didn't?'

'No. She was suitably staid, both in behaviour and clothes.'

'If you only knew how much that trouser suit set her back, you wouldn't be using words like "suitable".'

He did not answer. Annie's clothes had seemed nothing out of the ordinary. Very well cut, but not, he'd have thought, exclusive.

'I've invited them in, Annie and Laurence and his wife. They'll come in for dinner about six thirty. It'll give them half a chance to straighten up and to get rid of lingering guests. Some of them would stay until midnight, as long as there was drink around.'

'They might think she needed company.'

'Pigs might fly.' Peg pulled a sour face. 'I was a bit puzzled about one thing you said about Harry.' She waited for an answer which did not come.

He wondered what he'd said that did not seem right to Peg. 'What was that?'

'You said he always prepared himself for everything. No, well, I suppose that was fairly true, but you said he was ready and waiting for death.'

'It came quickly. We none of us expected it.'

'I don't think he'd given death a second thought. Why should he?'

'He was seventy,' Stone mumbled.

'That's no sort of age these days. If you'd have said he was stoical about it, that he'd put up with it, made the best he could of it, that would have been nearer the truth.'

'That's what I meant by "prepared".'

She gave him what his father would have described as 'an old-fashioned look' and moved off, humming, to her kitchen. Then he knew he hadn't done too badly. He was no Bach or Haydn who could knock off a work of genius for any trivial occasion, but he'd not made a fool of himself.

He laid the dining-room table, fitting new candles into their holders. Annie and her son and daughter-in-law, on time, had changed from their mourning clothes and had dressed modestly, casually. They had, they claimed, straightened the house (the catering people had been very good) and now seemed relaxed. They mentioned Harry over their sherry; Stone apologised to Karen that he had no knowledge of cocktails, but she raised her

176

glass of dry sherry to him. 'It's what we come to England for,' she said.

They expressed their pleasure at the gentle formality of the meal. Annie said that, left to themselves, they would have phoned for pizzas, but this was perfection.

'Did your father like formal meals?' Karen asked Laurence.

His mother answered for him. 'He liked his food and didn't mind how it came. If the Builders or the Rotarians had a dinner, he didn't mind fetching out his evening clothes. And he always insisted that I bought a new outfit for the occasion.'

'He was proud of you,' Stone said.

'Have you brought that photograph round?' Laurence asked. 'Show it to Peg.'

Annie bent to her handbag and fetched out a photograph, unframed but in a silver-edged folder. Peg looked closely and approvingly at it, before she passed it to her husband. It showed Annie and Harry on their wedding day at the church door. The bride and groom were of the same height. She wore a full wedding gown, veil now thrown back from her face, and she carried a large bouquet of white and red roses. She stood proudly, as if demonstrating her happiness, and she looked extraordinarily pretty, pert, young and yet already in command. Harry boasted a new lounge suit with a striped tie and an over-large button-hole. To Stone's surprise the young man was handsome, without the weathering and wrinkles that obtrusively marked his later years. His hair, greased down with a dead straight parting, seemed to shine. His brow was slightly puckered, but his mouth smiled, like a child's about to take a first lick of an ice-cream cornet.

'What a good-looking pair.' He spoke his judgement with satisfaction.

'Time doesn't do much for appearance,' Annie said.

'I don't know,' Peg said. 'You both look so young and innocent. Your faces are so clear and clean, as though you've yet to show real character.'

'He was thirty-two,' Annie said.

'And you?' Stone asked.

'Twenty-two. And a virgin.'

'In the swinging sixties?' Laurence raised his eyebrows.

177

'Don't you believe all you read,' his mother warned.

Karen had been scrutinising the photograph, which she held carefully between the palms and stretched fingers of both hands. 'It's beautiful,' she said, breathless, her American voice adding sincerity. 'You're both so handsome. Much, much better than Laurie and I on our wedding day. We look frightened to death, but you both seem so confident in what you've accomplished. We look like schoolchildren caught out in naughtiness, expecting a call-out to father's den for a reprimand or a spanking.'

'Did he spank you?' Laurence asked.

'No, not really. He made out he had to please Mamma.'

'Father's favourite?' Stone asked.

'I'm afraid so.'

Karen went out of her way to make a fuss of Stone and he enjoyed every minute of it. All the Fisher family admired 'The Headmaster' as they called him, or so Laurence confessed to Peg, and Karen had caught the disease.

'Aren't Americans much more polite to their elders than we arc?' she asked.

'I haven't noticed it.'

They drank wine with their meal, though not to excess. After a long, animated conversation over coffee, in which Laurence defended his view that there was no life after death against his wife's fervent faith, the visitors left for home at about nine thirty.

'It's been a long day,' Annie said. 'I shall be thinking about it all night.'

'Grieving for Harry?' Peg asked.

'No. Though I've done plenty of that. I accepted his death at once when I saw him in that hospital bed. I tried to look it straight in the face. But it keeps coming back and swamps me from time to time when I'm not expecting it. So I'm not sure. But I think I'll be going over in my mind all the people I've seen today. Some of them I haven't met for years.'

'And had they improved?'

'Not in looks, but otherwise they were on their best behaviour, concerned to say the right thing. And that's what I'd do in a similar situation, so I can't blame them.'

'You're a brave woman, Annie.'

'You always knew the right thing to say.'

178

The two kissed.

The Stones waited outside their front door until the Fishers, negotiating the two parallel front-garden paths, reached their own front door. Both families spoke their final farewells, calling out in the sharp air. The front doors closed together.

'Do you think Annie was fond of Harry?' Peg immediately asked her husband. She often baffled him with an unexpected question.

'I'd guess so. They'd been married thirty-odd years. Harry was by reputation a bit of a philanderer, but I don't suppose she'd mind. Otherwise he made a good living, let her have her own way, with holidays, for example, and decorating the house or planning the garden. She found plenty to do. I don't think he was a very demanding man. As long as he'd plenty of work to occupy him and his women to fill his leisure, in the bits Annie left him, he was ideal, did as he was told.'

'Presumably she wasn't jealous?' Peg asked.

'Or learnt to put up with it. Nobody likes his partner, or hers in this case, carrying on elsewhere.' He felt his cheeks flush.

Peg did not seem to notice. 'What will she do now?' she asked.

'That I don't know. I think women are better at coping with changes of this sort than men.'

'Some.'

'If anything happened to you I'd be lost,' Stone said.

'You'd manage. One way or another. You'd find a second wife. Or that would be my suggestion.'

That seemed to halt the exchange. She left the room, busying herself for a few minutes tidying the kitchen, perhaps to give him time to digest her advice. She returned, herself now spick and span, to the large sitting room where her husband occupied a comfortable armchair and, unusually, held no book in his hand. He seemed to be staring at the drawn curtains.

'Would you say that was a satisfactory day?' she asked brightly.

'For whom?'

'You. Who else?'

'Yes, it all went well. The only snag was the absence of Harry Fisher.'

'You weren't as fond as all that of Harry,' she objected.

'He wasn't my sort, exactly. No. But he was a man who was

179

still doing useful things in the world. Doing them properly. I think if I'd been deciding the matter I'd have given him another five years.'

'Sometimes,' Peg said, sounding almost aggrieved, 'you surprise me.'

Stone left her with the last word.

XIII

At the end of the week Peg's sister May telephoned the Stones from Scotland. Peg took the call and came back, after a long conversation, obviously bursting to confide. She waited, however, for a question from her husband before she began.

'Who was that?' he asked.

'My beloved sister.'

'It's some time since she rang last, isn't it?'

'Three or four weeks. At one time she phoned us every weekend.'

'Is it the men, the suitors, who are occupying her?'

'The lack of them would be a more accurate description.'

Stone closed his book, marking his place, laid it on his knee and gave his wife his full attention. 'She had two last time I heard, a lawyer and a parson,' he said.

'And now she has nobody.'

'Is she upset about it?'

'It's hard to know with madam. They haven't deserted her; she's given them both their marching orders.'

'Why was that?'

'They began to be a nuisance. The parson was a bit younger than she was and so had a few more years' duty to complete. That meant she would have had to join him in his active life, a minister's consort, at the beck and call of all his congregation. "Two for the price of one," she said.'

'Was he a widower?'

'I believe so. And young for his years. But it was the other one, the lawyer, Ronald Murray, whom she kicked out first.'

'And what was the cause of his fall from favour?'

'I'm only guessing. May's account of her life is full of holes, sometimes she'll labour some trivial point until you could scream and at the next minute she'll glide over some important matter. In this case she was beginning to be interested in the Reverend

181

Dr Duncan McPhee, seriously interested, and she didn't want Murray queering her pitch there. So she thanked him for all his kindnesses, his attention, but told him straight out that nothing further could come of their friendship. She hoped they could remain friends and that he would visit her, because she would always be grateful to him, but . . .' Peg thumped the word.

'Oh. And how did he take it?'

'Well, she said. Or he didn't make a fuss. But she put that down to his interest in someone else. He'd met on one of his recent visits to Edinburgh a girl who'd been his secretary there years ago. And her husband had conveniently died. He apparently invited her up to his home and all became true love.' Peg's irony was open. 'Or so it is said. People up there were apparently a bit loath to speak to May about it. They'd already got her written off as the second Mrs Murray.'

'How old was this girl?'

'I asked that. And again May was hoity-toity. How should she know? She didn't poke her nose into everybody's business. In the end, she thought the woman was in her fifties. Her two boys were grown up and on with their careers. She was back working as a secretary at some college of education.'

'And is Ronald happy about it all?'

'She didn't say.' Peg sounded amused.

'And that left the field open to the Reverend Duncan McPhee?'

'It did. But by this time she had begun to realise what she'd let herself in for as a minister's new wifie. McPhee had gone back to his parish, if that's what they call them up there. He'd been recuperating from pneumonia by the loch-side with a relative. So what with one thing and another she began to think she was much better off as she was.'

'What did she do? Write to him and tell him so?'

'No. He took a couple of days off from his duties and called in on her. Why, I didn't find out. Only gave her an hour's notice. Called her on his mobile on his way.'

'And that didn't suit?'

'It did not. She likes plenty of warning so that she can appear at her best.'

'Is her house likely to be in a mess, then?'

'You know damn well it isn't. Anyhow, he duly arrives in his best bib and tucker. He tells her that he's not going to beat about the bush, drops down on one knee and proposes to her.'

'Did it surprise her?'

'No, or so she says. He'd written several letters to her in a pretty torrid style. Anyway, she hears him out and says "No".'

'Just like that?'

'Not May. From what I can gather she put on her most queenly manner and thanked him for the honour he had done her by his proposal. She felt, she said, that they had interests in common, but others which separated them too widely for any hope of success in the alliance he was proposing. He was an excellent minister; everyone said so. He was likely to hold in his final years, or so she had heard, some high position in the hierarchy of his church, an office that he would carry out with great skill and dignity. Now her own attitude to religion was, if not quite Laodicean, luke-warm, at least it lacked the enthusiasm that would be necessary in the wife of a minister. Therefore she must decline his offer. They would not make a suitable pair, given the nature of his calling.'

'What did he say?'

'Apparently he stayed down on his knees and made a declaration of his love for her. He was quite passionate, with a red face and tears in his eyes, and very eloquent. If she turned him down he did not know how he would manage the rest of his life. She herself was so gifted, but too modest to realise how well she would appear as his wife, his helpmeet. She would find herself tested in some ways, but she would surmount the obstacles and become a different, greater, more noble woman for the sacrifices of her own personality, her own inclinations. She would blossom beyond any expectation of her own.'

'That would please her,' Stone ventured.

'I don't know. She'd be flattered that she'd made such an impression on the man. Or on two men within so short a time.'

'And so?'

'She told him to get up from his knees. She said, according to her, "Dr McPhee, please stand up. It embarrasses me to see you down there." He scrambled up, not very elegantly, puffing and blowing. When he'd recovered he tried to argue his case again, but she wasn't having any of it. She told him that she would make them cups of coffee, which she hoped they could drink together like the good friends they were.'

'Which they did?'

'Exactly.' Peg pulled a wry face. 'He tried, apparently, to broach the matter again. This time it was more in the style of a seminar. He does some teaching at the university. Theology and philosophy. She heard him out with barely a word. She ate two chocolate biscuits. And I bet she made that worse than a direct snub, especially as he'd refused them. She made him a second cup of coffee and then turned him out.'

'He went quietly?'

'Talking fast all the way to the door. She said nothing until she had him outside, then she told him, "Thank you for your proposal. I am honoured by it, but you must understand that it cannot be." He started to argue but she shut the door quietly in his face. Then – very typical of her, the sly hussy – she nipped upstairs and watched him through the lace curtains. She was frightened, she said. She thought he might do something rash. He stood on her path for quite a time. She thought he might come back and hammer at the door, or throw a brick through the window to get her outside. In the end he walked off, carefully closing the gate, but then stalked up and down in the street for a time, just five or six yards one way and then back before he got into his car. It was as if, she said, he was thrashing it out all over again in his mind. After a time he stopped this perambulation, crept into his car and drove off, but not in the direction of his cousin's. She didn't go out at all that day, or the next, in case he was still hanging about the town, and she kept the door locked and bolted. If anyone called she checked first before she opened up.'

'He must have made an impression on her.'

'I'm sure he did. He delivered it with such passion, as if he hadn't quite got control over himself. Not at all like Ronald Murray who was dry as dust all the time.'

'When did all this take place?'

'A week last Wednesday.'

'And has she not heard anything from him since?'

'No.'

Stone sat quietly, turning the news over in his mind. 'Does she not regret any of this?' he asked.

'She said not. Both, as far as she could tell, were decent men. Both would in their fashion have made good husbands, but their fashion would not have suited her, so that she ran the risk of being unhappy.'

'Was she unhappy with Ian?'

'Why do you ask that?'

'Well, looking at it now,' he said slowly, 'I wonder if either of these two wouldn't have made a more suitable husband than Ian.'

'You mean they would or they wouldn't?'

'They would.'

'Go on, then,' she said. 'Let's hear why.'

He paused before he spoke again, noting the scepticism in her voice. 'Both are educated men.'

'You think Ian wasn't? He had a degree in engineering. When he was younger he was extremely lively, with his anecdotes and tall stories, bad jokes. We met him first on a holiday up there. My mother and father were both fond of Scotland. He seemed old to me, my father's age. He wasn't, but he was more than twenty years older than I was. He had a wife when we first knew him, a Scottish lady, daughter of the manse, and she often sat with us, pale and quiet. She died in her forties and he'd be much the same age. By the time he came to propose to May he was fifty, and fifty-one when they were married and fifty-three when John James was born. My parents were worried by the big difference in the ages, nineteen years, between the two. There were great arguments at home about it, but May was over thirty and so had her own way in the end. She was doing very well at her career as a teacher, but she gave it up willingly and went off to Scotland. She must have known what she wanted. It wasn't as if she was stranded, on the shelf. She'd had plenty of young men; she was a very good-looking girl: statuesque, quick-witted. You knew that, if you bothered to, because we'd been married seven years when they named their day. Our Thomas was born just after, so I was enormous with him at the wedding. You'll remember Ian, the life and soul of the party.'

'They lost children, didn't they?'

'Two girls. One stillborn, one at three months. If you remember, I took Tom up there once to play with little John James while I looked after May. I guess that's when he started his extramural goings on. I'm not sure about that. I noticed nothing untoward while I was staying with them. Just talk, perhaps.'

'Local women, were they?'

'I've no idea. In fact, I don't know how bad it was at all. My impression was that he was nowhere near as wild as Harry Fisher. From what Annie said you couldn't leave Harry alone in a room with a woman without his trying it on. Perhaps she was exaggerating. I don't know. May was the other way inclined; she'd say nothing, wouldn't even question him. And if she found anything out she'd not go telling the wide world. Stiff upper lip; Scottish starch.'

'Didn't it upset her?'

'I never decided. She'd be quite composed in public, even when she realised that people were talking about her husband. But how she really felt about it I couldn't guess. Ian, for all his faults, saw to it that she went short of nothing. He amassed a fair amount of money. He had some patents on the go as well as his engineering firms. He was clever in his way.'

'Did May apreciate it?'

'I'm sure she did. She spoke of it to me often enough. But there was something wrong with their home life. Ian didn't show, or so it seemed to me, any sort of real interest in the domestic scene. If May wanted something and she asked for it, furniture, new clothes, holidays, he'd listen and just say straight off, "Fine. You please yourself."'

'A good many women would like that.'

'Women like to share. He showed no pleasure. Or not spontaneously. If she had chosen the exact opposite he would have agreed. One meal was as good as another to him. That's perhaps not surprising because May was really good in the kitchen and she enjoyed experimenting. If she'd served up stale cheese sandwiches he might have complained, but on the other hand he might not. She looked after the house, the garden, trips abroad. That was her duty and she did it well.'

'What about John James? Had Ian any time for him?'

'Oh, yes. He loved the boy, was ambitious for him when they found out from his infant school teachers that he was clever. He went to parents' evenings and fell in behind May to sit through the school play or the prize distributions. There were no complaints there.'

186

'And do you think this made her as she is?'

'That I don't know. Ian's been dead ten years now. So she's had time to get over any disappointment she may have felt. Ian died just before John James went to university and she's had all that time to herself. My guess is that living comfortably on her own suits her and though she likes men to notice her or make a fuss of her, and these two aren't the first, she doesn't want to give up her independence. She's a somebody where she lives and is a bit unsure of what might happen if she risked marriage again.'

'Is that sensible?'

'That's a daft question. There are drawbacks and advantages to anything you try. She's made her mind up.'

'And broken the hearts of two of Scotland's finest minds?'

'You can laugh,' Peg said. 'What would you do if I died?'

'I'd be lost. I wouldn't know where to turn.'

'Twaddle. You'd manage perfectly well. You'd have to think about a hundred and one things that I take care of nowadays, but that wouldn't trouble you. You'd get by. No, what I meant was would you marry again?'

'Who'd have me?' he asked.

'Dozens of women. Annie-next-door, poor soul. Or some of those clever misses you had on your staff. They'd be thirty now and pretty still, but mature. They'd make you take them out to concerts and plays and on Caribbean cruises or diving holidays on the Great Coral Reef.'

'Is that what you want?'

'No, my love, it is not. I'm an old woman.'

'All of fifty-nine,' he answered drily.

'What I'd fear is that left on your own, you'd stay at home all the time, make a hermit of yourself. Potter about in the garden, or read your books. Never go anywhere interesting. But I can assure you I'm not thinking of dying yet. I'm hoping to have a few more long years to pester you out of your inaction.'

'Oh, dear,' he said comically.

'You'd do worse, if I died, than to marry our May. I don't think she'd make any bones about taking you.'

'That's got me sorted out, then.'

She kissed him and moved swiftly out of the room to one of

those countless chores that she held in reserve for such moments. She closed the door after an ironical wave.

Stone sat in his chair. He enjoyed Peg's chaffing; she was a smart woman. He looked at, then picked up, a silver-framed photograph of the pair of them on holiday, he without a tie, she with an extraordinary coiffure, achieved by a new hairdresser never employed by her again. They both smiled, upright against the darkness of trees behind them. Thomas, their son, must have taken it. They looked young, he thought; everything went in their favour. Now they were on the decline. He dismissed his melancholy.

'Is May coming down to see us?' he asked when Peg next appeared.

'She hasn't said so. She doesn't much like travelling in winter.'

'I'd ask her if I were you. All this must have taken it out of her.'

'I guess she enjoyed it, but I'll do as you say.'

She marched on to the next task.

XIV

Peg did not have long to wait to make contact with her sister, for the next morning May rang. Again the exchange lasted nearly half an hour. When Stone returned from the errands on which she had dispatched him, she checked his purchases and announced cheerfully that May had rung and thoroughly interrupted her own morning's work.

'What had she to say for herself?' he demanded.

'Wait for your coffee and you'll hear it all.'

When they settled ten minutes later, both waited for the other to make a start on the real topic. As usual it was Stone who yielded. 'Come on, then,' he said. 'Let's hear all about May and her troubles.'

'It's not her. It's John James. Linda's left him.'

'When?'

'Last weekend. She announced it two days before and then decamped Saturday morning.'

'What about sleeping arrangements? On the two days?'

'They weren't mentioned. I believe they have two bedrooms. Whether she moved into the other I've no idea. For all I know they slept together as usual until she went. He knew when she was going. They might well have had sex together. Young people have such outrageous views these days. To some of them sexual intercourse is just about the equivalent of eating a Mars bar or drinking a Coke. It helps pass the time pleasantly.'

'Oh. Who moved her stuff?'

'She hired somebody with a van. She'd hardly any furniture proper. With the exception of one or two pieces she left her belongings back in her own flat, which she let furnished. So it wasn't a long job.'

'Was JJ there while all this was happening?'

'He was.'

'And there weren't any words? Or blows?'

'No. Fairly civilised. So May claims. It wasn't a long job. Linda had made lists and got everything together. The man and his son, a schoolboy, arrived about noon and it was all over within half an hour. They drove off to her new place. It's about the same distance from the bank but in the opposite direction.'

'Won't they meet at work?'

'Not necessarily. Or so May guesses. But she doesn't think chance meetings will bother Linda much at all.'

'Then why's she leaving him?'

'That's different. Their constant clashes and spats have made her life too uncomfortable. They quarrelled too often, she says. She put this to Jay, but he wouldn't learn sense.'

'Something of his mother about him?'

'Or his father. No, I imagine she's had enough of the life. The hours she works she needs a housekeeper and a couple of maids so she's nothing to do when she comes home but just have a bath, eat her meal and flop out on the sofa. May said she could easily afford that, but she couldn't put them up in the poky little flat she's taken all in a hurry. A bit different from this massive Victorian vicarage they were thinking of taking on only a few months ago. The only advantage to this place is that it has a garage.'

'She won't stay there?'

'They don't know, or May doesn't. She has the opinion that Linda doesn't much care where or how she lives provided there's a minimum of warmth and convenience. She's never been used to luxury, though again the flat she lets out is spacious and in a yuppy area. Perhaps when she started to earn big money she splashed out for once in her life.' Peg sighed and Stone thought it human weakness. 'Anyway, she's gone now. Apparently when she was about to leave she held her hand out to JJ and kissed him and said in a very steady sort of voice, "I'm sorry, Jay. This will be better for us both. No hard feelings?" and she turned on her heel and was gone. May said that if JJ had been at all given to violence he'd have murdered her there and then.'

'And how is he doing now?'

'He's just about coping. He was tearful over the phone for a start. But he's coming to terms with it now. Some days he's worse than on others. Linda had done such a lot for him, it appears.

Not only with his work, but in other ways. He's clever enough academically, but she helped him grow up. May was apprehensive when he said he wanted to live in London. She didn't think he had the nerve and drive and ruthlessness to get on, but Linda has seen to that. She wouldn't allow him to let other people walk all over him. She was good for him and May hoped that it would last, that maybe they'd marry. But the sort of girl she is, or has learnt to be, didn't want, won't ever want, to lead a domestic life. She wouldn't tolerate somebody like JJ for too long; he needed overmuch mothering. Neither would she put up with some domineering character who'd be dictatorially laying down the law from morning to night.'

'She'd need somebody in between?' he asked, rather foolishly, he thought, but it gave his wife a breather.

'May doesn't think such a person exists. She'll never be satisfied. She'll want to rule the roost, but then will incessantly complain about her husband's weakness.'

They considered this contradiction for some time, citing examples from people they had known. Stone was left unconvinced by their assertions. 'Is May doing anything about it?'

'Yes. She's coming here next Monday and then spending the weekend with JJ.'

'She won't be able to do anything for him, will she?'

'No. But she'll see for herself how he is. And get over her own troubles if they're still nagging at her.'

The front-door bell rang.

'You go,' Peg ordered.

He obeyed, and found Annie Fisher and Karen, her daughter-in-law, standing outside, bright as buttons. He invited them in.

'We're not interrupting anything, are we?'

'No. You're just in time for coffee.' He led them to the kitchen and announced them theatrically with a stentorian shout, 'The Mesdames Fisher.'

Peg already had the mugs out and stools ready. 'Sit down,' she called. 'We're not doing anything important.'

Annie apologised for breaking in on them without warning. 'We were going out for the day, but the weather's so cold we came back home. Karen's flying this Saturday from Heathrow and I follow a week later.'

'You soon got tired of England,' Stone teased Karen.

'No. I could stop here for years, but I didn't think it fair on Laurence.'

'There he is, slaving away all day, and when he comes home there's nobody there to make a fuss of him.' Annie, smiling broadly, offered this gloss.

'He had to get back fairly soon. He's up to his eyes in work, but he insisted that I stayed. "You'll be company for my mother," he said, "and you'll see a bit of England outside London."'

'But, oh, she's missing him,' Annie said, vulgarly loud.

'I admit it. I am. I guess it seems foolish to you.'

'You've not been married long, have you?' Stone asked, knowing the answer quite well.

'Eighteen months. Both Annie and Harry came over for the ceremony. It hardly seems any time.' A huge tear for Harry Fisher rolled down her cheek. She showed no embarrassment, did not attempt to wipe it away. 'This is lovely coffee,' she said, recovering in no time.

'We've been doing churches, this last day or two, cathedrals. York, Lincoln, Southwell,' Annie said.

'It's like stepping straight into the Middle Ages,' Karen echoed. 'Each building's so fulfilling that I feel I've garnered a plethora of new unique experiences within a few hours. I shall certainly be back before long.'

'Don't you find these buildings rather small, squat, when you compare them with the skyscrapers in New York?' Stone asked.

'No, not at all. And they're so old. There they stood, looking much as they do now, before Columbus crossed the Atlantic. The Pilgrim Fathers could have seen them. I think we can boast about our skyscrapers, but they in no way compare with your cathedrals in beauty. Size is certainly something; don't mistake me. We should be proud of what we've accomplished, but we don't know how long they'll last, do we?'

'You're very taken with England,' Stone said.

'She is,' Annie agreed breathlessly.

'There's only one thing wrong with it,' Peg said.

'What's that?'

'There's no Laurence here.'

They all laughed over-exuberantly at Peg's little witticism.

'There are so many things I admire,' Karen confided. 'For instance, I love the way you and Mr Stone talk. I could listen to you all day. I've told Laurence that if he loses his English accent I shall leave him.'

'Can you tell the difference between one kind of English accent and another?' Stone asked her.

'Sometimes. I could tell that Harry sounded different from Annie, and both of them from Laurie. But I couldn't say exactly how. I couldn't imitate any of you. Sometimes I couldn't understand Harry at all and Laurence would say, "Come on now, Dad, speak English. Karen can't make head or tail of you."'

'And could he alter it for you?' Peg asked.

'Oh, yes. He could make it plain.'

'Good,' Stone said.

'He told me it wasn't any use speaking properly to his workmen. They'd laugh at him, talking hoity-toity to them. He had to be as rough as they were if he wanted anything done.'

'Do they have different accents in the States?' Annie asked.

'Oh, yes. It would be remarkable if they didn't in a country the size of ours. And we've had so many foreign-speaking immigrants so quickly and for so long, many of whom keep, let's say, Spanish as their first language.'

'And are some accents regarded as superior?'

'Oh, yes. But it depends who it is who's judging.'

'As in England.'

When they had finished their coffee, Karen asked Stone to show her around the garden. The older ladies declined to accompany them, saying it was too cold to dawdle about outside.

'Is Karen a keen gardener?' Peg asked when the pair had gone out.

'I wouldn't know. I haven't heard anything. But I believe gardening's different in New York. You can't have private gardens if you live in flats, though some of their well-to-do friends have them right outside the city. But she was telling me that it's only a fine weather pastime. In the winter months they just close the place up, protect the plants that are delicate and snow will cover the rest two or three feet deep.'

'Are they thinking of having such a place?'

'I don't know. They're just settling down to work and married life. But I wouldn't be surprised, once they've really settled. Karen's the sort of girl who lives her life to the full. She'll always be on the lookout for improvements, new ventures, interesting visits, concerts, operas. Gardens. That sort of thing.'

'Does it suit Laurence?'

'Oh, yes. She whirls him along with her. She can do no wrong.'

'Will they stay in America?'

'Almost certain they will. I shouldn't be surprised if Laurence hasn't already taken out American citizenship. I think it takes some time. If their marriage lasts.'

'Why do you say that?'

'When you see how many divorces there are. More than one in three marriages break up. I don't understand it. Harry and I didn't always see eye to eye, you know. But we never even thought of separating. Or not seriously. We pressed on, kept out of one another's way until the skies cleared. Besides, there was Laurence. I always thought a child needed a father and a mother. Seems common sense if it can be managed. Karen's such a sweetie. She goes out of her way to please everybody. I love her.'

'Were you like that?'

'When I was first married? No. I was not. I was quite a bit younger than Harry. And I belonged to the family that owned by far the major part of the company when they finally amalgamated. I had a substantial number of shares in Langton's. My father wasn't too keen on my marriage to Harry. He thought I could do better. He was almost exactly the same sort as Harry was, grammar school educated, but rough-spoken. A good businessman. He expanded the firm he inherited from his father. He was happy to have Harry as a partner, but not a son-in-law. My mother took the contrary view. "Annie'll straighten him out if it's straightening he needs," she said. They were quite the opposite of what people would have expected.'

'Did Harry know any of this?'

'Oh, yes. He was no fool. And he made sure that my father found him a good partner. But I must have told you all this rigmarole before.'

'No. It all comes as news to me.'

'Well, there we are.'

Peg, slightly out of character, gave Annie a brief account of her nephew's domestic troubles. 'I can't think what to do or say,' she confided.

'How old is he?'

'Twenty-seven.'

'If he can't sort himself at that age then there's something seriously wrong with him.'

'Do you think so? I knew a man who when he was nearly twice that age couldn't make his mind up for himself. Any important decision taken in that house was left to his wife. Not that she minded. I suppose he had fallen into the habit of leaving it to her.'

'What did he do? Work, I mean?'

'He was a university lecturer. In some sort of chemistry. He did quite well, became quite famous. Or so they tell me. He became a professor. She pushed him into applying. He was satisfied with his laboratory and his research, but she wasn't having it when people not half his talent were promoted over his head.'

'Wouldn't he have to make decisions in his work?' Annie asked.

'Presumably so. And presumably he was good at it. But anything to do with their home life, the children, holidays, changes in the house, she had to take responsibility.'

'And,' asked Annie sternly, 'how did it all turn out?'

'I don't know. They moved away. They lived next door to my mother. They went to America to some prestigious job. We exchanged cards at Christmas. He retired years ago. And she died last year. I sometimes wonder how he's shaping.'

'And this nephew of yours? What about him?'

'My sister's very worried. Asks my advice.'

'And what do you tell her?'

'Exactly what you'd tell her. To leave it to him. But she thinks there's something she ought to do or be able to do.'

'She'll learn. We all have to. I didn't think I'd miss Harry as much as I do. He was never in when he said he would be. And when he was at home he'd be outside in his workshop or his office. I used to tell him that a house wasn't any use to him except for sleeping in. Yet now I'm listening for him. I hear a door open or bang shut and I think he's back. I never worried about or even noticed such things when he was alive.'

'You'd like him back if it were possible?' Peg asked.

195

'I know that's impossible. But it's in that moment while I'm immersed in something else that it slips into my mind. I think I'd like him back. We'd got used to each other. It's been a habit for me to get meals at the times he got home.'

'Even if he didn't turn up on time?'

'Yes. And sometimes he'd bring me a present in. The last thing he gave me was a beautiful mirror. He often called in salerooms. One part of the business cleared houses as well as built them. He'd seen this mirror; it was oval and golden, and the frame, if that's what you'd call it, was intricate, complicated, ornate, with naked goddesses and nymphs among the bushes and trees. "There they are," he said, "showing you all they've got."'

'Is that what attracted him?'

'It played its part, I don't doubt, but he could recognise a work of art. I hung it in the breakfast room.'

'I've never seen it.'

'I've a photo with me.' Annie jumped to her feet with the excitement of a child. She rummaged in her bag, thrust the picture forward. Peg stared at the large photograph. Annie tapped a piece of intricate carving, branches interlacing with branches, with the nail of her forefinger. She pointed viciously at a figure. 'That was Harry's favourite. He said to me, "There's a man showing you his willy," and when I didn't say anything, he laughed. "Not demonstrating much effect with all these nude women about, is he?" is what he said. I think he was trying to shock me.'

'But you weren't? Well, whatever his motive, it's a lovely piece.'

'Let's look out of the back and see what Karen and your John are up to.'

Again, hurrying took them to the window. They could see Karen and Stone standing in the middle of the path. The young woman's coat was shapely, belted, plum-coloured. He wore a scarf and mackintosh, and his hands were deep in his pockets. The wind blew the thin strands of grey hair about his scalp. He was clearly explaining something to her as he pointed downwards. Bare branches moved in the breeze. When Stone's explanation was over, the girl burst into laughter and laid a hand on his arm. Sunshine suddenly splashed across the shrubs, picking out a gnarled flowering cherry tree.

'Harry put that in,' Annie said. 'I wouldn't let him plant it too near the house. And those poplars at the bottom are even further off.'

'Was he a gardener?'

'Not really. He didn't have the time when we first came here. He'd plant a few vegetables, potatoes and cabbages, that sort of thing at the weekends.' Annie's voice changed, became softer, more intense. 'Don't they make a lovely pair? They might be father and daughter.'

'They might.'

'When you first came here you were pregnant and I hoped it would be a girl. The girl next door. And that Laurence would marry her.'

'I lost her. She was a girl. She lived only a few days, but we gave her a name. Lucy.'

'I remember. I shouldn't have mentioned it.'

'It's a long time ago.'

Annie lifted her head to look again at Karen and John. The man signalled, a priest-like gesture, to acknowledge their interest, but Karen waved violently, her mouth smilingly wide. She looked like someone who'd made an important discovery and wanted the women to rush out to share it. Peg saw it as a picture of perfect happiness.

A month later Annie, in New York in the young Fishers' apartment, listened to Karen's praise of John Stone, a man of perfect manners, the girl said, who'd had a very successful career as a schoolmaster and had retired, but had continued to learn more about geography and geology, gardening, education, literature, music. He had, Karen claimed, all the enthusiasm of a young student, but had acquired maturity of judgement, social grace without exaggeration, an openness to life, an interest in new discoveries, wide and different experiences. Annie, interpreting this as a New World over-expansive eulogy, made a murmur of agreement but this was not sufficient, it appeared.

'You don't agree with me, do you?'

'Yes,' Annie answered vaguely. A desire to contradict flashed in her. 'What would you say if I told you that he and I had an

197

affair?' As soon as she had spoken she knew she'd made a bad mistake. Karen's face was stricken, frozen as if she had been kicked with pain beyond bearing. Later, when the mother-in-law thought about this, she decided that the signs of hurt on her face had the intensity of her laugh, her looks of delight. Perhaps she overdid her shock at the revelation as she seemed often to exaggerate her pleasure.

Annie was slightly surprised at her daughter-in-law. She thought the girl would dismiss the confession as of little consequence. Mulling it over, she decided that the condemnation was not of the adultery itself but of old people's sexual antics. They should have been past it. These new experiences that Karen had earlier praised did not include copulation with a woman in her sixth decade. Or perhaps it was that she wondered about Laurence's fidelity to her, if his mother not only practised illicit sex but boasted about it.

Immediately after the confession Annie stood, blushing over her whole body, needing to lean on a chair back.

'Was he a good lover?' Karen asked. The voice was normal, without stress. This was the sort of modern, unshocked question Annie had expected.

'Yes. I didn't complain.'

'It's over now?'

'I'd think so.'

Karen turned her back as if to claim for herself a moment's thinking space. They then continued with their plans for the day and made no further mention of Annie's confession. Annie felt uncomfortable, sure that the girl would tell her husband, Laurence, about his mother's adultery. He, at least, did not speak about it to her; nor did he show by behaviour or body language that he disapproved of her in any way. Annie decided that Karen, demonstrating her common sense, had kept her mouth shut. Whether this tact would last Annie did not know. Perhaps, when tempers grew short, the young wife would fling her husband's mother's lewdness in his face and he would turn on the wrongdoer. For the rest of her stay in New York Annie was uncomfortable, fearing an accusation from her son, but their outings, meals together, the party in her honour, their attendance at a Sunday morning church service, discussions on a hundred and one topics brought her no embarrassment. Once again Karen had proved herself the perfect young wife.

Now, a month before this, Peg and Annie looked out over the wintry garden at the intense couple.

'There are still some roses out,' Peg said.

'And it's not long before Christmas.'

'Will you be back before then?'

'Just. The day before Christmas Eve, if all things go to plan.'

'The trip will do you good.'

'I want to try to clear Harry's clothes and private things out before I go. I don't relish the job.'

'I'll help you if you like.'

Annie kissed Peg's cheek and the pair clung together.

Outside, once the back door had been opened and they heard Stone's level voice explaining that 'tomentum' meant cushion stuffing in Latin, each in her differing fashion was proud that she knew a man with such abstruse knowledge.

When the two returned from the garden, Peg asked Karen, 'Does England get better or worse the longer you stay in it?'

'Oh, better. I learn something new. Your garden, we call them yards . . .'

'I believe the Scots do,' Stone interjected and was rewarded with a wide smile.

'. . . is really interesting – even now in winter. Ours would be just a series of heaps of snow, deep snow.'

'Not all over America, surely?' Peg said.

'No. I'm speaking about our stretch. The north-east.'

As they walked back to the kitchen Annie plucked Peg's sleeve. 'Look at your husband,' she whispered. 'He's like a cat who's got at the cream. It'll do Karen good. Her pregnancy came to nothing.'

XV

May MacGregor was struck down with influenza and thus had to postpone her visit to England.

When Peg rang on Christmas morning her sister still seemed shaky. Her voice lacked its customary curtness and there were long pauses as if she did not quite know what to say next. She had had the doctor twice, and they had arranged for May's cleaning woman and a nurse to call in each day. May had spent over a week in bed.

'I've never felt so ill in my life. I could have howled. My temperature rocketed up and I sweated like a pig. Every bone in my body ached. I couldn't breathe and I hacked and coughed all the way through the night. I didn't want to eat; I just lay there. I couldn't get comfortable. When I switched my bedside radio on it sounded in my head like a riot. Even in the ordinary way my headaches were so bad that I couldn't read. I shook and trembled. I heard myself groaning out loud, something I'd never done before. It frightened me.' May delivered this slowly, weakly, digging out each separate word.

'Hadn't you had a flu jab?' Peg asked, surprised.

'Yes. Last October. That made me more apprehensive, because I thought I was protected against flu and that I'd caught something much worse. I've had flu before, but nothing like this.'

'What's the doctor like?'

'He's a young man. Big, a rugby player. He sounded my chest and pulse, and took my blood pressure and all the rest of it. He told me to stay in bed and drink plenty, and take aspirin to kill the pain.'

'Did you let him know how awful you felt?'

'Yes. He just nodded and said, "Yes. Influenza can be pretty unpleasant."'

'That was all?'

'Yes. He gave me some cough linctus, but said it was no use prescribing antibiotics as this was a viral complaint.'

'He wasn't very sympathetic, then?'

'Oh, yes. He was just not for making a great fuss of me. He took his time, he was in no hurry, but he spoke plainly.' Peg heard her sister's long sigh over the phone. She guessed that May was unaware she had made any sort of noise. 'But I felt so ill, I sent for him again.'

'And?'

'The same thing. Thermometer. Stethoscope. Examination back and front. Advice. Keep warm. Try to eat a bit if I could. Drink plenty. He was sensible, but he gave the impression that I was making a mountain out of a molehill. "Be patient," he said. "You're not as young as you once were. These things take some getting over. You'll feel better within a few days, and if you don't you can send for me again. I don't think that will be necessary, but . . ." I heard him giving my cleaning woman instructions as they went down the stairs. "Keep her warm and where she is, because once she tries to get out of bed for any length of time she'll feel hopelessly weak." He seemed confident in his own judgements.'

'Yes. And what about JJ?'

'I've seen or heard nothing of him.'

'Didn't he know you were ill?'

'Yes. But he had three or four days off over Christmas and he'd arranged with some friend at the bank to spend them in Paris.'

Stone interrupted, brows knitted, when he heard May's news. 'He knew she intended to come down to visit him, didn't he?'

'Yes, but not at Christmas. I think he and this other young man had arranged this outing straight after Linda left him. He's selfish, May says, like all young people. And he'd no conception how sick she was. She was suggesting to me that she'd had pneumonia. The doctor did give her a prescription for antibiotics in the end, though he said it was to guard her against secondary infections.'

'But is she any better now?' Stone asked.

'Yes, though she feels utterly feeble.'

'You don't think she was in such a low state on account of

dismissing these suitors of hers that it made her feel much worse once the bout of flu started?'

'I don't think so.' Peg sounded dismissive. 'I guess it was a very bad case and different from the one or ones she'd been injected against. Usually she understates any illness or setback. Not this time. It must have been pretty potent.'

'And what's her next move?'

'She'll come down here once she's feeling anything like normal.' Peg's face grew stern. 'I'll get her up to scratch here before I send her down to London on the first weekend she's fit enough. Then she'll have two whole days with JJ. I don't know how welcome he'll make her, so she needs to be in good health. Don't you think that's right?'

'Yes.' Stone had difficulty in visualising May as one in need of being built up before she could talk at length to her son. Perhaps she needed to marry again.

The Stones spent Christmas quietly enough, eating well but in moderation. Peg had hinted that they might perhaps have their Christmas dinner out at a hotel, but he had immediately set his face against the suggestion. 'I know it will give you a rest, but I object to paying extortionate prices even in such a good cause and having to put up with all the bogus goodwill. I know I'm a miserable old sod, but I'd sooner cook the meal myself than put up with a hotel.'

'I'm not having my Christmas spoilt by your attempts at cookery.'

Peg wondered why he had been so obdurate about this. They could afford to eat out every night of the week. She did not mind; she enjoyed cooking and they invited the jet-lagged Annie Fisher in for Christmas dinner. The Stones had spoken on the phone on Christmas Eve, Christmas and Boxing Day, to their son, and these long trivial conversations with Thomas and his wife Catherine in Melbourne, and their announcement of an expected child, left Peg flushed and happy. When, one week into the New Year, she announced to Stone the impending arrival of May she seemed cheerful.

'You're going to sort her out?' he asked facetiously.

'Somebody's got to. I just don't know what's gone wrong with her.'

'In what way?'

'You know what our May's like. She can make her mind up in two minutes and act immediately on it. Now she's impossible. She decides and then changes her mind in no time and for no reason that I can see. I don't know what's wrong with the woman.'

'According to your account she's felt very ill and it's knocked all the confidence out of her.'

'Well, make sure you give me a hand putting it back.'

May arrived in mid-week in appalling weather. Sleet blurred his windscreen as Stone drove her back from the station. She sat straight-backed in her seat and said nothing, apart from a curt enquiry about his health and Peg's. He described their Christmas and asked about hers, boasted about the expected baby, but she seemed unwilling to say much.

'You usually go to midnight service on Christmas Eve, don't you?'

'Yes.'

'But not this year?'

'No.'

Once safely in Laurel Avenue, a flicker of warmth showed on May's face as her younger sister flung her arms round her.

'Good journey?' Peg asked.

'Not too uncomfortable.'

'Did you travel first class?'

'No. I was fine in standard. I don't believe in coddling myself. Besides, it's expensive enough as it is.'

'You're a real Scot,' said Peg in a mock sort of Doric accent.

Stone carried the visitor's luggage upstairs. When he returned May lay on the settee propped with cushions, her feet up. 'I'm not an invalid,' she was protesting.

'I'll believe that when you've proved otherwise.'

Peg dashed out for a cup of tea using her best china.

'She's a good girl,' May ventured.

'A gem,' he said jovially.

'Don't you find her a wee bit headstrong?'

'If I did, I daren't say so.'

May closed her eyes tight. Humour was not in favour.

Within a couple of days May had recovered. On two mornings she and Peg went shopping into town. Stone drove them in; they found their own way back. All three visited a museum of textiles and they had only been in the place for ten minutes when May was in animated discussion with the curator, a young woman who looked like a picture from one of the Sunday broadsheet magazines. The girl gave as good as she got and loaded her desk with books to corroborate her argument. May enjoyed every minute.

'I didn't know you were an expert,' Peg said, outside in the twenty-first century.

'I'm not. But I'm interested in what I make or buy.'

The older sister walked at a good pace and her cheeks glowed healthily pink. On Thursday night she rang JJ to warn him that she'd travel down on Saturday morning and return on Sunday evening. 'Is it convenient?' she boomed. 'You'll have to put up with my questions for the whole weekend. You realise that, don't you?'

When she arrived back from her London visit she claimed to be worn out and went early to bed. Next morning she seemed energetic, if rather grim-faced. Peg gave her no further time for recuperation but cross-examined her sister at once about JJ's state of mind.

'The impression I gained,' May said imperiously, 'is that he's escaped completely from Linda's influence. It hadn't been easy; he'd been desperate at first, but now he's come to see that the world still turns without her help. I would have said he seemed' – she sought for a word – 'well, cheeky, cocky, as if he was pleased with himself to have got her out of his system. He's doing well at work, and this friend he accompanied to Paris and he go out once during the week, and once if not twice at the weekend.'

'Where do they go?'

'Theatres. Concerts. That sort of thing. But I also got the impression that they went to some not quite so salubrious places. Soho strip clubs. Lap dancing.'

'Do you think that's wrong?'

'Of course I think it's wrong. I don't want my son catching AIDS or some other sexual diseases.'

'I expect the prostitutes are not so keen, either.'

'No. But they might have caught it unawares. Some of them are not exactly cautious. They can't afford to be.'

'Is that so?' Peg asked cynically. 'I don't know any, myself.'

'Neither do I, you silly puss,' May answered. 'But you can read.'

'Does he see anything of Linda?'

'It would appear so. They run across each other occasionally at work. They don't deliberately avoid each other. They're both very polite.'

'And seeing her like that doesn't upset him?'

'So he says.'

'Is it a good thing that they've parted? In your view?'

'Probably. There's no doubt she brought him on, especially at the bank. But I think he's confident there. And living with her has made him grow up.'

'Does that mean you approve of young people living together outside marriage?' Peg asked mischievously.

'No, but such seems to be the rule rather than the exception these days.'

May left for Scotland at the end of the week. She appeared much like her old self. Peg had advised her to take a holiday, a cruise, but May seemed disinclined. 'Single women on cruises are vulnerable. To conmen. Even to real suitors in marriage. There are all sorts of sharks about.'

'How are your two ex-suitors?' Peg asked daringly.

'Both of them were good men.' May spoke sternly, making it clear that this was no subject for trivial knockabout. 'Ronald is now engaged to his old secretary whom he will marry this summer. Duncan I don't hear anything of. It's very likely he'll find someone more suitable than I am and marry her.'

'And you don't miss them?'

'Why should I?' May sounded indignant. 'I liked being made a fuss of, but I didn't fancy the conclusion: marriage. I've grown used to my own ways. I should have made neither man happy and I'd have been uncomfortable myself.'

May was herself again.

The Stones saw little of Annie Fisher who spent, it appeared, a fair amount of her time away from home. She'd wave from her car as she drove off, but never called in or stayed a minute longer than necessary on the garden path to exchange greetings and news. She dressed well and seemed happy, if preoccupied.

One afternoon Peg turned a quizzical eye on her husband. 'Have you heard any local scandal?' she asked. 'Recently?'

'Not that I can remember?'

'Not about Annie Fisher?'

He cringed. Who had been talking? 'What about her?'

'She's acquired a young man.'

'Who's that?' He interpreted 'young man' widely.

'By "young" I mean "young",' Peg said. 'A toyboy.'

'Where did you get this from? We've seen nothing of him here.'

'I was talking to Joyce Williams. And she started asking me mysterious questions about Annie. Was she away a great deal? Did she seem different? In the end it all came tumbling out. They both belong to a private ballroom-dancing club and for the past week or two Annie had brought along this man, Alex, years younger than she is.'

'Is he a good dancer?'

'Yes. Very good. Professional standard, Joyce says.'

'Isn't that the answer, then? She pays some man to come along and dance with her.'

'I said that, but apparently she's been seen elsewhere with him. At the theatre, the cinema, at a dinner that Langley, Bell and Fisher gave for their employees in the New Year and so on. And the two make no attempt to hide their attraction for each other. They're like a pair of newly-weds.'

'He's as bad as she?'

'As far as I can make out,' Peg answered.

'She makes no secret of the relationship?' Stone asked.

'No. Apparently not.'

'If it were the other way about – I'm talking of ages – that would be acceptable, wouldn't it? How old is he?'

'Thirty, perhaps, at the outside.'

'And she's what? Fifty-five, fifty-six?'

'That's nearly twice his age.'

'Yes,' Stone said judicially. 'I can see that might give rise to talk.'

'"Might" is hardly the word.' Peg frowned. 'I had been told that she was free with her favours even when Harry was alive.'

'Had this affair started before Harry died, then?'

'I've not heard anybody say that. It appears to have begun after Christmas when she came back from America.'

'He's not American, is he?'

'Don't know.' Peg seemed to resent her ignorance. 'I know no more about him than you do.' She paused, then continued in a softer voice, 'You don't think she'll do anything foolish, do you?'

'Your friends obviously think she's already doing it.'

'It doesn't seem sensible, does it? Even to you?' Peg looked away. 'What I meant was this: would she make her money or property over to this man?'

'Why should she?'

'You read such things in the papers these days. Conmen playing on the susceptibility of lonely widows, old and disabled people. Why should a man pay court' – she blinked at her own phraseology – 'to a woman of her age? I know she looks smart and younger than she is, but I never think of her as anything but middle-aged.'

'You've known her for a long time. This man may genuinely have fallen in love with her.'

'It's possible.' She sounded unconvinced.

'In those same newspapers you'll read about men of influence and power, millionaires, notable politicians who marry young girls or take them as mistresses. And that's usually not regarded as exceptionally criminal behaviour.'

'Women are normally more sensible than men.'

'You don't find Annie sensible?' he asked.

'I did. In many ways. She spent too much on her clothes, in my view, without much improvement in her appearance. But she understood what people told her about, let's say, money or charity work – she did an afternoon a week for Scope – or people's behaviour in illness. And when I heard that she had affairs I thought that, at least, she kept them out of the public eye. She never mentioned them to me. But then she never told me what she did at the bridge club. They were more like one-night stands than long passionate affairs. I'm only guessing. But we all knew that her husband indulged himself with other women and what's sauce for the goose . . .'

'And who were her men?' he asked, greatly daring.

'I don't know. She used to talk to one or two other women at the tennis or the golf clubs, and one or two of these were indiscreet. She went on a cruise, she said, and fell for one of the passengers.'

'Was he young?'

'I don't know. I only got this at seventh hand. Now I come to think of it, he was her sort of age and had a wife who was an invalid, or partly paralysed, something of the sort.'

'Why did she boast of that particular affair? Annie, I mean.'

'Because Harry behaved so badly. She'd be making up to herself for all the embarrassment or jealousy he caused her.'

Peg hummed to herself and did some small chore in the kitchen. There always seemed some article to be put away in its right place or squared up, though the place was as scintillatingly tidy as a show kitchen at an exhibition. She had fallen into this habit of seeing matters to rights only recently to cover pauses in conversation. She turned towards her husband. 'It's not a matter of life and death now, is it?' Peg began.

'Why do you say that?'

'We're here talking about her misdemeanours as though they were the end of the world.'

'You'll find in those newspapers of yours,' Stone said, 'cases every week of jealous people murdering their wives or lovers. They considered, if "consider" is the right word, that what their erring mate got up to was important.'

'People have been slaughtered for a few shillings.'

'Yes. But that's not likely here. We're tittle-tattling about it because we're inquisitive and don't mind amusing ourselves with other people's misdoings.'

'It makes us feel holy, do you think?' she asked.

'You speak for yourself,' he said. 'Their behaviour is not what we'd expect from respectable middle-aged people in a provincial city and so we chatter about it, laugh at it, feel superior to it.'

This time Peg sat still, made no move to return some misplaced object to its rightful spot. When she finally spoke it was more slowly, as if she did not quite know what to say. 'I like Annie,' she said. 'She's not altogether my type, but she's a decent sort. I don't really think I'd mind if you were the man having an affair with her.'

'I'm not young,' he said. He wondered if this was a trap, to coax a confession out of him.

'I know that. What I mean is that if it did her good, eased her mind in some sense, I could even approve of it. And you might enjoy it.'

'You wouldn't be jealous?'

'I don't think so. We're not passionate about each other. We seldom make physical love.'

'That's not the only sort of love.'

'No.'

'And people are very often obsessed with what belongs to them. Or to the idea of it. If somebody tries to steal it it hurts, even if the object stolen has no value. I'm yours. I belong to you. Therefore nobody else should try to snatch or wheedle me away from you.'

'I'm not so sure about that. I think I'd rather be worried that you would do something silly, making a fool of yourself in front of our friends and neighbours.'

'That's a bit cold-blooded, isn't it?'

'It's not meant to be.' Peg looked serious. 'When I say I wouldn't mind if you had an affair with Annie, I meant that you'd both be sensible about it, tactful. You'd try to shield me from damage. You wouldn't go over the top. It would be a minor pleasure, agreed between the two of you, to pass away a few hours pleasantly, not an earth-shattering event.'

'I'm a dull old stick,' he said.

'That's right, that's the advantage.'

'I don't think Annie would be breaking her neck to take me as a lover.'

'Now don't run yourself down. She'd be tickled pink. You're a highly educated man, involved in culture, attending meetings at the Council House or County Hall and all the rest. And she'd see it as no end of a feather in her cap to have you rolling about in bed with her like any other human being.'

'It would be my status not my physical attraction?'

'It would play its part.'

'Um. I'll consider it,' he said.

'But not too seriously, I hope.'

He moved across the kitchen to kiss her on the lips. They hugged briefly and he scratched her shoulder bones.

'Keep your eye open for Annie,' she said.

Stone did not have long to wait. The next afternoon he was renewing a small piece of stonework in the front garden when Annie Fisher called out to him, 'That's what I like to see: a man at work.' She stood on her path, feet apart. A male figure stood by her.

Stone scrambled to his feet, brushing his hands together.

'Isn't it too cold to be working in the garden on an afternoon like this?' she asked.

'This bit is sheltered and I can keep myself warm if I work hard enough.'

He realised that he was dressed in filthy, stained overalls and battered, clay-caked wellingtons. Only his third-best brown trilby was anything like respectable.

'You haven't met Alex, have you?' she asked. 'This is Jack Stone, my neighbour. Alexander Wentworth.'

The young man, in a smart overcoat, returned Stone's greeting. He was too far away, with a wall between them, for hand-shaking.

'What are you doing down there?' she asked.

'There's a small well here,' he said, 'and I'm replacing a couple of stones from the wall.'

'A small what?' she asked.

'A well.'

'I never knew that. Do you use it?'

'Never. I've outside taps. They're easier.'

'Is it deep?'

'Ten feet or so. But it's getting blocked up. That's why I'm mending the wall. The cover is in good order except for these two holes where the blocks have been displaced.'

'How did that happen?'

'That I don't know. The well's hidden in these shrubs. I'm the only person who ever works in this part of the garden, so I can't blame the window cleaner. It's too far away. All I can suggest is that some animal might have knocked it out. The mortar had gone. It would need to have been a biggish creature, at least the size of a labrador or an alsatian.'

'Did it do much damage? Round about?'

'No. It must have been some time ago. I noticed it first in the autumn, when I was pruning. I've only just got round to mending it. I did wonder if it wasn't perhaps a burglar who'd stumbled into it. It's all rather overgrown. Or was until I chopped some of the branches off.'

'That's interesting. Perhaps he thought you had mantraps in

your front garden.' Annie seemed to be in no hurry. Neither did she attempt to include her companion, Alexander Wentworth, in the conversation. 'Could I come round to have a look?' she asked.

'It's none too clean here, but if you want.'

'Yes, please.' She sounded childishly happy and immediately left her garden path. Wentworth stayed where he was.

'This way,' Stone advised as she came through his gate. 'Keep by the hedge for a start.'

'You lead the way.' She put out a hand for him to hold. He took it, as she eased herself past a huge pyracanthus tree and a half-hedge of beech, and stopped by a large rose bush, rosa rubrifolia. She breathed deep and inspected his work. He had repaired a low wall, quite neatly she judged, but had not yet replaced the wooden lid.

'Here it is,' he said.

She peered down, still holding his hand. 'It's not very big,' she commented.

'Big enough to get a bucket down and up.'

'Who dug it? Do you know?' she asked.

'I've no idea. I don't think there were any cottages up on the hill here before our houses were built and so I guess it was dug in an allotment or something of the sort.'

'Did they have them at that time?'

'Yes. Socially ambitious people often had gardens well away from where they lived, and built huts or arbours on them and came and spent their weekends there. There's no sign of any such places here, but their nearest ones are less than a mile away. So it's quite likely there were utilitarian vegetable-growing gardens, or perhaps orchards. It would be out of the way then. There weren't any tarmacadam roads up here.'

'Have you any proof of this?'

'Not really. But there are signs of old hawthorn hedges about. There's an enormous hawthorn at the bottom of your garden.'

'Is that the lid?' She pointed to a round wooden object with a lifting handle.

'Yes. It's a bit like the copper lids people had in their sculleries or wash-houses.'

'Is that the original?'

'No. I doubt it. I guess the builders left the well and some-body had the cover made to prevent accidents.'

They heard voices from the path.

'That's your gaffer arriving,' Annie said with a giggle. 'Come to see what we're up to in the bushes.' Peg eyed them from the path as they emerged. 'We've been looking at your well. I didn't know you had such a thing.'

Annie stamped about the path, vibrant. 'You haven't met Alex,' she said. 'Alexander Wentworth.'

'Don't stand there,' Peg called. 'Come on round.'

He did as he was told, with overdone hand-shaking and intro-ductions. On Peg's arrival the young man came to life, began to chat, accused Jack of keeping a hidden wishing well in his garden. 'I think he goes in there and asks for what he wants.'

'Ah, but does he get it?' Peg said, then immediately to Annie, 'Have you time for a cup of coffee?'

The invitation was accepted without reference to Wentworth. While Stone changed his boots and cleaned the soil from his hands, Peg showed the visitors into the large sitting room and made instant coffee in her best china. Stone found that he had cut a little finger and went upstairs to the bathroom to wash the wound again and plaster it. When he returned he found Peg in full flow describing her house.

'So Annie's grandfather built it?' Wentworth asked.

'Yes.'

'And you rent it from the family?'

'No,' Annie answered for her. 'My father thought the house unlucky and sold it off.'

'Why unlucky?'

'My mother died here. During the war. Soon after I was born. There was an air raid and my mother was found dead next morning.'

'It was bombed?'

'No. She had a weak heart. I was here with her. We had a girl who lived in to look after me. She called the ambulance.'

'I take it you don't remember any of this.'

'Of course I bloody don't.' She seemed immediately to regret this snag of temper and continued more gently, 'He sold it off to some man at the university and moved into his father's house by the main building yard. That's where I was brought up. I never

212

came near this place till Harry was left the house next door and decided to move in.'

'Who lived here before?' Wentworth asked.

'Three of Harry's sisters. One died, and the other two decided the place was far too large for them and retired to a bungalow. Two of them worked for the firm; the other was a secretary at the Polytechnic.'

'It's very quiet up here,' Wentworth said. He seemed quite fascinated by chatter about the house. 'And with all these big sycamores and limes about you might well be out in the country. Are the two houses exactly the same, mirror images of each other?'

'Roughly,' Annie answered, 'but I can't be exactly sure. Builders were laws unto themselves and so they did as they liked. And they're over a hundred years old and occupants might well have altered things. The houses are big enough for such.'

'En suite baths?' Wentworth asked. 'Butler's pantries?'

'That sort of thing. And broom cupboards and store closets and cloakrooms and downstairs loos.'

Wentworth, it appeared, was an architect by profession, trained at the university.

'Did you know Cecil Jayston?' Annie demanded.

'Yes. He was the prof in my time.'

'He lived here before the Forbeses who preceded Peg and Jack. He must have retired now.'

'He's dead.'

'I expect he is. Harry never spoke of him recently, though he did quite a lot of work for him at one time.'

Wentworth proved a good teacher as he described his latest work on a chapel in York Minster. 'I'm thought to be an expert on Gothic architecture. I wrote a little book on it, but I never expected to get the commission at York. It was more of a hobby.'

'What are you designing now?' Stone asked.

'A comprehensive school in South Yorkshire; two petrol stations; I'm glancing at a competition for a Catholic church in Ireland and a private housing estate outside Grimsby.'

'There's plenty of work about, is there?' Stone asked.

'We're lucky. A few years ago it was tricky. Nowadays there seems more spare money available and in the hands of people willing to spend it. My partner and I have both won prizes, so the firm's well known. Mind you, I was utterly taken aback to be offered this York Minster job.'

'That was well paid, was it?'

'I wouldn't say that, but in any case it was my own fault. I put an enormous amount of my spare time into it. I learnt a great deal, but I guess that if I worked it all out, I'll have earned rather less per hour than we pay the woman who cleans our house.'

'But it was worth doing?' Peg asked.

'Yes. Purely out of self-gratification. Gothic is one of my hobbies. I read a great deal and looked about me when I could. Once I had received the commission, it got me and the firm a lot of publicity. And you can't do without that these days. Though my partner says if I get too many more commissions like that we'll be ruined.'

'Was he serious?'

'No. Not really. We've plenty of work. I'm down here now for a couple of months lecturing at the university. And I live and sleep and work in our office here. It's turned out very favourably for us all.'

Wentworth described the nature of his lecturing. Partly he taught medieval stuff. That's what got him the job in the first place; their hist. of arch. man was away on a sabbatical, and the fact that he was a practising architect several of whose buildings were to be seen not a thousand miles from here was regarded as a bonus. He spoke well, fluently but modestly, and conveyed distinctly what he could do for his students. He seemed quite different from the silent man on the garden path. Annie had found an excellent partner. The Stones approved.

'Well, then. What do you make of him?' Peg asked her husband as soon as the visitors were through the door.

'Very good. I'm quite impressed.'

'Is he the sort of man you'd have expected Annie to choose?'

'No.'

'Go on. Let's hear your reasons.'

'He's a bit more of an intellectual than I'd expect.'

'Who made the choice? He or she?'

'It's reciprocal according to your friends. Though they didn't show much lovey-dovey.'

'They respected your susceptibilities. Do you think they'll marry?'

'I'd have to question them a bit before I could answer that. I'd need to know more about his background. Otherwise, at a guess, they'd do well enough. I've seen worse matched couples managing to make a go of their marriage.'

'He's older than Joyce said,' Peg told him.

They raised the topic often during the next days. Annie seemed hardly at home. Where she went they had no idea. Wentworth's character was dissected in an imaginative way from the few snatches of information they had accumulated.

'I guess he's a lot older than thirty,' Peg said again. 'He's young in appearance, but I bet he's at least forty.'

'How do you know that?'

'From the bits and pieces of information he let drop. And his face.'

'If you're right, does that make the marriage more likely? A difference of sixteen years instead of twenty-six?'

'Yes,' Peg answered. 'You'd be surprised how much attention people pay to these matters. The professional classes are pretty hidebound. They really are.'

They enjoyed these exchanges, but lacked the information to make them worthwhile. Stone said he wished Annie would bring him in again. 'She's not been near her own house, never mind ours, for nearly a week.'

'I wonder where they are.'

They could not guess. Wentworth must have been about the town to be able to give his lectures at the university.

That weekend May rang from Scotland. Peg returned from a half-hour's conversation to trip immediately upstairs to her husband's study. 'That was May. JJ and Linda are back together.'

'In his flat?'

'Yes.'

'How long have they been apart?' he asked.

'Just under two months, May said.'

'Go on, then. Tell us all.'

'According to May it was Linda who broke first. She was the one who suggested they try again. One evening about a week ago JJ was at home in front of his TV set when there was a bang

215

at the door. It was Linda. He was a bit shocked, and brusque with her. She explained that she had called round to see a friend, some girl she was at school with, but when she arrived the place was bolted and barred. Obviously the girl had forgotten all about the arrangement. That didn't surprise Linda. This girl was always something of a feather-brain. Anyhow, she realised she wasn't ten minutes' walk from Jay's flat, so she left her car and walked across.'

'And?'

'She explained to Jay how she came to be there and when he didn't make any sort of move she enquired if he was going to ask her in. "It's cold outside," she said. "I'm freezing." He invited her in, made her a cup of tea. It sounds very dull, flat.'

'And thereafter all went well?' Stone asked sarcastically.

'Well, I'm not so sure. In May's version, or JJ's, they were a bit inhibited for a start. There were silences. Then JJ let it out that he missed her. I don't know exactly how he put it. May's not altogether good at dramatic dialogue. She said – that's Linda, not May – that she'd been off colour ever since she left. It didn't matter so much at work, even on those days when she ran across him, but she found no satisfaction in her own company at night or at the weekend, especially when she was ill. She didn't know whether it was depression or ME or flu or what, but she felt like death. She sat at home, that is in her little flat, with no telly or radio, not bothering to eat. She said, "I didn't think personal affairs could have such an effect." Typically, she tried to climb out of this by looking around for a new job. She hadn't yet sent her enquiries or application forms off. I don't quite know how you change jobs at her level. However, she hadn't yet done it.'

'Was John James surprised by all this?'

'Yes. He said he'd begun to look around. For jobs.'

'Was this the truth?'

'I believe so. But straight away Linda was herself again, the businesswoman, the consultant. She advised him not to do any such thing. It would be unwise at his stage of advancement. He was doing nicely, but he'd several things to learn, which he'd pick up more thoroughly where he was. His boss and his colleagues were ideal coaches; he couldn't have chosen better. He'd serve himself well by staying where he was and working hard while he was there. If he hung on, he'd make it. The top man thought highly of him already.'

'And how did he take this?'

'I think he recognised it as the truth.'

'And?'

'One thing led to another.'

'Sex, you mean.'

'You don't expect May to have told me that now, do you? She still preserves an appearance of the ladylike. They then walked out together to collect her car. They went along hand in hand. There's a touch of authentic detail from my sister. And here's a further touch. He drove her car back, not she, and she stayed the night.'

'Did May say so in so many words?' Stone wanted to snigger.

'I don't think you're taking this with proper seriousness, my man.' She pulled a comical face. 'But yes, she did. After that it's not quite so easy to follow the story. They aren't living completely together. Sometimes they spend the night in her flat, sometimes in his. At other times they'll be apart, depending on circumstances.'

'They haven't committed themselves?'

'No. It's early days. And it's like getting blood out of a stone, getting information from May.'

'I've never found that.'

'No. Well, there's some excuse this time. She instructed JJ to keep her up to date with developments and he swore on twenty bibles that he'd do so, but she's not heard a word since. She's rung both flats, but nobody's been at home.'

'It can't be much over a week. A fortnight at the outside.'

'A week's a long time in love.'

'Now who's not being serious?' Stone said. He guessed that Peg had enjoyed her sister's discomfiture. They sat together, he with hands on knees, and said nothing.

Finally Peg broke the silence. 'I can't make it out,' she said.

'Was May pleased with the story so far?' he asked.

'She varied. Sometimes it was the best thing that could have happened and the next Linda was a villain, unreliable, out to cause mischief. She's worried and JJ's silence has had its effect.'

'How's May's love life?'

217

'It didn't get a mention.'

'What are you going to do about it all?'

'Not much I can. I'll ring her at the weekend and if there's no joy there I'll try to get in touch with either JJ or Linda.'

Stone stroked his face. 'I was talking to a man after the Frederick Stevens School Governors' meeting. He was a decent fellow, a retired engine driver. And he said to me that running a school had its dangers. "It's like young love," he said. "Or driving an express. Both are marvellous things in their way. But suddenly they cause some desperate trouble. I killed two people," he went on, "as a driver. One threw himself off a bridge. There was blood all over the windscreen. I hardly knew what had happened. There was this bang and I glimpsed the body hitting us. It was awful. And the other case was worse, in that I saw the man step forward and actually put his head on the line. I braked and used the siren, but you can't stop a train doing over a hundred miles an hour inside a short distance like that. I was in no way to blame, but by God, it affected me. They gave me counselling and time off. I knew it was not my fault, but that made no difference. I'd killed somebody. I was doing a useful job, one I enjoyed and did well, and yet these things happened."'

'That's interesting,' she said.

'Yes.' He pursued his own thoughts. 'I rather liked Linda. She's had to make her own way without any influence, and in a man's world. John James was a fool not to take better care of her.'

'I dare say he'd no idea that this sudden break-up was a possibility.'

'No. Once she'd moved in with him that was as good as any marriage lines. She was his, and his for ever.'

'Is that how men think?' Peg asked, assuming simplicity. 'Do you, for example?'

'No. But he's young. He still believes in Santa Claus.'

'He's a good-looking boy.'

'Yes, and intelligent and polite. But having parents like May and Ian may not have been good for him. They knew their minds and got on with whatever they decided to do. He looked for the snags, always, and hesitated. That might have appealed to Linda for a start, but she grew out of it.'

'That sounds too simple by half,' she answered.

218

'Of course it is. Human beings are complicated. I'd like the fairy-tale ending, but it's not likely. May is not likely, either, to be wooed by a billionaire who worships her and fulfils her every wish. In my view, that's what she deserves. She does good works in an unobtrusive way; she put up with Ian's macho lifestyle; she brought JJ up sensibly, saw that he got a first-rate education. They had interesting family holidays; she kept a very comfortable and at the same time beautiful home. She was good to your parents and old MacGregor. But I don't expect she'll profit from it.'

'Except in her mind.'

'I doubt that. There's this hidden streak of self-criticism, uncertainty which she has to hide, depression perhaps, which won't allow her to enjoy even what she does outstandingly well.'

'She hasn't turned to religion for her comfort,' Peg said, slightly turning aside.

'No. She's sceptical, would believe that she was making heaven up just to comfort herself.'

'Is that nature or nurture?'

'Don't ask me,' he answered. 'You should know better than I do. If I had to guess I'd say nature, because I imagine your upbringing was the same as hers, but she's something of a pessimist, whereas you're quite different.'

'My parents spoilt me. I was the younger.'

They left it there. Stone looked forward to May's next phone call, but none came. He pressed Peg to ring, but she refused. 'Yours is just vulgar curiosity,' she said.

On the next Saturday he came back from a meeting of the local History Society. The sun had been shining when he set out but now darkness had descended and the February wind raked his bones. He hoped Peg had excelled herself over dinner, but he feared his uneven temper would not allow him to enjoy the meal. The meeting had been a waste of time.

Peg greeted him cheerfully. 'What's gone wrong today? I can tell from your face.'

He explained how the editor had turned down an article submitted to the society's magazine. The author had then made a formal complaint to the committee, claiming that personal animosity by the editor towards him was the cause of the nonacceptance.

'Is that true?' she asked.

219

'Oh, I wouldn't be surprised. They certainly don't get on.'

'Was the article any good?'

'I haven't read it. If it was like other stuff he's submitted it would be worthy but dull. This was about clergymen in the thirteenth century at some churches in the north of the county. He'd ferret out any information that was going, but he wouldn't make it interesting. There's hardly anything known about these people. It's useful to find out who they were and where they came from and where they were educated, sometimes, or any parish business or feuding that was recorded.'

'That sounds quite interesting.'

'Do you think so?'

She placed a large cup of tea in front of him. 'And what decision did you wise men arrive at?'

'It was decided to put it to adjudication by Professor Symes at the university.'

'And will that settle it?'

'I doubt it. Symes is the editor's head of department. So he's tainted from the start. And he's no medievalist. So.'

'I thought you enjoyed these childish little quarrels?'

'So I do. But both are worthy men. The editor wants the journal to be full of interesting topics, which the local, or with luck the national, press will take over and publicise. The author wants to root out facts from the Middle Ages and have them published so that they're easily available to other researchers.'

'And if you had been the ombudsman, what would you have said?'

'Publish and be damned. But in pretty small print.'

Stone took a mouthful of tea. 'Excellent,' he said. 'Excellent.' He drank again.

'Now,' his wife began, 'are you ready for my bit of news?'

'You've heard from May?'

'No. From Annie.' As usual, she made him wait.

He did his best to appear uninterested as he concentrated on his mug of tea. 'What had she to say for herself?' Stone asked in the end.

'Guess.'

'She announced the forthcoming nuptials of Anne Elizabeth Fisher to Alexander Wentworth FRIBA.'

220

'You're too fond of the fairy-tale ending. Alex has finished his course of lectures and has gone back to headquarters.'

'Where's that?'

'Newark and London.' Peg sat down, looking serious. 'He's gone back home for the present, though there's some big job in London in the offing. But his family lives in Newark. Don't ask me why he didn't drive back every day.'

'Family?' Stone played up to his wife.

'Yes. He's forty-one years of age and he has five children, the oldest of whom is eight.'

'So all this stuff your friends were making up about them was fiction?'

'They went around together in their spare time. They enjoyed each other's company.'

'And sex?'

'She didn't mention it straight out, but I did have the impression that sexual intercourse was part of the entertainment.'

'Did Annie know about his wife and family from the word go? Or did that gradually emerge?'

'I think she did, but I'm not sure. Does it make any difference?'

'I'd have thought so. She could have been bitterly disappointed. She meets this attractive professional man and they seem to hit it off. It's quite likely thoughts of marriage crossed her mind.'

'That's old-fashioned. People don't behave like that these days.'

'Don't you believe it. Annie would like nothing better than a smart, successful, professional man as a husband.'

'So you say. Anyhow, she didn't seem unduly upset. Rather relieved than otherwise.'

'Is he coming back?'

'For a few lectures before Finals. And he's marking one of the papers. And judging some of the submitted work.'

'Does his wife mind his coming away and leaving her in charge of the home?'

'Apparently not. She's the domestic type. She gets daily help.'

'I'd think so, with five small children. Does he seem fond of them?'

'From what she said, I gathered he was, so long as they didn't get in his way.'

'An ideal marriage. For him.' He looked up. 'Why have they had so many children and so quickly?'

'She didn't say.'

'And you never remarked on it? That was very forbearing of you.'

'It'll come out in the end. I shall hear all about it before long. I'm patient.'

'Did Annie meet Mrs Wentworth?'

'No. Don't think so. You can't leave five small children to fend for themselves.'

That was that. Peg set about the dinner, which was excellent. After the meal they drank whisky, but didn't talk much. Peg, in fact, fell asleep. Even while she was sleeping her face appeared mischievous. Two or three times during the next few days he tried to revive the Annie–Wentworth conversation. His wife joined in without reservation, but he learnt little more than he already knew. She did not presume to dot 'i's or cross 't's without further evidence. She had seen and talked to Annie, and had, she claimed, observed her neighbour closely. To the best of her knowledge Annie had not suffered on account of her parting from Alex.

Stone met her himself one morning walking back from the shops. He offered to carry one of her bags.

'A gentleman,' she said. 'This handle's cutting my fingers off.'

'What have you bought? Lead shot?'

'Bottles. Listen to them clink.'

'We've taken to drink, have we?'

'No. Toiletries. Bath foam. Shampoo. And for drinking purposes two huge bottles of lemonade.'

'Are you keeping busy?'

'I can occupy myself. I do a bit in the garden and I've employed a regular gardener since Harry died. Not that this is a busy time. He'll be fully occupied in a month or two. I see your camellias are nearly out.'

'Yes. I hope they're not too early. If you get frost at night and sun in the morning it ruins them.'

She asked him a sensible question or two about horticulture. He promised to lend her a book on the cottage garden.

'I'm thinking of going away. I hate this time of year in England.'

'May I ask where?'

'Portugal. The Algarve.' She laughed. 'It will be dull there, but warmer than it is here.' She described the kind of life she and her old school friend would spend together for a fortnight. 'And then,' she concluded, 'the weather will have begun to behave itself. Ask Peg if she'd like to come. We've a spare bed.'

'I will.' He elicited dates from her, flights. 'Come in and see her. It seems a good idea to me.'

They talked, trailing on up the long hill. Suddenly she said, 'I didn't know you had a wishing well in your garden. Alex was very taken with it.'

'I don't see why. It was, is, a straightforward allotment well. All the gardeners dug them.'

'He thought it was magic.'

'That's the young man with you the other day? The architect? He seemed very quiet. He made a wish, did he?'

'He did.'

'What was it?'

'Ah, he didn't let on. You're supposed to keep it to yourself.'

'And you can't guess what it would be?'

'I bet I could. Pots of money.'

'Is that good or bad?' He drew his breath with difficulty as they talked and climbed the slope.

'He earns a fair amount as far as I can make out. You need it with a family his size. He never seems short.'

'Clever man, is he? At his job?'

'I imagine so. Not that I know anything about architecture. He suffers from the same complaint that many older men do. That's his trouble.'

'And what complaint is that, may I ask?'

'He thinks he's God's gift to women.'

'And he isn't?'

'He is not. Not as far as I'm concerned. He's amusing enough, and good company and all the rest. But he thinks I'm at his beck and call at a minute's notice. He had to learn otherwise.'

'And he wasn't pleased?'

She shrugged. The conversation was not exactly as she wanted it. Or he, for that matter.

'Did you know him before?'

223

'Yes. Vaguely. A few years back he was architect to a large civic building project in the Potteries. And the firm built it. So he came over twice to see Harry and had lunch with us.' She stepped forward more sprightly. 'So when he took on this university job, he called in to commiserate with me on Harry's death, which people had told him about. He came in for a meal or two in the evening and we went out together several times. He always seemed to have time on his hands to enjoy himself.'

'And you were pleased?'

'Flattered. And he knew how to make a woman feel wanted. There was a difference of fifteen years in our ages. The other women at the ballroom-dancing class were envious. That was obvious.'

'But you weren't serious?'

'Serious? What do you mean by "serious"?'

'Well, some people mentioned, well, er, wedding bells.' He spoke hesitantly.

'What people?'

'Acquaintances. Friends of Peg's.'

'Name them.' Now her voice sounded hot, desperate.

'I shan't do that. I can't remember and might well get them wrong. Peg mentioned to me that there was talk and asked me if I knew anything about it.'

'And you didn't?'

'No. I did not.'

'Just you tell that tattling wife of yours that she should have known better. Alex and I enjoyed each other's company. I knew he was married. I knew how many children he had. I knew how long he was likely to be living here.'

'That's not fair to Peg.' Stone used his most cool, headmasterly tone. 'She knew you must miss Harry and would have been delighted if you had found a suitable second husband . . .'

'In next to no time.' She spat out her words. 'And it's very good of you to defend your wife. Does she know what you got up to with me from time to time?'

'No. And that's all the more reason for you to be fair to her.'

'You're a bloody hypocrite, Jack.'

'I admit it. And you're angry for some reason, so we'd better drop the subject.'

224

They were now steaming up the hill. He felt the redness of his face. Sweat gathered where his hat pressed his forehead. He was weak with rage and could barely keep up with his companion.

'I shouldn't have said what I did,' she muttered and stopped to face him. 'We'd all pass on snippets of gossip of that sort. We know so little of other people these days that we make their lives up for them.'

'There's something in that.'

'And I shouldn't have called you a hypocrite, Jack.'

'Forget it.'

'I was angry suddenly. I don't know why. I bridled. I could have killed somebody. It was as if something got possession of me. A devil. Why was I so cross? Come on. You're a clever man. Why was it?'

He frowned to indicate thought. 'I could think of a reason, but if I told you you might be more furious than ever. And it may be nowhere near the truth.'

'Tell me. Right or wrong. You've made me curious.'

'Well, I'm not sure of this, but I thought perhaps that in the first place you thought in the same way that your friends did.'

'What's that mean? I don't follow.'

'That when you first met Alexander Wentworth again you saw him as an attractive, intelligent, lively man and you thought that he'd possibly make you a good husband. You found out, sooner or later, I don't know which, that it wasn't likely and you were disappointed. And when I tell you that these friends of yours confirm your initial notion that you would have made a good married couple your disappointment, your frustration, boils up again and you're angry with me.'

Annie seemed to consider this. 'Well tried,' she said. 'But I knew all along he was married. He was when we met before. He had a child or two even then. So marriage never crossed my mind. Perhaps it was these women's idle curiousity. Why can't I enjoy a man's company without half the people of Beechnall gossiping about it?'

'"What great ones do, the less will prattle of."'

'What's that?'

'Shakespeare. *Twelfth Night.*' He'd done it for School Certificate all those years ago.

225

'You bloody schoolmasters.' Her temper had not altogether subsided. He touched her arm and she allowed it. 'Look, there's something I want to ask of you. Please don't mention a word of any of this conversation to Peg.'

'I wasn't thinking of doing so,' he answered humbly.

'You never know,' Annie said. 'People spill all sorts of confidential knowledge as carelessly as they empty their rubbish into the dustbin. Just to catch somebody else's interest.'

'I'll be as silent as the grave.'

'I'm sure you will. You know, Jack, you're the sort of man I should have married. I know I'm not the sort of woman you'd have wanted to marry, but there.'

'I'm not without faults,' he said, grinning.

'Committing adultery?' she queried.

'Just with you. Nobody else.'

'And whose fault was it?'

'Mine,' he said glumly.

'No, you're wrong. I went after you as hard as I could. With the whisky bottle. Partly to see if you were as randy as other men.'

'And I was.'

'Yes, in one way. You did it.'

She prattled on. He did not listen, immersed as he now was in his own black thoughts. It was twenty-six years since they had first made love. He remembered the dull October day when Peg was visiting a sick aunt in the Lake District before going on to her sister's. God knows where Harry was. Peg had arranged for her husband to have lunch with Annie, since it was his fortieth birthday. On that celebration Saturday he and Annie had drunk more than they should, so that what followed came easily, surprising him. He had yielded without resistance as he might take a second helping of summer pudding. No more; no less. And yet guilt had racked him as soon as he was left to himself. Peg had set out straight after breakfast, after she had handed out his cards and presents. 'I shouldn't leave you alone on your special birthday, but poor old Amy really is on her own. There'll be nobody in to see her if I don't go.' He had felt wretched about his misbehaviour. Now it suffocated him. His love life with Peg was eminently satisfying, but once Annie had made

226

her first move he'd acted like a sex-starved adolescent. Yet they continued.

The whole affair seemed half-hearted.

He'd thought it over time and again, and doubted whether in the whole twenty-six years they had made love more than eighty times. He often calculated, or tried to estimate, the number. Thrice a year. It seemed feeble, the moral and numerical equivalent of sending seaside postcards to a friend. But it was not even the crude, snigger-inducing postcards of fat women with oversized breasts and buttocks berating henpecked husbands who had risked a lewd glance at the bikini-unclad girls that came to mind. He had broken his marriage vows primly, sedately, over a quarter of a century, more like those glossy photographs of the marine gardens, the beaches with children, buckets and spades, deckchairs and sandcastles. The comparison – he'd often made it before – did nothing to comfort him. A throe of remorse racked him on the corner of his own street, a spasm of guilty disappointment in himself. He could barely move. Breath seemed locked inside him. Annie chattered on. Paralysis of will imprisoned him. He had risked his marriage to Peg for the equivalent of a packet of postcards. And yet he'd yield again.

He thought he might choke.

She drove a heavy elbow into his ribs. 'Come on, dreamer,' she said. 'It's too cold to be hanging about on street corners.'

They set out again, he still bemused, choking, full to the throat.

At Annie's gate he wordlessly handed over her bags. She thanked him, set off along her path. He took the necessary few steps but could not turn in at his own gate. He staggered along, fighting his emotion, finally to reel in at the garage drive. Nobody was about. Frost still coated the grass verges. He looked about him again and there in the deserted street a loud sob burst from his chest, with the sudden violence of a hiccup. Now tears streamed and he toppled. The gate saved a fall. The muffled sounds from his mouth and nose seemed driven by some physical stimulus, quite unpredictable, fitful, unconnected with his emotions. He leaned on the closed, barred gate of his drive, snivelling, moaning.

How long he hung there he could not say. Gradually his weeping ceased and reason re-established itself. He had to take

the car out that afternoon. He opened the gate clumsily, thighs
trembling, still unable to contain completely the faint sounds of
distress from his mouth. He fastened the gate back and drew from
his pocket an unused handkerchief. Before he mopped his face,
he stared at the clean square of linen in his hand as if he did not
recognise its use.

It took some seconds to wipe his face clear and he feared, so
violent and inexplicable had been the outburst, that he could not
trust himself to regain immediate control. He breathed deeply;
the cold air did him a little good, then cut unfriendly into his
lungs. It was as if his body had become a moral dictator, deciding
that he had done wrong, and set about this punishing catharsis.
He left the gate open.

He walked back to his front door slowly. He fiddled with his
key as if the task were beyond him. As he usually did, he called
out to Peg to announce his arrival. His hello echoed round the
hall. He was surprised at the strength, the normality of his voice.
She did not answer. He tried again even louder. No result. Peg
would perhaps have gone out into the garden, to the dustbin. If
there had been some small domestic crisis that had forced her
out of the house she would have left an explanatory note on the
kitchen table. He lugged his bag towards it. Nothing.

Again he felt weakness invade his body; his shoulders shuddered, almost as if the flesh were disintegrating. Breath held, he
waited for the next outburst of tears. Not easily, gradually, he
became himself again. His relief held him straight for the moment.
He, with a sense of real purpose, found himself a glass and filled
it from the tap. His heartbeat grew unevenly quick. He sipped
his water, felt his pulse. At first he could not trace it, then it
surged under his middle finger. The merciless attack of grief,
penitence, remorse in the street obsessed him, silenced him still.
It had felled him as he imagined a stroke would. One felt off
colour, not uncommon with older people, then suddenly part of
his body lost its life, mobility, sensitivity. One was crippled,
dumbed, within seconds. His spasm had changed his body, trans-
mogrified it, some such daft, unusual word, into that of an infant
unable to contain or hide its tears, its cries. All adult control had
gone. Certainly he did not scream, but only his physical weakness
precluded that.

Now he was relieved that no such hysterical fit had been thrust on to him. He had sobbed openly out in the street, and moaned in public, though no one had observed or passed him. Now he propped himself against the sink. He was drawing a second glass of water, his hand shaking, when the kitchen door flew open and Peg appeared.

'You're back,' she said. 'I didn't hear you.'

'I called out.' He could keep his voice steady.

'I was down in the cellar. I wanted a small piece of wire.' She held up the loop. 'Did you get the coffee?'

'I did.' He pointed at his shopping bag.

She lifted it energetically to the table, emptied out its contents, banged the coffee jar prominently in front of her, having examined the label to her satisfaction. 'Right,' she said. 'No complaints. Fill the kettle, please.'

His small task complete, he looked his wife straight in the face. Her hair was ruffled. She had, he thought, been crying. 'Are you all right?' he asked.

'I've been talking to May on the phone.' A distinct tremor sullied the clarity of her voice. He waited. Even in everyday affairs she did not like him to hurry her. 'She's in trouble again.'

'The children?'

'No. They hardly rated a mention. They're still together.'

His lethargic mind groped for an explanation. Some accident? Loss of money? Cancer of the breast? The cervix? He made no attempt to guess. The kettle screamed. Peg efficiently filled two mugs with coffee. She pushed one towards him, pulled out a stool and sat. 'It's Ronald Murray.'

'I thought he was marrying his ex-secretary this summer.'

'He was. He isn't now. She broke it off. And he's driving May mad. Always round at her house wanting comfort. He's like a child, she says.'

'How did it happen?'

'There seemed no reason. He'd just spent Christmas with this woman in Edinburgh and three days after he'd got back he received a letter saying that she couldn't go through with the wedding.'

'Did he go back to see her?'

'Yes, he did. She had enclosed their engagement ring. And he took it back with him. She saw him. They met at least twice, but

229

he couldn't shake her. Her mind was made up. She was like brass. That was his expression. She'd thought it over and decided they would both be unhappy. She had no complaints against him. He'd been perfect and generous and kind. But they would only make themselves unhappy if they tried living together.'

'Was there some other man on the horizon?'

'No. Apparently not. And they'd seen enough of each other since they'd got together again. He was always going down to Edinburgh and she went up there several times.'

'Did people in the village meet her?'

'I believe so. At one or two functions.'

'May?'

'Yes.'

'And did she find her a reasonable woman?'

'Yes. Very ordinary, she said. Pleasant. Lively. And they'd decided they'd keep her little house in Edinburgh as well as living up there. In fact, he'd said that if she wished it, he'd buy a larger place in Edinburgh and spend quite a bit of time there.'

'I see. Then why this sudden change of mind on her part? Family?'

'He doesn't know. Her sons seemed to like him. Her friends. His old colleagues. The two of them were ideally matched, enjoyed each other's company, went to concerts and plays, were both churchgoers.'

'It all seems unlikely to me.'

Peg stiffened. 'We don't know half of what other people think or do. But it's not that that's worrying me. It's the effect on May. He's down at her house two and three times a day, and his behaviour is that of a madman. He's weeping and shouting. He seems a different man from the smart lawyer he once was. He lies on the carpet, kicking and screaming like a spoilt child in a tantrum. He carried on on one occasion so violently he wet himself.'

'What did she do?'

'Fished out an old pair of Ian's trousers.'

'Perhaps the other woman had seen signs of this sort of behaviour.'

'I don't know. But it's half killing May. She sobbed like a baby on the phone. She's usually in control of herself, but this has gone beyond all reason. She sounded mad.'

230

'And what advice did you give her?'

Again Peg looked hard at him. 'I invited her down here. She said she couldn't come. He might commit suicide. It upset me. We were both crying.'

'Have another go at her.'

'Will you? I got nowhere. She might listen to you.'

Peg ordered him out of the kitchen. He sat in his study, an open crime novel in front of him, though he read nothing of it. Their lunch was silent, numb. If he attempted conversation, Peg snapped at him and disappeared almost immediately. He washed the dishes, miserably enough, and decided against going out as he'd intended.

Peg rushed in as he tidied the kitchen. 'When are you going to ring May?' she asked unpleasantly.

'Now,' he said. 'As soon as I've finished here.'

He was as good as his word.

The exchange with his sister-in-law was far easier than he expected. He repeated Peg's invitation and said she'd oblige him by coming immediately. She could make some pretext up for Murray's benefit. She had stuttered through a few feeble excuses, which he soon disposed of, then she seemed almost grateful that he had bullied her into the visit.

'I don't want this upsetting both you and Peg.'

That settled her. She recovered something of her old efficiency. That afternoon she'd find out train times; she'd pack her bags and would ring him at about seven thirty that evening so that he could meet the Edinburgh train in Newark on the next day.

'Good girl. Seven thirty, then.'

He left it at that; he feared she'd change her mind, though in fact she did not.

Peg was not about again when he came away from the phone. He called out and she emerged from their bedroom.

'She's coming tomorrow. She'll ring at seven thirty tonight to give us details.'

'Well done,' Peg said and slowly descended the stairs, hanging on to the rail. When she reached him she said, oddly, 'Tell me again.'

He did so. She nodded as if she had finally grasped the answer to some difficult problem.

'Will she come, d'you think?' he asked, voicing his fears.

'If she promised, she will.'

'We're beginning to get old, Peg,' he said. 'We aren't quite so athletic or intelligent or even hypocritical as we were in our prime.'

'She'll come,' she announced with confidence and smiled before she stretched up to kiss him. 'Now I'll go and make up her bed.'

'Do you want any help?'

'No, thank you. You go and sit down quietly somewhere, and get your breath back.'

She marched upstairs. He, in the sitting room, stared out on to the wrecked ruins of the winter afternoon streaked greenly grey across the sky.

Peg had smiled at him. It probably meant little. He straightened his tie.